"Let's set up the flytrap." I whipped along behind the backdrop. Barbara's dark head was barely visible where she was leaning against the piece. "Barbara, excuse me. Want to get off now? We've got to wheel it out. Barbara?"

There was no answer. How I hated to stir her up. I flipped the latches off the anchors and touched her arm. "Barbara? Barbara, please move."

Her arms slipped away from me. I assumed she was moving.

I pressed the pedal, releasing the brake, and shoved, turning the tree slightly. As I turned the flytrap, I saw that Barbara wasn't just standing; she was propped against the flytrap, her head on her chest. How could she sleep so soundly?

I grabbed her arm and shook it hard. "Barbara!" Then I saw the golden cord around her neck, holding her in place.

———————————— ★ ————————————

"...fast-paced and well-written. Jorgensen's endearingly quirky characters will hold readers' interest as does the clever plot..."

—*Booklist*

Previously published Worldwide Mystery titles by
CHRISTINE T. JORGENSEN

A LOVE TO DIE FOR
YOU BET YOUR LIFE
CURL UP AND DIE
DEATH OF A DUSTBUNNY

DEAD
ON HER
FEET

CHRISTINE T. JORGENSEN

WORLDWIDE.

TORONTO • NEW YORK • LONDON
AMSTERDAM • PARIS • SYDNEY • HAMBURG
STOCKHOLM • ATHENS • TOKYO • MILAN
MADRID • WARSAW • BUDAPEST • AUCKLAND

To Jim

DEAD ON HER FEET

A Worldwide Mystery/April 2000

Published by arrangement with Walker Publishing Company, Inc.

ISBN 0-373-26344-9

Acknowledgments

I would like to thank Denise and Natalie Turnbull, who took time to acquaint me with the theater that became the model for the Magic Circle Theater and who answered my many questions about theater operations and terms. Their help was invaluable.

There never is an adequate way to say thank you to all the people who patiently assist in the writing of a book.

In this case, the help and encouragement of Leslie O'Kane, my reading buddy, my critique group and my husband, all of whom were more than generous with their time, were crucial to the completion of this book.

ONE

"THE PRICE OF crickets has gone up! Eight cents a head now," I said.

"Let them eat wax worms."

Fluffy and Lips, my pet chameleons, actually green anoles, are definitely spoiled. They turn up their little noses at wax worms, leaving them to pupate on the terrarium floor. Desperation for cash had made me jump at the chance to earn what Zelda, the *Daily Orion's* receptionist and power magnate, so charmingly called "four hundred dollars of dead easy money."

One year earlier I had quit my secure but boring job as an accountant and talked my way into writing an astrological column for the lovelorn for the *Denver Daily Orion,* a once prosperous newspaper now devoted to happy neighborly news on a weekly basis. Now I loved my job, but I wasn't earning enough to live on, especially if my chameleons were going to feed on crickets at the exorbitant price of eight cents a head.

Jason Paul, the *Daily Orion's* one reporter and my lovelust, was on the other end of the telephone, his voice not quite purring out of the receiver into my ear. "You're practically dead on your feet, and I've hardly seen you since you took that theater job. Did you know it was going to be this much work?"

"It's only for three more weeks."

"The theater scene in Denver is very tight. You didn't have enough experience to get that kind of job—"

"Maybe not, big boy, but I got it, nevertheless." I stuck

my tongue out at the phone. "They chose me because Zelda recommended me, and I convinced Ogden Bane, the director, that I was forceful."

"Oh, my God." I heard him sucking air. "This is trouble. I can feel it. There's something wrong with the job."

As soon as he hung up, I opened the window to look at the moon, silvery cool in the warm night sky. May in the Rockies was a time of soft breezes, warm showers, fat robins, fragrant wild iris; even the moon was full. Everything was full, except my bank account, which is why I had taken a second job. *And* why I was so tired I had simply thrown myself across the bed without even undressing.

The phone rang again.

"Stella, baby, I'm warning you. Barbara Steadman's a dead woman!"

This time it was my best friend, Meredith Spencer, in a snit. It seldom occurs, but this was her first starring role in the little theater, and she was fired up. "I'm saving up my money and hiring someone named Guido to kill her. You know that, don't you?" Sometimes she overreacts.

"It's not that bad, Meredith."

"It's worse than bad. It's lethal. She's the primo stage mother of history, and it's your job to get control of her. You're the assistant director. If you don't do it, she dies. And it's all your fault."

I closed my eyes and rolled onto my back. My head was pounding, every bone in my body ached, and I was so tired I couldn't begin to think. The only thing that felt good was the breeze from the window cooling my forehead. I pulled the sheet over my feet and snuggled up to my down body pillow. "How much do you think Guido will cost?"

"Don't laugh at me. I don't care if she is the playwright and owns the theater, she's going to ruin the play. I know you're falling asleep. Don't you dare."

"Okay, I'll do something." Then I hung up, and fell asleep to the tune of some very expensive crickets chirping in the terrarium.

I woke later in a sweat, strangled by my shirt, fighting a bad dream I couldn't quite remember. The night-light lit the room in a strange glow, casting shadows on the wall by the window. The bedroom seemed odd, foreign. The window was open, and the drapes were moving. My first thought in my dream-soaked paranoia was that someone had just stepped through them.

Everything was strangely quiet; not even the crickets in the terrarium were chirping now. It took a minute before I remembered I was house-sitting and realized it was only the chill night breeze rustling in the drapes. After three months I still wasn't used to the town house and the quiet neighborhood. Shivering, I closed the window.

Too wide awake now to go back to sleep, I decided to check on Fluffy and Lips. Lips had gone from plump to thin two weeks ago, and I was worried about her. She flinched when I flicked on the grow light but otherwise didn't respond. She was sleeping on top of Fluffy, her little front legs wrapped around his shoulders. No impersonal body pillow for her. Seven crickets, fifty-six cents' worth of beef on the hoof, snoozed on the hot rock.

I started to flick off the light when I caught sight of a small cream-colored oval, like a TicTac, wedged in the crotch of the Swedish ivy plant in the terrarium. Lips opened her eyes, stared at me, and flicked her tail toward it. I swear she smiled. She had laid an egg.

How long had it been there? I hadn't noticed it before. I was so excited I almost called Meredith. I didn't, of course, because her biological clock is ticking very loudly right now, and this would only make it worse.

I also felt a pang of envy. Lips's love life was considerably less complicated than mine. Fluffy opened one eye, then closed it again. Chameleons need their solid twelve hours of sleep a night. They aren't wakened in the night by worries. Although I knew it was ridiculous, now that Lips had laid an egg, I felt even more desperate.

I went downstairs, wandered out into the backyardlette, a tiny swath of grass sandwiched between the house and the garage, and slumped into a plastic lawn chair. My savings were gone, I was house-sitting to save on rent, my credit cards were hanging out there, and I had a $350 car payment due in two weeks. The temporary job with the theater would barely tide me over until next month. I had to have a significant cash infusion—a raise at least, maybe even syndication—before life became a real nightmare.

And then I remembered what I'd been dreaming about when I woke—Barbara, the primo stage mother.

I'd taken the job of assistant director at the Magic Circle Theater, a small family theater privately owned and operated by Barbara and Lawrence Steadman, to keep the wolf from the door and because it sounded easy. I merely had to assist the director, Ogden Bane, for the three weeks of rehearsals and the two weekends of performances. The fact that Zelda was a volunteer costume maker for them had made the job sound easier.

I had gone to some of their previous productions, and the fact that I'd even met Barbara and Lawrence a couple of years ago all made it even easier. Moreover, I knew their sixteen-year-old son, Phillip, and liked him, although he was clearly into body-piercing adolescence.

So how was I to know that Barbara had turned into the stage mother from hell? She had always been one of those dynamic, intense women whose eyes burn when they're excited and whose voice could lure snakes from their holes. But what had been dark, flaming beauty before had become mercurial temper, and the voice that once lured snakes now sounded like one. Supremely irritating. Most unattractive. And my problem was to keep my temper when she was losing hers. I would only get paid if I kept her quiet and out of the way. So far, I had not been successful.

Ogden Bane was sarcastic. Cammie Dinkum, the stage manager, was harried but hanging in there, and Phillip the sixteen-year-old star was hanging on only because his two best buddies, Linc and Judd, were always around. I didn't know Linc and Judd very well. Mostly they seemed to be interested in the pyrotechnical aspect of the theater. Smoke bombs were their favorite. The police had already come once because they blanketed the neighborhood with thick black sulfur smoke.

Truly, I thought, my only problem was Barbara and how I would manage to keep my cool with her and keep her from interfering.

The air was unusually warm and soft, and the moon looked like a lemon meringue pie. Everything I looked at reminded me of food—even Barbara. Thinking about her, her heavy chest and skinny-legged shape, reminded me of a pork chop. Round, pink, and ridiculous. The image made a nice warm glow in my insides. Maybe if I thought of her as a pork chop when she got on my nerves, I'd keep my cool. It was worth a try. I had three more weeks to go, and I didn't have any other ideas.

THE NEXT MORNING, Friday, I was a bit tired from lack of sleep, but on the whole, far more optimistic than I had been the night before.

I put on a bit of eyebrow pencil so I'd look more forceful and wore my favorite power teddy under a bright turquoise-and-yellow shift. Color always makes me feel good. There's something about really wonderful lingerie that just lifts the spirits. Unfortunately it's also lifted my credit card bills, but it's been worth it. My hair dragged to my shoulders, but it still had a bit of an auburn rinse so it wasn't its usual blah brown. I tied a ribbon around it, sweatband style, to keep it out of my eyes and set off, hopeful that if I handled it right Mr. Gerster would come through with a good raise and maybe even help with syndication. Syndication was the only way I could support myself.

The *Denver Daily Orion* is located in central Denver on Pennsylvania near First Avenue in an area that has recently begun to fight off the encroaching apartment buildings. The silver maples are old and shade the streets, while Victorians and Denver squares are interspersed with ten-year-old three- and four-story yellow brick apartment buildings. The musty one-story brick building of the Orion fit into the neighborhood with crumbling ease.

Zelda was already at her desk, the sun glinting off her blond hair, piled in lumps and curls on her head. She was in her romance heroine mode, her blazing red fingernail tracing a path across the printed page as she read.

"Zelda, can you fit me into Mr. Gerster's schedule this morning?"

She didn't look up. "No."

"Why not? He's here, he's in his office, he doesn't have any other appointments—I can see his daily schedule from here."

"He said no appointments this morning."

"Then this afternoon."

She finally looked up and shook her head slowly back and forth, her lips pursed and a little frown across her brow. "He said no appointments until further notice."

"No appointments? What's going on?"

She dropped her gaze. "I don't know." Of course she did, but she wasn't going to tell me.

"Zelda, it's important. Please tell him I really need to talk to him."

"All right, but if it's about money, you can forget it." She thrust an inch of manuscript bound in a rubber band at me. "Here. Take this. This'll keep you busy."

"What is it?"

"The revised play."

"I already have the script."

"What you have is the first act and the blocking. You'll need this for tonight. You've only been working off the first act. Read it. This is the complete and latest version of the play. Barbara just finished it."

"When did you get this?"

"Brought by messenger a quarter hour ago."

I took it. Something was attached to the bottom. Immediately my fingers tingled, and a chill ran along my arms. My face grew cold, my lips stiff, and the room began to grow dim and gray.

My breathing sounded loud in my ears, and through a mist I saw white manuscript pages floating like feathers in the breeze.

Then I saw a vague shape, a body twisting from a noose, one way, then slowly back again, as though blown by the winds of hell. A nasty metallic taste filled my mouth.

The taste of blood.

TWO

My BODY WAS trembling lightly; I tried to see through the mists clouding my vision. I couldn't even tell whether the form was male or female. I strained to see some feature—any distinguishing mark—that would tell me who this was.

These strange spells began when I was a child and discovered I just "knew" certain things, at first just minor, almost funny incidents, such as who, on a dare, ate all of Mrs. Baumeister's goldfish. Then a bit later I began to "see" them, clearly, as when I "saw" Mr. Katzenwald put Mrs. Katzenwald's mean old parrot in the fridge for a couple hours so it caught pneumonia and died. I explained it as catching someone else's thoughts.

As I grew older I also had what I called "gray spells," when I began to see things dimly in a gray haze. But if the gray spells were not so clear, they were also not so light-hearted. I felt like such a freak for this that I never talked about it or told anyone other than Meredith, except once, when I was very young and told my mother. She dismissed it as the product of an overactive imagination, and I never mentioned it again—not even to Jason, although he has been very curious about my "intuition," as he calls it.

The minute I felt Zelda's hand on my arm, shaking me, the vision faded. All that was left was the memory of the metallic taste and a fine, cold sweat along the sides of my face.

Zelda stared at me as if I'd been slobbering on my shirt. She shouted, "She's gonna faint. She's got a look in her eyes!"

I blinked and looked around, shaking myself a little to loosen up my joints. The cold sweat on my face disappeared.

"Zelda, stop it!" I said. "It's nothing."

"It's not nothing, you're white as a sheet. Get in here, Jason. Get ahold of her, before she crashes to the floor."

Jason raced toward me; Zelda shouted, "Hurry!" Even Mr. Gerster came scurrying down the corridor.

"Stop it. I'm a bit dizzy. I skipped breakfast, that's all." But I was shaken. What had precipitated this? I glanced down at the manuscript. Was it set off by the manuscript or by something else? I turned it over. Caught in the rubber band were a couple of scraps of paper. One was a telephone message for Jason. The other was an article about Barbara Steadman's Magic Circle Theater. I started to shiver uncontrollably.

Jason put his arm around my waist. "Let me help you. You look like death." His body heat warmed me, and the sunlight streaked his hair, dancing off the sun-lightened strands.

I'd been managing just fine until I felt him, warm and strong, standing beside me, his voice in my ear, caring. I melted into his side and let him lead me over to the hard wooden waiting room chairs. He started to take the manuscript from me.

I clutched it tighter. "No, it's all right. I'll keep this."

Jason looked at me strangely. "What happened?"

I find even the idea of discussing my spells with anyone very disturbing, I think because I don't understand them well myself. Of course, the fact that anyone I told would think I was loony tunes may have influenced me. I leaned heavily on Jason, putting my lips close to his ear. "Can I tell you later? I don't want to talk about it here." I wrinkled my nose and said, "Female stuff," which was enough to make him acquiesce in a flash.

Mr. Gerster tentatively eased closer to me. Instead of the hard-driving, glamorous newsman of legend, he is a quiet, dry wisp of a man, pressing sixty, who wears suspenders because he has no hips on which to hang his trousers. He looks eternally anxious and surprised because he ties his bow tie too tight around his neck. He stopped beside me. "Uhm, Stella…"

"Yes?"

"Maybe you need the afternoon off. You can actually work from home, you know."

I looked up at him, focusing my darkened and forceful eyebrows at him. "Mr. Gerster, I'll be fine. What would make me feel better is an appointment with you."

He hates appointments in his office with me and will do nearly anything to avoid them. I figured I'd better strike while he was in sight. "I'll see you at two in your office. Thanks so much for asking me." And I'll have our eyes on the same level, or mine higher than yours, I thought.

"Oh, er, fine." He turned and fled.

I glanced down at the manuscript and saw again the pink telephone message caught under the rubber band. For Jason. I didn't recognize the name of the caller, but I noted the area code, 212. New York City.

He also saw it. "Here, I'll take that," he said and took the message, reading it with exaggerated interest. Then he whistled and reread it.

"What's so great about the message?" I asked.

"You wouldn't be interested," he said, waving it in the air. The veiled look in his eyes made a liar of him.

"I tell you when I get a story. In fact, I always do."

"You *almost* always do."

"So how long are you going to wait before you call back?"

He folded the message and slipped it back into his breast pocket. "No hurry." He leaned over, his crispy masculine smell wrapping around me. "Hey, Stella with the dark brown eyebrows," he said and touched my cheek. "Looks to me like you're up to something."

I smiled and kissed him. "It's my mysterious gypsy look. Forceful."

"Please don't be mysterious. You don't need any look. You're wonderful just as you are. I've got a proposition for you. Dinner, movie, and a good time afterward, tonight. My treat."

I shook my head. "I've got another rehearsal tonight."

He straightened and ran his hand through his hair. "When am I supposed to see you? This is not good. It's trouble, I know it." He glanced impatiently around. "Gerster won't put up with you getting into trouble."

"Well, there's no reason for him to worry. There won't be any trouble. And you know he can't fire Zelda; the place would crumble in a week without her."

Jason pulled his chair over and took my hand in his. "Stella, you wouldn't need that money if you'd move in with me."

"And then what? I'd siphon off whatever's left of your salary, and we'd both just live on love? You think that's a good way to start a relationship?"

"Stella, this is the same excuse you've used before. What's really bothering you?"

"Okay, here it is. One, I'm not going to go into any relationship one down or dependent. Two, I'm barely beginning my columnist career, and it's important to me."

"And what else?"

"Nothing."

"There's more. I know it."

"All right. Three, you also are starting a career, and you need to be in a position where you can go where you need to go without worrying about anyone else."

"Translated from Stella-speak, that means you think if I get a good offer, I'm going to simply take off without worrying about anyone else?"

That was unvarnished. I swallowed and nodded. "On that order."

"Thanks for being tactful and sensitive, Stella."

"You're the one who said it."

"You agreed."

"We have such a mature relationship, Jason. It's astounding."

Jason is twenty-eight years old, a somewhat bothersome six years younger than I am. A year ago he was a green-around-the-gills reporter with no more notion of what to do with a pencil than your average Doberman pinscher, but since then he's learned very well. Under my excellent tutelage, of course.

He's the other reason the *Daily Orion*'s circulation has expanded. He can write a human interest story with the best of them and has gradually developed an inquiring mind, so the stories have a tantalizing interest line besides.

Our relationship occasionally borders on childish and competitive, but most of the time it is friendship, and all of the time it is lust. I'm in the process of trying to find out if true lust also equals true love, and I've almost decided he's really settled enough to hook up with and genuine when he says he loves me.

I picked up my considerable stack of mail and went to my desk. At the back of the ancient newsroom the early-morning sunshine streamed through the little square windowpanes, creating a perfect, peaceful golden glow, like a backdrop for a Renaissance painting. It was a soul-satisfying scene. I absolutely loved this job; if I could just earn enough money, it would be perfect.

I settled in to work on my correspondence. By eleven Jason was off on a story, while I picked up another envelope from the top of the stack and slit the envelope with a flourish, using my new letter opener with turquoise and lapis lazuli inlay on the handle—a May Day gift from Jason. It was quite sharp and a bit wicked, really a dagger, but it was Jason's gift, so I was very fond of it.

I shook out the letter, a simple sheet folded in half with block printing.

Dear Stella
See if you've ever had a problem like this one.
    Our dog sleeps in bed with my wife and me. I thought it was funny at first, but now I think I like the dog better. No kinky sex. The dog adores me and doesn't tell me I snore. My wife says this is a problem. What do you think?
    The dog and I are Leos, and she's a Libra.
                              Sam in Grand City, Colorado

Well, that was a new one. I wrote a quick answer.

Dear Sam,
    Let's cut to the quick here, Sam.
    Make a bed for the dog on the floor, and give your wife attention. If she gets her needs met, she'll sleep more heavily and not mind your snoring.
    Libras tend not to speak up directly for what they want, while Leos tend to be too proud to seek help.

This can be a combination that works well, but it can run into a lot of problems, especially in communication.

Good luck,
Stella the Stargazer

It was hard not to sign it "Arf-Arf," but I managed.

The next one was a pink, flowery envelope. For some time I've noticed people use stationery that reflects their personalities and their problems. At first glance this one looked like sweetness and light. Then I noticed the handwriting—a rough juvenile scrawl, almost masculine and curiously at odds with the dainty stationery. There was no return address, and the postmark was unclear. Not a good sign.

I slit open the envelope and pulled out the letter, written on pink onionskin paper with background daisies. Lovely, except the pen strokes had torn the paper in places. I held the paper in my fingers lightly, then smoothed it out and began to read.

Dear Stella,
I've got really bad trouble, and I don't know what to do. I've got a friend who sometimes jokes and laughs and seems real normal, but then sometimes he'll be real sour and say he might not be around much longer, like he's going to hurt himself. What should I do?

Scared.

P.S. I'm a Scorpio if that helps. I don't know what he is.

Not knowing an astrological sign was the least of Scared's problems. Because there was no return address and no name on the letter other than mine and Scared's, it would have to go into my next column, which meant I had to squeeze it in pronto. I logged the letter in my book and started a reply.

Zelda's husky voice shattered the quiet. "Stella? I've got to see you."

Zelda stood in the doorway, her great white purse swinging from her shoulder, her skirt tight above her dimpled knees.

"Zelda, I've got a critical letter to answer and get in the column before deadline. Can you wait?"

Her brows furled in an uncharacteristic frown. Usually she keeps her face free of expression to discourage wrinkles. She minced over and lowered herself into the chair opposite me. "I control the deadlines. *Listen* to me."

Zelda is so mealymouthed.

"My letter is important, Zelda."

She brushed my complaints aside with a wave of her perfectly manicured hand. "Dog hockey. *This* is important." She leaned forward. "I've got a problem."

My stomach growled. "Everyone has problems, Zelda."

She glanced around, as if making sure no one was listening. No one was there. "Have you read the script yet?"

"No, I've been working."

"Well, I did. I can't really explain it. It's just that it's all wrong…no, that's not quite true. The truth is, I've got a terrible feeling about this play. I had bad dreams about it all night. There's something really spooky about the play. Ogden said it's supposed to appeal to children on one level and adults on another, funny on the outside and dark and meaningful on the underside. But it feels like there's a threat in it."

A chill crawled down my neck. "What do you mean?"

"That Venus's-flytrap set is evil."

"Zelda, this wouldn't have anything to do with the fact that you've tried four times unsuccessfully to make the slip-cover for the thing, would it?"

"No." She smoothed her skirt. "Well, maybe."

THREE

By THE TIME two o'clock came, I was really hungry, really cranky, loaded for bear, and ready to fight. I'd worked out a game plan. I'd soften Mr. Gerster up with a request for a raise, then when he said he couldn't afford it, I'd come up with what I really wanted, syndication.

I marched myself down the dark corridor to Mr. Gerster's office, knocked, opened the door, and swept inside with all the authority I could muster, which was considerable, given that I was wearing forceful eyebrows, my power teddy, and my vivid turquoise-and-yellow shift.

Mr. Gerster blinked as though my appearance and the sudden color hurt his eyes. He reached for his eternal bow tie, one of the mannerisms he uses to reestablish his sense of security. "Stella, how nice…" He paused, then rose from his chair nervously. His bow tie bobbed again. "Zelda told me you're working a second job now. It must be tiring."

"She must have mentioned that I'm house-sitting to save money on rent. My earnings from the column barely feed Fluffy and Lips, my pet chameleons. And now that Lips is pregnant…" I let the word hang in the air.

"I see." He pursed his lips and pushed his chair farther from the desk. "So you want to talk to me about a raise."

"Mr. Gerster, I came to work here a year ago with little experience and a great deal of enthusiasm and a bank account to tide me over until I was earning enough to live on. I've amassed a sizable audience of correspondents, my column's popularity has soared, and circulation of the *Orion* is up, primarily due to my column. Not only do I think I have earned a raise and deserve it, but I want your help to syndicate the column." There. I'd said it.

"Well." He straightened his bow tie again. "I agree with most of what you've said. You've proven there are many more troubled and unusual people out there than I ever suspected, and I think you've earned a raise. My offer is ten cents a column inch, starting next month."

"Ten cents?!"

"I thought you'd be pleased your work was being recognized."

"My work is recognized each day by my correspondents; what I'm talking about is fair compensation for it. I'm not even earning benefits here. I'm the cheapest help you have, and I've increased circulation. That should be worth something."

"Actually, you've increased costs too. More paper, more ink."

"I've brought in advertising—"

"I don't think you realize, but paper is a huge expense."

"Well, it can't be that great— you only put out one edition a week, and it's small."

"Even ink is going up."

"And so is the price of crickets, eight cents a head now—"

"Maybe you should get goldfish instead."

"I've got a possible solution. Help me get syndication, and that will bring more money to us both."

"No."

I was shocked. "What?"

"I can't do that."

"Can't or won't?"

"Won't."

"Would you expand on that, please? I don't follow."

"It's more complicated than I can explain right now. Besides, syndication brings deadlines, responsibilities, demands—"

"I don't have any trouble meeting deadlines. I'm always in early with my column."

"You'd be distracted—"

"From what?"

"If you feel you absolutely must have more money, I'll increase your raise to fifteen cents a column inch."

"Make it a dollar a column inch."

He shook his head. "I can't do it."

"Fifteen cents, even a dollar, won't cover the cost of crickets for Fluffy and Lips for two weeks. Crickets cost eight cents each. I'd make more money raising insects! Maybe a worm farm with bugs on the side. I'll have to leave."

"You have an obligation to give a month's notice. This is a professional-level position."

"I'd say it was a horizontal position, as in foot wipe!"

He blanched. He must know of another kind of wipe. "That's four more columns you owe me before you leave."

"Fine." I walked to the door, fuming, and jerked it open. I turned back to him, slowly, for dramatic emphasis. "You know, Mr. Gerster, if you had any foresight at all, this paper would have a chance. There's only one reason why it's grinding to a low end here, and that's because you're living in some kind of distant past. For whatever reason, you're stuck about twenty years ago. If you could bring yourself to move into the present day and deal with reality as it really is, you could put out a small neighborhood newspaper with real news and some relevance to people today. As it is now, it's a blooming wonder this paper grinds out once a week and not once a year!"

He was rigid at his desk, bow tie slightly crooked, lips

so thin I couldn't see them, completely emotionless. "Is that all?"

"Probably not. But it's enough for now."

It would have felt so good to slam the door, but leaving it open would disturb him more, so I left it wide and swept out and down the hallway.

Zelda's jaw hung somewhere around her lap.

"You can turn off the intercom now, Zelda."

"Did you mean to do that?"

"No. Yes. I don't know." I marched past her to the newsroom, sank into my chair, put my head in my hands, and closed my eyes. I had finally done it. And I felt pretty sick. Where was the triumph I should have felt for saying what I thought? My eyes stung, and my breath was hard to draw. There was a lump in my throat. I had just quit the job I loved most of all. Now what?

I opened my eyes and looked around. Afternoon sun was drenching the room. It was hot. Messy. Not even particularly clean. The two unused desks were stacked with back issues of the *Orion,* clippings, stuff we thought we might want to keep and probably would never use again. The overhead lights were dingy, bug-filled, and ancient. Not even up to code. I blinked hard to control my tears. It was all old, tired, and out of date. And I loved every square inch of it and all it represented. Independence. Individuality. Inefficiency.

A great big fat tear slid down my cheek in a cold liquid trail.

I had had run-ins with Mr. Gerster several times, but we had always managed to avoid any words that would be impossible to take back. That meant I'd tiptoed around what I really thought many times. However, I'd kept my job.

Today I'd gone in there cranky, but planning to be so controlled and articulate, and all I'd done was impulsively blurt out words that would be impossible to take back. My cheeks were wet with sorrow. Whatever happened next, this was a milestone passed, and it felt very irreversible.

Jason had the phone stuck to his ear, his gaze on his desk pad, writing furiously. Wasn't that handy, just when I needed to talk to him.

I picked up the phone and dialed that oh so familiar number. I was greeted with a recording. "We're not home right now, but if you'd like to leave a message, we'll get back to you as soon as we can. If this is my daughter Janie, please come visit, we've forgotten what you look like. There's Jell-O in the fridge. Love, Mom."

Mom loves me. She still calls me Jane, the name she and Dad bestowed on me at birth. Now my eyes filled with tears of love, humiliation, self-pity, and hunger. It had been a long time since Jell-O made my mouth water. I decided to get out of there before Jason finished his phone call. I wasn't ready to talk about this after all.

I shoved a stack of unopened envelopes into my purse, swigged down the last of my coffee, cold, wiped out the cup, and was nearly out of the room when he whooped and called out to me.

"Stella, guess what that was! I got an offer—from New York City. The Big Time wants Jason."

I turned, stunned, and watched him climb onto his desk.

"Me, Jason. You, Jane. We go to New York." He beat his chest and whooped again.

"You got a call from a New York paper offering a job?"

He beamed. "Well, shucks, ma'am. Just little old me. Not much. They want me to apply for an opening as a reporter." He laughed and climbed down. "Now what do you think of your old hometown boy?"

"It's a joke."

He stopped, shook his head, and grinned. "Not a joke, Stella. It happened."

I was stunned. Was this what the trance was about—
Jason, his job offer, my job loss?

It was a struggle to smile over the yawning pit in my
stomach, the buzz of disbelief in my head. I love him, but
I'm not blind. He's good, but to get an offer from NYC? It
didn't make sense. "How did they hear about you way out
here?"

"They read one of my stories in the *Post.*"

Jason occasionally sold a feature to the *Denver Post,* a
legitimate daily that prints real news, as opposed to the
Orion, which puts out news Mr. Gerster would like to read.
"Jason, are you sure it's legit?"

"I called them, area code two-one-two. That's the big
city, kid. A million stories, and they want me to write them.
I have to apply, of course."

"They called you to come and apply for a job on their
paper? Jason, there are hundreds of good reporters already
in New York; why would they call you?"

"Could you be jealous? Are you sure you aren't envious
because you thought you'd get syndication?"

Anger swept over me. "Do you pride yourself on under-
handed listening in on my private conversations with Gerster, or is it a genetic flaw?"

"You *are* jealous, because I got an invitation to apply."

"Yeah, well, I'm not jealous, I'm incredulous. And you
haven't got the job yet."

I raced through the front office, where Zelda was also on
the phone. Listening in, I might add. She called after me.

"Don't forget rehearsal tonight."

How could I? Suddenly the theater job was much more
important. Besides one more measly *Orion* paycheck, it was
my only income. One way or another, I needed to keep it.

And given how difficult Barbara was, I'd better get cash in advance.

It occurred to me that the word *hearse* lay in the middle of *rehearsal*.

FOUR

I WENT BY MOM'S, picked up the Jell-O, left her a brief note, and then went home. Even my house-sitting would be over by the end of May, and then I'd be homeless to boot. Instead of me getting syndication, Jason got an offer from New York, and instead of me getting a raise, I'd resigned.

I wanted loving arms around me, a comforting shoulder to cry on, and lots of sympathy. I wailed to Fluffy and Lips. Lips crawled under a leaf. Fluffy tried to help me. He breathed heavily and blinked several times. Nowhere near the comfort I wanted. Lizards don't really emote all that much.

Finally I settled down and read the script for the play. It was titled *The Garden of Iden.*

After my first read-through I closed the thing and placed it dead center on the kitchen table. A kind of offering to the gods that be. We were going to need it.

At best it was a fractured allegory of the Garden of Eden story, featuring a misunderstood, neurotic snake who leads an ambitious young woman, Eve, to fatally overdose on a drug-poisoned apple and drives her weak lover, Adam, to pay for his sins by leaping into the mouth of a Venus's-flytrap. To enliven the action there are two singing mushrooms (read evil drugs) who also provide several dream-sequence banquets. Not quite Pulitzer prize material. Fluffy put his head under the log.

This was my dilemma. Two people, one snake, two singing mushrooms, two interminable acts, and lots of bathos. I couldn't tell whether this play would be an allegorical masterpiece, a pleasant child's play, or a disaster. There was as much chance of it folding as succeeding. If it didn't go well, it would take a miracle just to keep the audience in their seats through the performance. I decided it was essential to get my pay as soon as possible.

I darkened my eyebrows even more, spritzed up my hair a bit, then donned a scarlet bra and panties and a pair of purple crinkle-cloth trousers. Finally, I put on an almost matching multicolored top and jacket. It was a little on the psycho blue/purple side of sanity, but that's where I was at the moment, and it sure suited the play to a T. It was plain and simple use of color to make me look more forceful so I could intimidate Barbara.

Fluffy was breathing hard and flapping his jaws at me. He doesn't like the color purple much, but he does love to travel. He wanted to go with me. Evidently being the father of an egg didn't mean he had to stay home nights. I put him into his magenta harness so he wouldn't get lost and pinned his harness to my jacket. He's good company, and besides, I was still troubled by the little spell I'd had that morning.

THE MAGIC CIRCLE Theater was located in a renovated theater on Sante Fe Drive. This area is made of two neighborhoods, Baker and Lincoln Park, distinct from each other but sharing history.

These were among the original neighborhoods of nineteenth-century Denver, but by the 1960s both time and poverty had eroded them, leaving the large houses subdivided into tiny apartments and the once comfortable brick homes overrun with woodbine. The little bungalows burst at the seams, and plastic flowers grew in the dust.

In the last fifteen years, however, Baker and Lincoln Park had caught restoration fever. Many of the cottages were brightened with new paint, the woodbine cut back. Slowly the subdivided homes had been restored to gracious living behind strong new security doors. They were jumbled together with the tumbledown, time-scarred elements that stubbornly held out behind weed-filled yards and dingy windows.

The sun was rapidly sinking into a thick bank of clouds glowering from the tops of the Rockies. I drove down Inca Street, where the charm of color, a hint of Mexico, and a lot of energy have combined to make headway against the dust of neglect, then turned west to Sante Fe Drive, with its pink adobe facades and neo-quaint streetlights, only one of which was shot out.

The Magic Circle Theater is an old brick theater around Tenth Avenue with oak half-barrel planters holding marigolds, petunias, and geraniums in an attempt to soften the iron grillwork of the security door and barred windows. Unfortunately the eight-foot, industrial-strength Cyclone fence totally negated the effect of the flowers.

I pulled in, parked, got out, and locked my car, inhaling the scents of automobile exhaust, dust, and the sweet smell of a linden tree mingled with cumin and chilies from the restaurant across the street.

Threading my way between two other cars, I reached the stage door, propped open with a broken brick. Emblazoned across the center of the door was graffiti suggesting an impossible, unpleasant anatomical act. Fingerprints darkened the door handle. I slipped inside, accidentally bumping the brick. The door slammed shut behind me, plunging me into darkness. The smell of wood, paint, ether, and dust filled my nostrils.

Although I'd been here for two rehearsals already, I was still momentarily confused by the dark and unsure where to go. I remembered somewhere to my left there was a steep stairway leading to the basement storerooms and Zelda's sewing empire and costume racks.

I edged backward until I could feel the door and shoved it open, propping it with the brick. The fresh air was as welcome as the light.

For a long moment I considered giving up on the whole thing; then I reminded myself of the four hundred very necessary dollars and picked my way toward a hum of voices.

I was opposite Adrian Foster's workshop. Adrian not only was the leading man in most of their productions, he designed and built the sets. I glanced in and saw him with Linc, Judd, and Phillip. Phillip looked up at that moment, and a huge smile lit his face. "Yo, Stella!" He bounded up to me and gave me a big hug. He looked at my outfit, shaking his head. "Great threads. You're looking real cool tonight. Awesome eyebrows. Tattoos?"

I pulled away, laughing. He was so like a half-grown puppy, tall and lanky with the awkwardness of recent, rapid growth. I knew he wanted something. "Not tattoos, pencil. What are you guys up to?"

"Working with Adrian on the coolest smoke effects." The slightest shadow flitted across his face. "You got the new script, right?"

I nodded, not sure what to say. His mother had written the thing, after all. I didn't know what his take on it would be.

He glanced nervously around, as if he was checking to make sure he wouldn't be overheard. "It's a...different, isn't it?"

"I figure it's an allegory."

"Yeah, that's exactly what it is. Anyway—" He relaxed then and grinned. "I didn't want you to get...uh...discouraged and leave. We"—he gestured toward Linc and Judd—"we think you're doing a great job." He moved a little closer. "My mom's a little temperamental, you know, but she doesn't really mean it."

I nodded and smiled. He was clearly trying so hard to make me feel welcome. "I'm not leaving, Phillip."

"Oh, good," he said and smiled shyly. "You're okay. Cool eyebrows."

How could I not love him? I waved at him and went on, coming out in the wings of the stage.

Zelda stood at the edge of the stage apron, speaking to Ogden Bane, seated in the fifth row. "She said she'd be here. I'm sure she's on her way."

"Zelda?"

She glanced at me. Momentary relief flooded her face, then disbelief spread across it. "Stella! What happened to your hair? And your eyebrows—" Then she gaped at my electric green paisley harem pants. "You look like a traveling circus."

"What? I should shroud myself in black?"

She hesitated, staring at me. "You mean, you did this to yourself on purpose?"

"It's theater, Zelda. I'm dramatic."

A bellow rose from the fifth row. "Zelda, where is she?"

"She's here," Zelda called over her shoulder. She grabbed my arm, her fingers digging into my skin, and growled, "You're late, so go talk to the man. I don't know what's wrong. He's got a wad in his panties." She started to say more, then changed her mind and pointed at a set of three steps. "Never mind, get down there."

Ogden Bane unfolded himself from his too-small seat, rising to over six feet tall, a good five inches taller than I. He wore jeans and a dark T-shirt that emphasized his muscular shoulders. He looked like the brooding hero of a gothic romance with his dark hair and widow's peak, but up close he was every one of his forty-plus years and then some. He had deep-set dark eyes that flickered impatiently in my direction. They widened when he saw me advancing. "And tonight you are…Stella, the swami?"

Sarcasm, the weapon of the weak intellect. Instantly pissed off, I responded, "I'm your muscle."

The corner of his mouth twitched. His gaze traveled again over my clothes, my hair, my forceful eyebrows. "You look more like a fortune-teller than an assistant director. But so long as you keep Barbara off Phillip's back and out of my hair, I don't care if you dress like a woolly mammoth."

"I need to talk to you about payment—"

He jerked a thumb toward the balcony office. "Catch Rachel Vincent later. She'll get you set up on payroll. You brought your script, didn't you?"

I held it up. "Have you read it through?"

"Every word."

I read the title, *The Garden of Iden*. I laughed. "That's quite a typo in the title."

His aesthetic face compressed into an ice sculpture. "That's not a typo."

"Oh." A niggle of nervousness crept across my chest. "Ah, how would you describe this play? What exactly is the effect you're planning on?"

The vertical line in his cheek that ran to the corner of his mouth suddenly deepened, and his lips pressed together, as though he suspected I was being sarcastic. I hurried to reassure him. "I, uh, I just want to be in sync with your artistic interpretation."

"My 'artistic interpretation'?" His eyebrows rose, and he drew in a deep breath. "This play is the work of Satan, and my interpretation is that we are in hell."

FIVE

AT THE FIRST BREAK I made my way up the side to the balcony office and tapped on the door. A second, louder knock, and the door swung open. I think I expected another charismatic type, with a personality at least as large as a room.

Rachel Vincent was a small woman with quiet hair, a patient air, and beige clothes that drained the color from her face and her slightly protuberant, nearsighted eyes. She had a plain mouth, unadorned with color. Color would have helped. I guessed her age at very early forties and clinging, but not well.

"We're not open." She squinted at me. Her eyes traveled over my clothing, as though she was unaccustomed to bright colors. "I'm sorry, I didn't recognize you…er, Stella. Come in. Ogden said you'd be by."

I smiled, wondered briefly when Ogden had talked to her, and stepped in, noticing the extreme tidiness of the place. Rachel moved quickly to a small desk, picked up a stapled set of forms, and turned slowly to me. "You know this is a one-time-only job. It doesn't carry benefits or any guarantee of future employment."

I nodded. "I know."

She handed the papers to me. "I just wanted to make sure you knew. You need to fill these out. Sign and date at the bottom of both pages." She looked at me, blinking rapidly for a moment, then asked kindly, "Do you need a pen?"

I glanced around at the other, larger desk. "No. Maybe I can just use the desk here and fill them out right away?"

Concern shaped her face into a mixture of anxiety and irritation. "That's Lawrence's desk. I—"

"Lawrence isn't using it just now." I sat down, hauled out a pen, and started filling in blanks, ignoring her fussing. The forms were simply an emergency contact form and a tax-withholding form. I finished them in minutes. "Here are the forms, I finished them. I need to be paid cash in advance."

"Well, we don't do it that way," Rachel hedged. "I can't do it. Barbara has to approve each check. And this is a very difficult time for her—"

A deep voice boomed out behind me. "Maybe we can compromise."

I turned and recognized Lawrence Steadman, a large, broad man with grizzled hair, mustache, trimmed beard, a florid face, and appraising eyes that seemed to be tired, maybe a little defeated. Rachel hurriedly introduced us.

Lawrence smiled. "Phillip's been talking about you. Seems he thinks you're all right. Quite a compliment from a kid who basically thinks anyone over twenty-one is a moron." He looked sharply at me. "Tell you what. I'll give you one hundred tonight, two hundred next Friday, and the rest closing night—on condition that you keep Barbara happy and Phillip in the play."

"Thanks."

He held out his hand. "Glad you're here. This play is Barbara's baby. She wrote it, you know. Here, see this?" He turned and pulled a cord, opening the drapes over one-way windows. We could see the whole stage and part of the seating area. Meredith was seated on a cabbage-shaped bench, hunched over her script with Phillip next to her, cueing her, a look of adolescent adoration on his face. Meredith had another conquest.

Phillip, tall, thin as a rail, and awkward when he wasn't acting, was transformed onstage into a confident, even masterful actor. There was no doubt in my mind that he was a real talent. He had won my heart the first rehearsal by standing up for me when Barbara lit into me. He hadn't needed to, but it was very endearing. A few more years, and he'd fill out and look almost as good as Jason.

Lawrence pointed to the front rows of theater seats. "Have you met Cammie Dinkum, our stage manager?"

"Oh, yes." I looked down where Cammie, her blond hair caught in a bunch at the back of her neck, was talking to Ogden and gesturing emphatically at the back of the stage. "I met her the first night of rehearsal. She told me to stay out of her office and keep my hands off her sets, and we'd be friends for life."

Lawrence laughed. "That's our Cammie. One hundred pounds of pure spitting wildcat. But she's real good at managing the stage."

She was real good at fighting with Barbara, too, I thought, but I didn't say anything. I'd already said too much today.

Cammie had turned and was pointing to the back of the stage. A large set that looked like the tree from *Swiss Family Robinson* had been moved to the right of the rear stage. Zelda and Adrian Foster, the leading man and set builder, were attaching two huge wire leaves to the tree trunk. When they finished, it looked like a giant clam on a stalk. Then they fitted a green gauze cover over the leaves.

Lawrence was fascinated too. "Here, let's put on the sound." He flipped a switch on the wall next to the windows.

Zelda's voice boomed into the room as though we were only inches from her. "Jump into the damn thing, Adrian, let's see if it works."

He jumped. The leaves closed like a giant clam on a stalk eating a man. We could see him perfectly in silhouette. Zelda jammed her fists on her hips. "It works, but it still looks like a big moss-covered clam, Adrian."

They changed places. Adrian considered it. "If we put a couple more leaves above and cover the trunk, it'll be perfect. It's great." It wasn't perfect, but it might work if the audience were hallucinating.

Lawrence shook his head. "Impressive! I don't see how they can be so creative." I was impressed he kept a straight face; mine was nearly paralyzed, I was working so hard to keep from laughing. Clearly, he was a master of euphemism.

Lawrence scanned the stage. "Ah, there's Barbara!" He pointed to the wings. I couldn't tell whether he was relieved or anxious. I suspected he was as anxious and nervous as the rest of us whenever she was around.

In truth, most of the time Barbara was lovely and kind and generous, but she had such wild mood swings we all lived in fear of her. In an instant her moods could escalate into a rage that she could barely contain. It was astounding. She may once have been a beauty— may still have been one—but I had stopped being able to appreciate it.

Tonight Barbara was dressed in a high-necked, bat-wing gold-and-black blouse over pencil-slim tights. She was poised in the wings, with the intensity of a cat stalking a miller moth.

Lawrence pointed to Barbara. "Look at her. She's marvelous." He followed her progress across the stage to Meredith, seated on the cabbage-leaf bench, practicing her lines.

"She designed this setup, you know. It's perfect. The director can sit up here and follow everything perfectly—"

I translated that to mean she could be kept out of the way.

"—it can be used for recording, everything. All her idea. She plans to use it as a teaching theater next year."

"Oh?"

He nodded confirmation. "Linc and Judd are her first students."

"I haven't actually met Linc and Judd yet."

"Oh?" He shifted uneasily. "Well, they're Phillip's friends, but they've been in a little trouble, and Barbara and I have sort of taken them under our wing. Really it's Barbara who's done it. I don't seem to be able to talk to them the same way." He dropped his head. "I seem to have lost touch with Phillip, I don't know why. We used to be great friends."

Barbara's voice boomed into the room. "Meredith, repeat that, but with feeling this time. You've got to emote. Put yourself in Eve's place. Understand her pain...."

Lawrence flipped the switch off. I wondered if he was afraid she was going to rip into Meredith and he didn't want to hear it—or he didn't want me to. He cleared his throat noisily. "Barbara wanted to play Eve, you know. Would have, too, but Phillip said he wouldn't be in it if she was Eve. They're having a bit of trouble, but that will get better." His voice rose a bit at the end, inviting me to agree with him. I didn't.

He patted my shoulder heavily. "So she's not in this one. It's too much, you know, when you've written it, to be in it as well. It would tear her up. Couldn't let her do it. Glad you're here. This is going to be the best production yet. Glad you're aboard."

If he repeated "Glad you're here" one more time, I'd know for sure the play was even worse than I suspected. Lawrence grabbed my hand again, pumping it a bit too familiarly. "A week from tonight. That'll give you a chance to show your stuff. Then I'll get you the cash."

Rachel blinked rapidly and put a restraining hand on Lawrence's arm. "Don't you think you should run that past Barbara?"

"Oh, no. She's got so much on her mind, what with her projects, the play, Phillip's performance. It'd only distract her. Can't have that now, can we?"

Feeling a bit sorry for him, I fished for something nice to say. "Meredith is very excited to be in the play. I think she'll do well. We're going to go over blocking and lines before rehearsal starts again." I glanced at my watch. "Right now, in fact. I'd better be going."

Rachel's lips twitched in an imitation smile. I thanked Lawrence, thanked Rachel, and thanked my guardian angel, Don Bosco. Money… food…

MEREDITH AND I were onstage, and for the twenty-seventh time she repeated the line, "If I don't get the part, I'll just kill myself." Not particularly great dialogue.

Barbara's clear, ringing voice cut through the air. "I expect perfection, and this is trash."

Meredith and I looked at each other in alarm. Meredith's eyes were wide, even scared. I turned.

"Meredith, you're going to have to work harder at this. You were cast because of your promise and your looks, but it's going to take more than that. This is an important and meaningful play. It has to be perfect. You can't stumble through this like some gawkish old maid. It takes sensitivity and passion."

I thought Meredith was going to show her passion, so I rose and tried to step between them.

Before anything went further, Adrian called out, "Barbara, look here!" He appeared from stage left, holding out a length of gold-colored drapery rope. I figured he was distracting her. "Isn't this the cord you wanted?"

"What?" She whirled around, barely controlled. "Yes, that's it."

Adrian came close, put a hand on her shoulder. "You were right. It'll be perfect for the Venus's-flytrap."

She was distracted, and flattered. I realized she loved being told she was right.

"Where'd you find it?"

"In the basement prop room." He turned to me and dropped the gold rope in my hands. "Stella, please set up a prop table stage left behind the legs there." He pointed. "Against the wall will be fine." He smiled and made a tiny wink at me. "Come on, Barbara, I've got something to show you in the shop. Zelda's working her fingers to the bone for you."

His arm lightly and tenderly encircled her shoulders. She frowned for a moment, then miraculously the frown melted away, and she allowed him to lead her into his shop area at the side of the building, her head resting so naturally against his shoulder. Now, how did he manage that?

Meredith turned to me. "What do you say, shall we kill her now?"

THE NEXT DAY, Saturday, Jason flew to New York, promising to call as soon as he knew anything. I didn't hear a word until he called Monday night. I had barely stepped inside from a grueling rehearsal when the phone rang.

"Stella, you won't believe. It's amazing. I'd forgotten how exciting New York is."

"Have you seen your father?"

I heard a sharp intake of breath.

"Jason, have you even called him?"

I could hear him breathing, soft little puffs into the phone. When he finally spoke, his voice was gruff. "No. He'd do something to interfere and I'd never know whether I got the job on my own, or he wired it for me. This is something I have to do myself."

"You need to bridge that rift, Jason—"

He interrupted. "Have you made up with Gerster?"

Stalemate.

"Why don't we talk about the play?" For half an hour I told him how the play wasn't going.

"Barbara alternates between being a screaming witch and an angel. Lawrence tiptoes around wringing his hands. Rachel hides out in the box office, and Phillip slouches around with his hair in his eyes, avoiding contact with both of his parents and disappearing whenever Barbara has a fit."

"Where does he go?"

"Out the back door. I think he's got a refuge out there where he can smoke and hang out with Linc and Judd. Whenever they return, I smell tobacco and sometimes pot on them."

"So, are you going to quit?"

"I can't do that. But I've got a mantra to help. Pork chop. I just repeat it to myself when she starts in."

"So long as you don't say it out loud. If you do, Barbara will think you're calling her names." I missed the humor in that completely, but he practically guffawed at the thought. When he finally sobered, he asked, "Are you sure this job is worth it?"

"Yeah. If I can keep peace and keep Phillip in the play until Friday night, I get two hundred bucks. If we're all still alive on closing night, I get the rest."

And then we talked about more pleasant things.

SIX

BY THE NEXT WEDNESDAY, Meredith had developed a twitch on the left side of her face whenever Barbara's voice rang out from the box office, and by Thursday I had used the pork chop mantra at least a hundred times. And I had become a veritable snake charmer, trying to humor Barbara. Jason was still enthralled with New York City.

The only really good thing was that Fluffy and Lips's lizard egg was still lodged in the Swedish ivy and hadn't been eaten by the crickets. I tried without success to figure out when the egg might hatch and bought a book of names and started trying to find a suitable one. The prospect of birthing a lizard was daunting, but a lot more pleasant than contemplating the play or unemployment.

Friday evening, as I was locking my car, Lawrence drove into the parking lot. His car had barely stopped when Phillip exploded from the vehicle and raced inside. Barbara raced after him. It looked like the tail end of another family disagreement. Lawrence dragged himself out of the driver's seat, waving to me to wait up, then walked toward me with all the enthusiasm of a man going to the gallows. "Stella, I haven't forgotten your money, but I didn't get a chance to stop at the bank today, so I'll pick it up tonight after I drop Linc and Judd off at home. I always give them a ride to make sure they get there, if you know what I mean."

I wasn't sure, but I thought I knew what he meant. Linc and Judd had a real talent for trouble. They were like the Three Musketeers, or maybe it was the Three Fates, I wasn't sure. They were charming little time bombs, obviously just this side of the law, but their scenes would probably steal the show. I glanced around. "Are they here already?"

He nodded. "Adrian is showing them some of the special effects, smoke and fog and some of that stuff."

It occurred to me that the next headline we'd read would be, Juveniles Rob Bank Using Smoke Bomb for Weapon. "You think that's wise?"

He shrugged. "Adrian's pretty good with kids. He's picked up the pieces after Barbara's projects before."

"Lucky for Barbara."

Lawrence stopped for a moment. "I know it's been a tough week, and I want to thank you, Stella, for the job you're doing. I know it isn't easy. Zelda said you were good, and she was right, you are. And Phillip thinks you are top-notch. Talks about you all the time."

I closed my lips. Compliments make it hard to complain. I think he knew that. So I smiled, called myself a flipping chicken, and meekly said thanks, glad to escape.

If Barbara hadn't been so changeable and difficult, I think I'd have been totally in love with the theater. As it was, I loved the smell of the paint and the fragrance of the sawed pine Adrian used for the sets. Even the sharp stench of ether that he used as a solvent was growing on me. At least he said it was a glue solvent. He was so patient with Barbara, I'd wondered if he was actually zoning out on it.

Zelda had finally finished the Venus's-flytrap. It was a set to die for. Unbelievably ingenious. The old tree trunk was green now, and while the leaves still looked a little like a clam shell, Adrian had added long toothlike fangs to their edges, so it looked pretty darned ominous.

Anyone standing behind it appeared to be inside the plant. It was amazing. If the rest of the play was produced with as much originality, it would be a fine production. Unfortunately, it wasn't there yet, and I wasn't sure it would be.

Meredith was sitting on the stage. "Stella, help me go over my lines one more time, I just have to have them down. I can't stand it if Barbara reads me out again. It's humiliating when she starts in."

I gave her the line.

She frowned. "You aren't using the script."

"Meredith, we've been over these lines so many times—"

Ogden's voice boomed out. "Stella, get the mushrooms up here, it's time."

Phillip came onstage, smiling luminously. Smitten. "I'll go through the scenes with Meredith."

I left them and stepped backstage to look for the boys. Linc and Judd were in the shop, huddled with Adrian. Linc was maybe five and a half feet tall, fifteen, and had a mop of blond hair, some of which was twisted into dreadlocks. Most of the time he was as solemn and blank-faced as a stone, but when he smiled his features would reorganize in a slow, ironic shift to a very mischievous grin.

He held a little bag of chips in one hand and a travel-size can of hair spray in his left. "Look, man, this is the way to do it. You want sudden, awesome flames, we can do it. Show 'em, Judd." He tossed the hair spray to Judd.

Judd grinned and caught it with a flick of the wrist. He was small, wiry, and dark-haired, with the kind of eyes that instantly tell you you're never going to know all that goes on in his mind, and when you realize it, you feel relieved.

He flipped the hair spray can in the air and caught it with a flourish. "Lay your eyes on this, man." He sprayed with his right hand, flicked the lighter with his left. A bright streak of flame shot out. It could have been a fire-breathing dragon.

He laughed, delighted with my stunned reaction. "Here, look at this!" He picked up a packet of nondairy creamer, ripped it open, and sprinkled it on the lighter flame. A column of fire.

"Stop!" Adrian shouted. "Enough! You'll set off the sprinklers and have the whole damn fire department down here!"

I craned my neck. Sure enough, there were nice new sprinklers overhead.

Adrian, looking a little green, fanned the air to disperse the smoke. "That's not quite the effect I was looking for, but thanks, guys. Where'd you learn that?"

Linc rubbed his nose, a gesture I associate with diluting the truth. "Oh, around. From some of the dudes on the street, you know."

Judd, ever behind him in every way, nodded, a grin spreading across his wide, freckled face. "Yeah, we got a few more if you need 'em." He held out a cigarette that looked as if it had been emptied and then refilled. "Smoke?"

I swallowed. "Put your smokes away. Time to rehearse. You two are on."

Linc entered first, and Judd followed, both in their costumes. Zelda had made them into morel mushrooms, with huge spongelike tops and only their legs in flesh-colored tights visible beneath the costume. They were supposed to do a little bobbing and weaving, while humming tunelessly.

They entered simultaneously with a little soft shoe and sang a couple of ditties, now curiously altered, that I thought I recognized from my mother.

"Oh, I'm a villain, a dirty, dirty villain,
I put poison in my momma's shredded wheat.
I put the smudgeon on the family scudgeon,
Meat, *snort, snort*, raw meat!

"Carry on the carrion, oh carry on the carrion.
Carry on the carrion and let's begin the feast.
Ham bone is sweet, chicken is good,
Possum meat is mighty mighty fine, don't ya know,
But give me, oh give me, I really wish you would
A little bit of very rotten meat
Oh, carry on the carrion and let's begin the feast."

They followed that with a chorus of Barbara's Druggie Duet, sung in chipmunk voices:

"We are the druggie duet. We are Mary and Jane,
We'll ease your pain, see you never attain,
We'll blow your wits and your brain
We are Mary and Jane.
Oh, yeah! We are Mary 'n' Jane,
We'll lead you down the lane,
We'll promise you gold, give you mold
Lead your son to ruin
Your daughter to slaughter,
Oh, we are the promise twins,
We are the druggie duet. We are Mary and Jane."

I couldn't keep a straight face. Ogden's head dropped to his chest, his hand over his eyes. I waited for a shriek from Barbara. Nothing.

The mushrooms would steal the show. So far tonight, rehearsal had gone without a single interruption from Barbara. Too good to be true.

Adrian was congratulating the boys on their routine when Lawrence strolled onto the stage, jingling his car keys. He stopped at my side. "I've got several errands tonight after I run the boys home, Stella," he said. "I'll be back later with your cash."

This time Barbara's voice carried through the auditorium on the microphone. It absolutely sliced through the good feelings and left them shattered on the floor. "What cash, Lawrence? What's this about?" In seconds she was striding down the aisle and up the steps to the backstage area. "What are you doing now?"

Lawrence turned to her, his voice soft and placating. "Now, Barbara, I'm taking the boys home, running a few errands, and I'll be back."

"What errands, Lawrence?"

"Cleaners, grocery—"

"The cleaners are closed."

"Not yet."

"What cash for Stella?"

"Now, Barbara, this is nothing you need to worry about. You've got the whole play to sweat, you don't need to add to it. Come on, boys, let's—"

"Lawrence. Tell me what the cash is for."

"Barbara, it's Stella's pay. I forgot to go to the bank, so I'm going by the ATM for it."

Barbara flushed, her eyes narrow and angry. "Damn it, Lawrence. You don't have the right to be throwing my money around. Who pays the bills here, anyway?"

Onstage, Phillip jumped up from the cabbage-leaf bench. "Tell her to shut up, Dad. Just once, tell her."

Barbara spun around and advanced toward Phillip. "You've always been trouble. You think you're free and easy now, well, you're not. One word from me"—she stopped in front of him and jabbed his chest with her finger—"and you won't be going anywhere. And neither will your little friends there."

Phillip's face was pale, his arms awkward in his anger and humiliation. He glared at her, then shoved her aside and stormed offstage, calling over his shoulder, "Why don't you just die?"

SEVEN

In the silence that followed, the stage door banged shut. Barbara glared at me briefly, then turned and flounced back up the aisle to the balcony office. A loud slam resounded. A collective sigh of relief went up among us.

Linc and Judd shrugged. "Cool, man, maybe she'd like a joint."

Lawrence rubbed his forehead as though he was trying to erase what had happened. His voice was tired when he finally spoke. "She's under a lot of stress. She doesn't mean it....Oh, hell. She means it, but she's not herself right now. I don't know what's the matter, really. But I don't much care, either. Come on, boys, let's get out of here."

My sympathies at this point were entirely with Phillip. I wouldn't have blamed him one bit if he'd refused to go on with the play. Ogden called a short break and told me to start again in ten minutes. I shot out after Phillip. If he quit the play at this point, we were in trouble.

I'd noticed a set of shaky-looking steps at the back of the theater, almost a ladder, leading to the roof, and I figured Phillip, Linc, and Judd used the roof as a getaway. I climbed up carefully, gripping the rails and hoping the rungs wouldn't collapse beneath me; the top one was missing.

At the top I peeked over the wall and saw Phillip seated on the top of the facade, silhouetted against the western sky, his head resting on his knee. For a moment I caught my breath, wondering if he was poised to sail off into space, but then I saw the glow of a cigarette and decided he was just smoking.

"Hey, Phillip." I stepped over the wall onto the roof and walked to the front of the building. He turned his head and the light fell across his face, accentuating his cheekbones and shading his eyes. A sense of pervasive loneliness surrounded him. His face looked gaunt and hollow, like a tragedy mask. I blinked. The image was gone, but I was very cold. It had been a bit too real for comfort. Beyond the usual adolescent agony, this was a dark presence that peeked out every so often, giving a glimpse of a very complicated young man.

I sat down on a crate and leaned against the side wall, facing him. "Everybody's getting pretty tense now. I guess it's all part of getting the production ready."

He looked skeptically at me. "You mean, Barbara is getting even more bitchy than usual. She's the worst. I'm not going to be in this damned play. It's stupid."

"Sometimes when things hurt, it's easier for us to deal with them by getting mad instead of sad."

His face twisted with emotion. "Yeah, well...."

It was incredibly painful watching him struggle with his feelings. He was trying so hard to be tough.

"Phillip, the play means too much to her. And she's real worried about how Meredith will do."

He looked at me, his eyes dark, shaded by his drawn brow. "People always make excuses for her. Dad, Rachel, Cammie, Adrian, now you."

I wasn't making much headway. I decided to back off for a moment. "How come you call your parents Lawrence and Barbara, instead of Dad and Mom?"

He sighed and tipped his head back against the rough bricks. "Parenthood hinders their lifestyle, know what I mean?"

I knew exactly what he meant, but I didn't want to say so. I figured it would only make things worse.

He continued before I had to answer. "You know what I really like? Wrestling. I made all-city finals last fall. Think she ever had time to come watch a match?" He shook his head. "I made swim team as a freshman. She said the smell of chlorine made her sick." He looked at me. "When she did show up, she'd be all dressed in some stupid outfit so everyone would stare at her."

"She's dramatic."

"Excuses." He sighed again. "You know, most of the time I don't care, but she picks on me. She wants to hurt me."

"She doesn't. Some people don't know how to show their love."

He got up and shook himself. "It's okay. It doesn't matter."

But it did. His loneliness was like a blanket wrapping him in misery. I felt like putting my arms around him and telling him he was really okay, but that would probably have sent him over the edge. I didn't know what to say to smooth it over. "Your mom wouldn't pick on you if she didn't care about you."

"Get real, Stella." He sighed. "It's okay. I've got Linc and Judd. They like me the way I am." He smiled sadly at me. "You know, I used to lie awake at night trying to find a way to please them. Trying to make myself into a copy of the kid they really wanted. Someone who was good at sports, popular. Like—" He stopped suddenly, gulping back his words. I felt a lump in my throat for him. He continued. "Like someone they'd be proud of, but I guess I wasn't good enough."

"Phillip, that's not true. They're proud of you."

He stood and stretched, appearing taller and thinner than life itself would sustain. Then he folded himself back up and settled on the rooftop, his back against the facade, and closed his eyes.

"Your folks *are* proud of you. Your dad told me the first time he met me that you had real talent."

He was silent for a long minute, then raised his head. "I wish he'd tell me."

PHILIP ENTERED ON CUE, a bit disheveled, but amazingly still able to act. It was as if he were playing himself, he was so natural.

The last scene was the one that bothered Zelda, the dramatic crux of the play. Phillip had to throw himself into the Venus's-flytrap in a symbolic suicide. It had never rehearsed well.

He stumbled over the framework, fell against it, and ended up missing the flytrap and wrapping his arms around Meredith, who burst out laughing.

"Stop!" Barbara's voice roared down, and the next moment she came flying down the aisle, her bat-wing top billowing appropriately out at the sides. She looked a whole lot more like a rabid bat than a pork chop, but I repeated it to myself anyway. *Pork chop, pork chop.*

Ogden Bane snapped his pencil in two and snarled at me. "Stop her, dammit, before she eats that kid alive. That's what you're here for."

I jumped forward to block her while she was still in the aisle. "Barbara, stop. You can't do this." She stiff-armed me, and I fell back into the seat, muttering, "Pork chop, pork chop."

By the time I regained my footing and ran after her, she was already onstage, shouting. "You can't do this! It's terrible. You're terrible." She crossed the stage, reaching for Meredith.

Phillip protectively flung out an arm, catching Barbara's

shoulder, spinning her away. Ahead of me, Cammie burst onto the stage, going to his side. "Oh, Phillip—"

Barbara grabbed his arm. "You're in such trouble—"

Cammie whirled on Barbara. "Stop it, stop picking on him. He's fine. If I were him, I'd have smacked you by now."

Barbara leaned into her face. "Well, you aren't him, you're a stagehand."

Phillip pulled Barbara away from Cammie. "Don't yell at her."

I stepped between everyone and was horrified to hear myself say, "Pork chop, stop this right now. Pork chop."

Barbara aimed a fist straight at my face. I ducked as soon as I saw her shoulder move. Her hand breezed by my cheek. Phillip grabbed her wrist and twisted it into an arm lock, then walked her roughly offstage and up against the wall, his eyes blazing with rage. He put his mouth close to her ear and said, "If you don't stop this shit, I'll kill you."

"Phillip." I touched his shoulder. "Phillip, easy."

He stared wildly into my eyes for a moment, then his eyes changed, calmed, and focused on mine. Slowly his eyes softened, and he released her. His hands were shaking. He threw himself out the stage door.

I felt a fine mist of sweat break out on my forehead. "Barbara," I shouted, "this play is never going to be produced if you keep this up. Go home. Get out of here. This is my rehearsal, and you're messing it up. GO!"

Barbara turned around, her mouth open, shocked. Her lips worked, but gradually she calmed. She jammed her hands into her pants pockets. Her eyes clouded. She slumped against the wall, suddenly defeated, tears filling her eyes, a tremor in her chin. "I can't go," she whispered. "Lawrence has the car."

It was a great act, but I wasn't going to be taken in. If

she wanted to bluff, I'd call her. "I've got a solution," I said and dragged her over to the stage door. "Walk."

I shoved her outside and pulled the door shut, automatically locking her outside.

Barbara thumped on the door, loudly at first, then politely. I opened the door. Barbara stared at me, her face calmed, her eyes seemingly rational. "Sorry. You're right. Now let me in."

"No. You can't be here. You've ruined every rehearsal we've had. If this play stinks, it's because of you."

A streak of lightning lit the sky, and the first fat drops of rain splattered on the tarmac. She bent her head, raising an arm in a futile attempt to stay dry. "I don't have my house keys, and it's going to pour. I'll catch pneumonia."

A suitable solution to the problem, I thought.

"Please let me in. I'll stay out of it. Promise."

I waited, let her get a bit wet. I wanted her to wonder just a bit whether I'd let her in or not. Then I cracked the door and peered out at her. Ozone was heavy in the air along with the smell of wet, hot tarmac. Rain began to pelt the ground. Her hair wilted, then plastered to her head. She looked pathetic.

I relented. "You can come in, but you have to stay in the back left corner. Move one step out of there and you're out of here, and I don't care if it's snowing or hailing."

Barbara slunk in and started toward the balcony office. Once she got up there, she'd be nearly impossible to control. She could hear everything, yell through the microphone, and would be virtually impossible to remove. "Hold it, I said the left back corner offstage. You can sit on the Venus's-flytrap or the prop table. Nowhere else." At least from there it was reasonably easy to push her across the stage and out the door.

She started sullenly across the stage.

"Barbara!" She looked back over her shoulder. "Not one word. Not a peep. Anything you don't like, you write it down. If you make one, even one remark, I'll personally strangle you."

She actually went.

Ogden was still out, so I took over. The first run-through went amazingly well. Except for one time when Meredith made faces and complained of the smell of ether, another time when Barbara made several thumping sounds, and a third time when the overhead spot exploded, it was smooth.

After half an hour we took a brief break. Through the gauze of the leaves, I saw Barbara leaning against the trunk of the flytrap. She was so quiet I figured she'd fallen asleep. I decided not to stir her up by moving the prop into position and announced that we'd leave it offstage until the last scene.

By ten of ten, though, we had to shift the flytrap. The last scene, where Phillip throws himself into it, was always difficult, and we had to rehearse it with the set, although it meant disturbing Barbara. It had been so nice with her asleep.

I called to Adrian in the shop, "Let's set up the flytrap." I whipped along behind the backdrop. Barbara's dark head was barely visible where she was leaning against the piece. "Barbara, excuse me. Want to get off now? We've got to wheel it out. Barbara?"

There was no answer. How I hated to stir her up. If it hadn't been so important, I'd have left her alone the rest of the night. I flipped the latches off the anchors and touched her arm. "Barbara? Barbara, please move."

Her arm slipped away from me. I assumed she was moving.

I pressed the pedal releasing the brake and shoved, turning the tree slightly. As I turned the flytrap, I saw that Bar-

bara wasn't just standing; she was propped against the flytrap, her head on her chest. How could she sleep so soundly?
"Barbara!"

First she wouldn't shut up, then she wouldn't wake up.
It was too much. I grabbed her arm and shook it hard. "Barbara!" Then I saw the golden cord around her neck, holding
her in place.

EIGHT

"OH, MY GOD!"

The gold cord Adrian had found for Barbara was tied in a simple loop and hooked over the top of the Venus's-flytrap. Fatally simple.

"Adrian!" I shouted.

She was warm. I fumbled for her wrist. There was a faint, irregular pulse. We had to get her down as soon as possible.

I tried to reach up to loosen the cord, but it was too tight and too high. I grabbed her, wrapped my arms around her, and tried to lift her. She was incredibly heavy and awkward.

The rope didn't budge. She sagged against me. I nearly collapsed. I staggered back, then let her down just a bit and again felt for the rope to slide it forward. "Adrian! Somebody! Quick, help!" I could barely make a sound. It came out as a desperate croak.

I couldn't undo the knot, and Barbara was too heavy for me. I staggered and nearly fell. "Adrian! Somebody!"

I lifted her up again to take some of the weight off the cord. Even though there was little hope she was still alive, I had to try.

Meredith pushed in next to me, trying to help, but it wasn't enough. My arms and shoulders ached. My knees were shaky. I wasn't sure I could keep a grip on myself or on Barbara much longer. "Where's Adrian?"

"Here." He shoved Meredith aside. He groaned. "Oh, my God." He wrapped an arm around her waist, lifted and unlooped the rope. Together we laid her on the floor. She was blue around the lips and completely nonresponsive.

Adrian rocked back and forth over her, patting her hand. "Barby, what have you done this time?" He was near tears, loosening her blouse and patting her cheeks.

"Adrian, stop. We've got to try to pull her back." That seemed to jar him into action, and he immediately blew into her mouth. I started counting and pushing on her chest.

Meredith, face pale, shoulders shaking, started babbling, "I didn't mean it. Oh, I'm so sorry. I didn't mean it."

I figured action would give her something to do besides pitch a fit. "Meredith, call nine-one-one, get an ambulance." She ran. Zelda appeared, staring helplessly. "Zelda, stay with Meredith, we don't need another problem."

My arms were aching, and I wasn't sure how long we could keep it up. Barbara still hadn't responded. Adrian and I traded places. God forgive me, but I took the time to wipe off her lips and mouth, prayed she didn't have HIV, then blew into her mouth. "Has she done this before?" I asked between puffs.

"Rachel told me she threatened to kill herself if we didn't produce the play, but none of us took her seriously." He looked at me, helplessly. "And she was always very...dramatic. She's never really done anything, but lately when she gets upset she overreacts, sort of."

Overreacts! I thought of her tantrums, her mood swings, her incredible generosity. "Overreacts? I meant, has she tried to kill herself before?"

I shuddered. Barbara must have put her head in the loop and hanged herself. Between puffs I loosened the waist of Barbara's trousers, a remnant of some long-ago first-aid instruction. Keys clanked. I remembered her earlier plaintive whine. Were these the keys she had said she didn't have? Without hesitation I slipped my hand into her pocket and pulled them out. A triangular scrap of yellow paper came with them. They were definitely car and Kwikset house keys. So why had she lied?

I picked up the little scrap. It looked like the corner of a larger sheet that had been hastily torn away. Two pathetic words were scrawled across it. "Too much." Blinking back hot tears, I shoved the note and keys back into her pocket.

Looking up from the next puff, I saw Phillip across the stage, stricken, mouth open, face pale, and eyes huge and round. Without saying a word he crossed the stage, knelt, and touched her cheek tenderly, like a baby's caress. His voice was hoarse and shook when he spoke. "Mom?"

His whispered single word was more wrenching than any wail of grief could ever be. A lump burned in my throat, and I thought my heart would break for him. How could Barbara have even thought of leaving her child? Surely it was the cruelest thing a mother could do. What could possibly have driven her to this?

Phillip looked up into my eyes searchingly, then turned to Adrian, as if looking for answers none of us had. I don't know what he saw there, but he jerked back as though electrocuted, spun away, and ran. I wanted to race after him, but I couldn't leave Barbara. Adrian and I switched places again.

After what seemed an eternity, though it was actually closer to ten minutes, we heard the sirens of the ambulance and the police. By the time they took over, I ached all over and felt almost ill.

They found a faint heartbeat.

Adrian hugged me, and my eyes burned with tears. I've never been so relieved and happy in my life. My knees shook, and I sank onto the cabbage-leaf bench and watched as they began all the paraphernalia of resuscitation.

The police arrived and began to quietly organize everyone.

Cold shock fell over me. It wasn't merely that I'm one of those people who fall apart after everything is taken care of, it was that suicide had always been an abstract concept, safely distant. It was an event that circumscribed someone else's life in a vague and darkening way. Up close and personal it was awful. Overwhelming. Incomprehensible.

Her beautiful face was swollen and puffy. How could she do this? It was a nightmare.

Denial set in protectively. This couldn't happen. She'd never do something like this.... I don't know how long I might have remained sitting there, but a policeman shook my shoulder and brought me back to the sickening reality.

He asked me to describe the events, listened, and made notes on a little pad while another officer moved everyone else to the audience and began taking names and addresses. I must have repeated what happened four times, in detail.

As I finished the last explanation, I felt a breeze from the stage door and saw Phillip enter. Again, he stood at the side, his eyes huge and dark, his cheeks gray.

The emergency medical team put Barbara on a cot and rolled her out to the ambulance; she still wasn't breathing on her own, but she was alive. Phillip turned, followed them, and slipped back outside. As soon as the officer finished with me, I went after him.

Outside, I walked to the back of the building and made my way up the steps, clinging to the rails nervously.

"Phillip?" I called. He didn't answer.

I stepped over the guard wall and walked softly toward him. I could smell the smoke of his cigarette and realized with a slight sinking of my heart that it was a joint. Whether he got the stuff from Linc and Judd or elsewhere, it wasn't going to help. As my eyes grew accustomed to the dark, I gradually saw the dark hollows that were his eyes and the bitter twist of his mouth.

"Phillip? May I sit with you for a while?"

No answer. Figuring no answer was as good a response as I would get, I settled down across from him on a rain-dampened crate, leaning against a vent. The night air was cool and carried the scent of the city in early bloom. Cars on Sante Fe Drive made wet-tire sounds on the pavement, and I wished I'd brought my jacket with me. "I'm sorry about your mom, Phillip."

He drew deep on the joint, the ember glowing brightly, lighting his face momentarily. "She hates me."

"Why do you say that?"

He shrugged. "Long story."

"Phillip, your mother is an angel most of the time. She's been under terrible stress. She didn't mean the things she said."

"Oh, she meant them when she said them." He drew one last time on an impossibly small twist, held his breath, and mashed it out. Then he exhaled slowly and threw his head back, the light from the street below illuminating his thin cheeks and dark brows.

"Phillip, I came up here because I'm worried about you. I saw your face. I know you're in shock, and I know you're devastated by this."

"You don't know a damn thing, Stella. Nobody does. You don't have one idea of what it's like living with her. Half the time she's screaming and yelling at us, the rest of the time she's laughing or crying. They say you don't really know someone till you live with them, but I don't think I know her, and I've been living with her for sixteen years."

He lit a cigarette. He offered me one; I waved no thanks. I waited for whatever would come next. I wondered if we had all been assuming Phillip was simply acting out normal teenage rebellion, when it was more complicated than that.

I wished I knew more about teen psychology. Of course, if I did, I'd be a millionaire overnight.

"Stella, I think my mom's a druggie."

"Why do you say that?"

"Her moods. Her eyes sometimes. She has migraines, but I think it's more than that."

I closed my eyes. Of course, that would explain so much—the mood swings, the tantrums, the intensity. What would she have taken? Prescription drugs? It wouldn't be the first time a person got hooked on legitimate medications and went overboard. Sometimes physicians overprescribed. As far as that went, Barbara could have convinced the best of docs that she needed drugs. Or did she take street stuff? Surely she wasn't getting stuff from Linc and Judd? "Have you seen her take anything? Or found stuff? Prescriptions?"

"No. She complained about her doctor 'cause he refused to give her any pain pills for her headaches. That's when I started thinking about it."

"Does Lawrence think she's using drugs?"

He shook his head. Tears were so close to the surface, I thought he'd break down, but he didn't. I wasn't sure whether I should protest, agree, or just listen. In the end, I didn't have to decide.

He cleared his throat, gathered himself together, and in a pathetically defiant tone of voice asked, "So, what are you doing up here? Did they send you? Are you my keeper now that she's—"

"She's not dead. And sarcasm doesn't make the pain less," I said. "When someone tries to kill themselves, we naturally blame ourselves."

"Ah, that's it. Blame. They're down there saying I did her in, and you came up here to console me. Well, don't bother. In fact, maybe you'd better get back down there."

"In a minute. I thought we could go back together."

"Bringing in the outlaw? Dragging the guilty little sniper in? Get a reward for this, Stella?"

Matching his anger with anger would only make things worse, but I wasn't sure he'd be up to any attempt at humor, even grim stuff. "I came up here because I care about you, Phillip."

He was silent for a moment, thinking "You go. I'm hanging out here."

The choice of words worried me. "I'd feel better if you'd come in with me."

He grinned a painful, lopsided grin. "Why? Think I'm next?"

This juvenile bitterness was growing old. And it sure wouldn't wash well with the cops. "Look, Phillip, I like you. I just want to make things better for you, even though it probably doesn't seem like it right now."

I meant what I said and hoped it came through to him. It seemed to me he was so stunned and furious and confused, he was just lashing out at me because I was there. But I'm not a saint. I'll take being whipped just so long, then it's over. It was over now. Reasonable or not.

He was silent. I bit my lip. I'd probably blown it. I felt like a double dipshit. I hadn't recognized his mother's behavior as drug-related, and I hadn't been very sensitive with a kid in his hour of misery. Hell.

He reminded me of a pup I once found in the park, abused and abandoned. He had snarled and growled, then sidled up to me, tail barely wagging, eyes mournful, hoping I'd take him in. Of course I did. Phillip was looking at me as if he still expected I would strike out at him. I leaned toward him and lowered my voice. "Phillip, when you told your mom you'd kill her, you didn't mean it, did you?"

He shook his head. "No," he whispered.

"Well, your mom did the same thing. She said things to

you she didn't mean. We all say things in anger that we don't mean. It's a bad thing to do, but it doesn't kill people.''

He hesitated, then said, "I gave her a lot of shit."

"You didn't cause this."

He hung his head. "What if she dies?"

He was scared, really scared. All this silly bravado had been to cover up his terror. And there wasn't a thing in the world that I could do to honestly reassure him. What he needed to do was mature about seven years in less than fifteen minutes, and it wasn't going to happen, no matter how smart he was. I put a hand on his shoulder. "Phillip, your mom is a strong woman, not a quitter. She loves you, and the thing a parent wants most is for their kid to grow up and be happy." I'd have given the earth to be profound at that moment.

Phillip roused. "You really don't think I had anything to do with it?"

"Of course I don't! How could you? She's your mother."

"Dad will think it's my fault. You watch. He'll walk in, look at me, go all weird in the face, and say, 'What did you do this time?'" His voice thick with unwanted emotion, he broke off, and I heard a sudden catch of breath.

"Phillip—"

The shudder of his shoulders, the ragged breathing, told me he was sobbing. "Stella, I don't want her to die."

"They'll do their best, Phillip." And then my eyes filled until I was a mess myself. I think I was crying more for the tough-on-the-outside, hurting-on-the-inside kid who sat beside me. Sixteen is no age to have to deal with a suicide attempt.

When I dried up, I looked around on the rooftop, my eyes fully accustomed to the dark now. I could see the boys had spent a good deal of time up here. There was a small stash of empty cola cans, a large stash of cigarette butts and twists, and a plastic bag that looked like it held all kinds of supplies. An urban tree house.

Phillip wiped his face on the sleeve of his shirt and rose to his feet. At the steps he turned, stepped back, and waited for me to go first. "So, if you think it isn't my fault, who do you think did try to kill her?"

NINE

I NEARLY FELL OFF the rickety steps.

Who do you think did try to kill her? Phillip's words echoed in my mind. I forgot about the top step; my foot aimed at the missing rung and thumped to the next one.

He grabbed my arm; I grabbed the step rails. Maybe the confusion covered my surprise.

I climbed down three more steps, my mind in a whirl. I'd been talking about a suicide attempt; he'd been talking about attempted murder. Of course, Phillip didn't know about the note.

Now that I thought about it, except for that note, attempted suicide didn't compute. Hanging is not a pretty death. Why would a woman so particular about her looks kill herself in a way that disfigured her? Surely she'd have chosen to die peacefully on her bed of, say, an overdose. Wouldn't she at least have chosen some method that wouldn't leave her marred?

Initially I'd accepted the idea that Barbara had committed suicide without much question, because of the note. But now it seemed inconceivable that Barbara would kill herself just when her masterpiece was going to be produced, when she had so much riding on Phillip, and when she was as vain about her looks as she was.

But how on earth could anyone have tried to kill her? She was in plain sight the whole time. Well, almost plain sight. I thought about the exploded spotlight. I saw her most of the time. No, only some of the time. I felt sick. I'd been so

mad at her, I hadn't really watched her at all. I'd been con-
centrating on the rehearsal.

Still, she wasn't a quiet, mousy woman. She would have
fought like a fiend... Then I thought of the thumps I'd heard
during rehearsal. I felt cold. Had I heard her being killed?
Had she been calling out, and I didn't respond? I didn't even
look in her direction to see if something was wrong, because
I was mad at her. The thought was paralyzing. A wave of
nausea swept through me, followed by a numbing chill. I
nearly slipped from the ladder again.

Phillip was descending right behind me. "Stella, are you
all right?"

"Yeah, I'm okay." Of course, I wasn't. And neither was
he. Barbara was his mother, and despite everything he said
about her, he loved her. It showed in his voice, his bitterness, his awful struggle to be independent, and most of all
in his pitiful wish that she would tell him she was proud of
him.

If I was upset, how much more must he be? And if I felt
guilty because I hadn't heeded what might have been a cry
for help, how much worse must it be for him? He had threatened her. Their last words had been angry and hateful. What
more alienating thing could happen to him? Not much, unless he was blamed. Or she died. That would be the worst.
That might be enough to push him over the edge.

I needed to get my feet on terra firma, get my mind in
order, and think things out. The one thing that was clear to
me was that Phillip needed help, needed someone strong in
his corner. And he needed to see he wasn't abandoned. I
would have to tell the police that I believed this was an
attempted murder, but would that put suspicion on Phillip?
Surely not. Phillip was a kid, and all kids say rash things.
Phillip would see that people stood up for him. And

Lawrence would. He was his dad. Too many questions—too many to sort out right then.

We entered through the stage door as Rachel came down the aisle from the box office. Her face was somber, gaze cast down. Without so much as a glance at either of us, she hurried on toward Cammie's office in the rear of the building.

"See?" Phillip muttered. "She thinks I did it."

"I see a sad and frightened woman, that's all."

"Shit, man. You wouldn't say—"

"Cut it out, Phillip." He looked surprised at my sudden maternal orders, but followed along until we were sitting in the first row of the audience. He lowered himself into a seat and put his head in his hands, covering his eyes.

Ogden and Cammie sat in the second row, Cammie grim-faced and pale, Ogden with his head in his hands. Adrian looked up as we slipped in, his hair miraculously well combed, his face ruddy. Then I remembered he wore makeup, so his pallor wouldn't show.

Meredith and Zelda were in the fourth row, behind us, Meredith quietly crying while Zelda looked over her shoulder to the lobby as though she expected someone to come busting in any minute.

Lawrence, I thought. He'd come breezing in here, not even knowing about it. I felt sorry for him. He, too, had left her on bad terms. I wondered how he'd take the news. Would he be surprised by an attempted suicide? Or would he immediately suspect an attempted murder?

Fifteen minutes later Phillip hadn't moved. The front door of the theater opened and closed and I turned expecting to see Lawrence; instead I saw Zelda greet Detective Lee Stokowski of Denver's homicide division in the lobby. I was careful to conceal my surprise at seeing Stokowski. I didn't want to alarm Phillip.

I first met Stokowski a year ago when one of my correspondents was murdered, and since then we have had an
uneasy relationship. He is tough and humorless, but fair. I
figured Zelda *must* have called him. He has been dating her.

Stokowski has deep-set eyes, crisp dark hair, and a very
stubborn chin, and that night he looked older than his forty
years. He wore brown trousers, a tweed jacket that pulled
across his shoulders as though it was just a mite too tight,
a tired blue button-down shirt, and a teal-and-beige tie that
had outlived its fashion statement by about ten years. He
was grim and observant, but solid, and in a strange way,
comforting.

Why was he here? *Had* Zelda called him? Or had the
police called him because they too suspected attempted murder? Why would they? There was that little scrap of a note
that said, "Too much." Had I told the officer about the keys
and the note in her pocket? I must have. I squeezed my eyes
shut. Of course I had.

Were they suspicious about something else? Or was this
standard procedure when investigating an attempted suicide?

Phillip turned to see who was coming down the aisle. He
stiffened in his seat and muttered, "Sheeit. Stokowski. He
works homicide—"

I turned to Phillip. Why would he, a sixteen-year-old,
know a homicide detective? "How do you know him?"

He was slow to answer, and his voice was carefully ca-
sual. "I knew him when he was a traffic cop." I told myself
firmly that Phillip wasn't lying.

We watched Stokowski make his way in measured steps
to converse with the police officers and then to where Barbara had lain, mostly concealed from us by stage props. He
seemed to be memorizing the scene, staring for a long time
at the Venus's-flytrap.

Rachel returned to the theater, her face waxen, and seated herself behind us. Stokowski talked to the officers, examined a little bag, which I assumed held the note and keys from Barbara's pocket, then pulled a pad from his pocket and made notes. When he finished, he glowered in my direction, his gaze falling first on me, then on Phillip. His brows closed into a thick, sullen line.

I started to speak, but he waved me silent and beckoned Zelda to his side. While she was trotting up to the stage, he spoke briefly to all of us. "I'm sorry for the inconvenience, I know you're all shocked and this is hard for you, so we will proceed as efficiently as possible. I appreciate your patience.

"I'll be calling each one of you up here for a brief interview so that we can make sure we understand the situation. Until then, I ask that you not leave and not talk to each other. Thank you."

He spoke briefly to Zelda, listened to her response, which I couldn't hear but tried to, then turned to the officers for reports, also unfortunately out of earshot. After he finished, he looked around and asked Adrian to come talk with him. He had not left the stage area when the front door of the theater opened and shut with a bang. Hurried footsteps down the aisle followed. Lawrence bellowed out, "What happened here?"

Stokowski looked around at the sound of his voice.

Rachel stood in the aisle. Quietly she reached for Lawrence's arm. "Lawrence, please. Come here. It's too sad." She hesitated, seeing his puzzled glance in her direction. "Barbara tried to hang herself."

"What?" He looked around, his massive head twisting on his neck like a buffalo searching the winds. "What do you mean?"

"It's true," Rachel murmured. "They've taken her to the

hospital. She's still alive, thank God, but she's very serious. She nearly killed herself." Two tiny tears leaked down her cheeks, leaving twin shiny trails. "It's too unbelievable." Then she slid back into the seat and dabbed at her eyes with a tissue.

Lawrence frowned, disbelieving. "What did she just say?" he bellowed.

Stokowski had been watching this interchange with interest. Now he stepped to the stage apron. "Please have a seat, Mr. Steadman. I would like to talk to you in a moment."

"The hell I will. I'm going to the hospital. She's my wife."

"You can go in a moment. Please be seated."

"What the hell are you doing here?" Lawrence roared.

I was shocked. Did Lawrence know him? Why?

Lawrence squinted in our direction, his gaze finally landing on Phillip. His lips moved, mouthing disbelief, then in a crescendo he asked, "What in the name of God have you done now?" For a long moment Phillip barely even breathed, then he blasted out of his seat and dashed up the aisle, shoving Lawrence out of the way as he went.

"Phillip, wait!" I yelled and ran after him.

He was disappearing out the door when I caught up with him. "Come on, Phillip. Your dad was just upset. He didn't mean it."

"The hell he didn't. He meant every word. He doesn't give a rat's ass what I do, but anytime anything goes wrong, it's my fault. I told you so."

I grabbed his shirtsleeve to keep him still. "Phillip, I don't believe you did anything. Now, come on, this makes you look guilty."

"Everything I do makes me look guilty."

"Come on, Phillip."

"You said you believe in me, well, you're the only one in this whole effing world who does. So if you really believe me, then you do something. Nobody else will."

I gripped his arm, refusing to be shaken off. "Phillip. You're your own worst enemy. Running from your father isn't going to get you anywhere. Come on. Your dad is a mess right now. And your mom needs you, and she needs you to be strong."

Silence.

He turned slowly to me. In the glow from the streetlights I saw his eyes were reddened, watery looking. "You better be telling me the truth."

We walked in silence back to our seats.

Stokowski was talking to Lawrence when we sat down again in the now nearly empty theater. Lawrence clomped leadenly down the steps and threw himself into a seat. When Phillip walked past him, answering Stokowski's beckoning, he mumbled an apology and tried to grasp Phillip's hand. Phillip yanked himself out of reach.

Nearly a quarter of an hour later Lawrence and Phillip left in stony silence, Phillip following, his elbows awkwardly flopping, his feet dragging.

I WAS LAST ON Stokowski's list of people to talk to. He came down from the stage, stopped at the row where I sat, and rubbed his face and the back of his neck.

He shook his head and began gruffly. "For God's sake, Stella, what have you got yourself into this time? Couldn't you just live a normal life? What do you have against the human race? Every time I get a call and you're involved, it turns out to be a disaster."

"Do you want to hear what I have to say?"

"Is there a place to get a cup of coffee around here?"

"So I'm not a suspect?"

"A suspect?" His eyelids lowered speculatively. "There are no suspects in a suicide. Are you saying this was something else?"

In a flash I shook my head. "Not me. I'd never think such a thing. Just because the homicide detective is here asking questions, and the forensic people have been called and are dusting everything that doesn't move, doesn't mean I suspect anything out of the ordinary. Not me. Innocent, sir."

That little attempt at humor went nowhere. I took in his fatigue-ringed eyes, the creases of cynicism growing in his cheeks, his stubborn chin, and let out a sigh. "It would be really nice to have a pleasant chat with you over coffee, Lee."

He grinned, one corner of his mouth higher than the other, as if he couldn't fully enjoy even this minor thing. "Yeah, well, that's life. Come on. You can confess over something strong and black."

"Grilling at the Grill?"

"Something like that."

We crossed Sante Fe Drive to José's Burro Bar and Grill and entered a dark room crowded with south-of-the-border music, chili scent, cigarette smoke, and people. The customers filled the booths that lined the far side of the room, and they filled all the tables and chairs. A narrow counter with vinyl-clad stools ran halfway back in the room. Lee pointed to an empty stool at the far end. I sat, and he stood beside me, waiting for the next one.

The bartender sized us up while he chased peanut shell crumbs around the counter with a gray rag that smelled like mold and disinfectant. His dark eyes were steady, challenging. "Do for you?"

He'd made Lee for a cop immediately. Lee stared back. It was macho eye-wrestling time.

Something changed; I wasn't sure what. Lee leaned forward, palm on the counter. "Coffee, two, black." He turned to me. "You want something to eat?"

Not really an invitation, but I was hungry, and he had asked.

"Beef burrito, smothered green, extra cheese and lettuce," I said.

"Indigestion alley."

I smiled. "Not for the pure of heart."

He looked deep into my eyes. An expression sadder than I'd ever imagined possible in him lurked there. It suddenly occurred to me that I always saw him as a cop, a strong, impartial, sometimes sullen and angry but always official person. But just now, for reasons I didn't understand then, he was a very human man with emotions like the ones I had, like Meredith had. Like everyone has, except that I'd always seen him as set aside from all that complicating stuff. Frankly, I was a whole lot more comfortable with the official person.

The woman on the next stool shoved money onto the counter and left. Lee sat heavily on the stool, crossed his arms, and leaned on the counter.

I couldn't figure out what was going on in his mind. Sometimes I can, but not this night. It was one of those awkward moments that sits on the emotional doorsill, refusing to let any brighter mood pass. I tore my napkin into shreds, my mind ever busy with possible causes. The only thing I was certain of was that he had some unpleasant thing on his mind. Most likely something that was going to be painful for me as well; otherwise he'd be talking.

Finally the food came, and I could eat. Food is a comfort for me, undoubtedly explaining why I'm not lithe like Meredith.

While he was contemplating his cup of coffee, which

smelled like burned aluminum and sludge, I worked on reasons why he had decided to bring me here instead of staying at the theater. The only thing I came up with was that he was trying to soften me up for something. I remembered how Fluffy would wait for a cricket, holding completely still until the unsuspecting thing crawled past his nose and he snapped it up. I felt a little like that, waiting for Stokowski to say something. Finally, when I'd eaten the whole tasty, stomach-satisfying burrito and he'd had a second cup of coffee, he leaned back and faced me.

"Stella, please listen. Why don't you just leave all this and go back to writing that little column of yours? Stay safe and out of trouble."

"Lee, I'm not meddling in anything. I'm the assistant director for the play."

"You were hired to keep Barbara Steadman out of everyone's hair, to keep her quiet and calm."

"She is quiet... Oh, my God. You butthead!" I blinked furiously. No way would I cry in front of him. "It isn't my fault this happened. It isn't."

He drew a breath. "But you don't believe it's suicide, do you?"

"No," I whispered. I gripped my now empty coffee mug in both hands and squeezed really tight. We sat in hostile silence. I wondered why it was I didn't leave. I should have.

"You know those kids, Linc and Judd, pretty well?"

"Sort of. Why?" I set my coffee cup down. Whatever Stokowski had been meditating over was coming. I could feel it, and I thought I knew what it was. "Look, Lee, I know both of them were into joyriding at an early age. In fact, Zelda said they were so little they couldn't reach the pedals and drive at the same time. One of them would steer while the other pushed on the gas. But they seem to be doing pretty well now."

He nodded slowly, a faraway look in his eyes. "I worked juvenile several years ago. I met them then. They were trouble, and in trouble. I'm the one who busted them, and I'm the one who sent them to juvy and ultimately to Lookout Mountain. They were two of three incredibly young, and smart, kids into serious crime."

"Joyriding isn't the worst. At least they didn't deal drugs."

"Now, who said they didn't?"

"Well, at least they weren't into violent crime..." He looked steadily at me. I got the message. "Well, they seem to be doing okay now." He continued to stare at me. "And they're so talented. You should see them onstage. They're wonderful."

"They've had plenty of time to practice, Stella."

I shook my head. "I think you're too cynical, Lee. People change, especially kids. When someone takes an interest in them, it can make a tremendous difference. I just don't know what this will do to them. They'll be devastated."

Lee snorted. "I don't think it will do more than slow them down for five seconds. You don't know what trouble those kids are."

"And you do?"

"Yes, I do."

"Well, maybe you're just wrong, Lee. It's a possibility. I'll bet you've been wrong before once or twice."

He got that funny sad look again. "Yes, I have." He straightened up. "Look, Stella. A little while ago you said you were pure of heart. I know you were kidding, but it's true. You're awful trusting underneath that flippant, cynical shell of yours. Especially if it's someone you know and like. Or a kid."

"I've been right each time. I've got good instincts."

He rubbed his chin, snapping his whiskers, which were

unbecomingly overgrown, in a gesture I recognized as one he used when he was getting really impatient. "Look, you've meddled in things before, and it's been sheer luck you weren't killed or maimed. It's getting to the point where if I hear you're there, I assume it's homicide."

This was taking a nasty turn. "You mean, because I was there, you think it's a homicide and you think those two boys, merely because of their pasts, are involved?" My voice had become a bit shrill, but he didn't answer. "Isn't that really jumping to conclusions? Isn't that going strictly against your belief in objectivity? What happened to your ethics, Lee?"

He looked at me, dark, glowering, distant. "What happened to your common sense, Stella?"

"My common sense is just fine. It's your attitude that needs adjusting."

He drew in another breath, harbinger of even more bad news. "Ever talk to Barbara or Lawrence about Phillip?"

"Nope. What I know of him is from him and from watching him, talking to him. He's a fine, bright, gentle kid."

He shifted uncomfortably on his stool and emptied his coffee cup. "Phillip was the third kid in the trio. He was the mastermind. He's the one who thought up everything."

TEN

DETECTIVE STOKOWSKI suspected Barbara's hanging was a murder attempt. He had worked hard to convince me that Phillip, Linc, and Judd were the nation's greatest potential sociopaths, and he probably believed he was absolutely right. I thought he was wrong.

I'd known Phillip for at least the last year, and I'd never seen anything sociopathic in him. He did perhaps have too much curiosity, some childish defiance, and more smarts than he knew what to do with, but that was part of what made him appealing. I did not think he tried to kill his mother. I thought he was genuine when he said he hadn't hurt her, even if he could act better than most professionals.

I called the hospital as soon as I was home and learned Barbara was still on the critical list. I had a terrible time falling asleep that night. The coffee I'd drunk made it hard, but the thing that really kept me awake was the thought that Barbara had tried to get my attention, and I'd ignored her because I was so angry. Talk about a guilt trip.

I woke around two a.m. in a sweat from a bad dream that involved Barbara begging for help. I went over last night's events in my mind: Barbara lying about the keys, the note that was barely a note, Lawrence blaming Phillip, Barbara's drug use, that weird play. Most of all, Stokowski's attitude toward Phillip disturbed me. Phillip's assessment of how blame would fall was looking uncomfortably accurate. I must have fallen asleep around three A.M., but it didn't last.

At five-thirty the sun was up and so was I, the remnant of another ugly dream clouding my senses. In my dream the letter from Scared worrying about his/her friend was somehow melded with Barbara's thumps. It didn't take a Jungian genius to figure out that both of them were cries for help that I hadn't answered well. In addition, I had promised Phillip I'd help him, but I'd also promised Stokowski that I wouldn't get involved.

I was looking for a loophole. I ran a hot, pounding shower, and while water streamed over my head, I figured out a way to keep both promises. Since Jason was in New York and I had to write a couple stories for the paper, I could do a story or two on the theater. I'd have to be careful to frame it in background, or Mr. Gerster would never print it, but that was easy enough. And if I were working on a story for the paper, I could interview people, get background, and of course, I'd have to go on location. It was perfect. And there was always the chance history might hold a motive.

I slithered into an adorable apricot-colored chemise and panties, then dove into my closet and came up with a pair of red crinkle-cloth pants, a multicolored top, and a matching scarf to wind in a turban over my head. The *Daily Orion*'s morgue is in the basement of the building, shared with generations of critters, none of whom I wanted bedding down in my hair.

Fluffy and Lips were still sleeping, Lips on top of the log and Fluffy on the top leaf of his favorite plant. Lips hasn't been the most enthusiastic mate for Fluffy, but his push-ups, head bobs, and throat swells must have won her over. I checked on the egg. It was still in the crotch of the ivy, still whole, and it looked thicker somehow. I didn't know if this meant a tiny lizard was growing or if it was drying out in the arid climate. I added water to the bubbler dish and sprinkled it around the terrarium. I was feeling very maternal.

Before I left, I called my mother, pleased that for once I

could get to her before she got to me. We always talk on Saturday mornings, need it or not. She had already glanced at the *Denver Post,* where a brief story on Barbara's "accident" had been inserted just prior to printing.

"That's the play you're working on, isn't it, Janie?"

She always calls me Janie, although I have been going by the name of Stella for over a year now.

"Yes."

"It says here you found her. You must have nearly fainted. You don't have to talk to the police, do you? I mean, since she tried to kill herself, don't they leave it alone? Or will that nice Detective Stokowski be there? I always thought he was interested in you. I don't suppose you two will get together someday."

"No. I'm dating Jason, remember?"

"Such a nice boy. He went to New York, didn't he? People don't come back from there, you know."

"I've heard that, Mom. They get off the bus and disappear right into the manholes."

There was a little silence on her end of the phone, then, "I don't like it when you tease me. I hope you're not wearing some wild outfit." This constituted a rebuke from Mom, who was clearly hurt.

I relented. "Jason's not so young, he can take good care of himself, and he said he's coming back." I said it with more conviction than I actually had.

She was quiet again, then spoke gently. "It's just that it's so distressing when I learn what's happening to you in the papers, instead of directly from you."

Another guilt trip. The great ones make it look so easy.

"It was late when I got home. I didn't have a chance to call... Oh, Mom! Linc and Judd. They weren't at the theater when she was found. They won't know. They'll see it in the papers." Mom doesn't like to have me ring off so fast, but she understood.

Through some oversight, I did not have the phone numbers or addresses of the cast, so I woke Zelda, who irritably gave me Lawrence's number, then fumbled the receiver back onto the switch hook.

Lawrence answered wearily on the second ring. "Of course they should be told, as soon as possible and in person, I guess. They're going to be real upset." He read off their addresses.

I drove through the early-Saturday-morning traffic from southeast Denver, where I was house-sitting, to the Five Points area of Denver, so called because in the center of it three streets come together to form a star. Five Points lies aging in the shadow of downtown, whose wealth has never filtered into this area. People there need about a gallon of paint a day to keep up with eradicating the graffiti, and turf issues are settled with gunshots.

There have been several programs to rejuvenate Five Points, and more than a few energetic souls have poured their time and energy into renovations, none of which have really dented the pervasive problem: poverty. Curtis Park Housing Project lies in the middle of it all like a huge drain, sucking down the hopes of the residents. Some of the families have a history of generations there, and underneath the seeming quiet is an undercurrent of resentment, despair, and drugs that gives the people watchful, guarded eyes.

Efforts have been made to lower the crime rate, with the result that the criminals have gotten smarter and moved inside. Decent people living there have learned to keep their mouths shut and their blinds down. And nobody sits in front of a window.

I fit in like an onion in a petunia patch.

Judd's home was a one-story brick bungalow built about

the 1920s. The yard was tired, thirsty, and untrimmed. The porch was surrounded by trees of heaven—weed trees, my father used to call them. He hated them. Judd's sister Juleen, a girl of about thirteen, answered the door wearing a T-shirt, cutoffs, and sandals. Her hair was tied attractively to one side. I explained why I was there.

She glanced back into the house, then stepped out on the porch rather than inviting me inside. Her voice was low, and while I could hear her, I was sure no one else could. "They weren't here last night. Judd didn't come home. They probably went to a party and stayed over," she said, but the troubled look in her eye told me she was far more worried than she was admitting.

I explained why I wanted to find him, and her worry increased.

Her hand was trembling lightly. "There's lots of nights they stay at the theater instead of coming home. Mizz Steadman pays them to be the janitors there, so they have keys to the place. Soon as you find him, tell him to get home. He's been doing real good, but the police will try to pin it on him, I just know it."

I tried to reassure her, but she looked at me as if I were speaking in tongues, and from her perspective, perhaps I was. She snorted and said, "If you aren't worried about the same thing, why're you here?"

I gave her my card and said to have him call me right away if he came home. And I told her I was on his side.

"You've joined a minority, then," she said and closed the door.

Linc's home was in a basement apartment of a crumbling brick bungalow. An elderly woman with her hair in rollers answered the door. She kept it open only far enough to see my face, but not so far as to suggest that I might come in. I asked for Linc.

"Why're you askin' for Linc?"

"I work at the theater with them...I need to talk to him."

"There's trouble, ain't they?"

"No, no, not for Linc. Fortunately he wasn't there then. I just wanted to tell him about it, so he wouldn't be upset."

"Upset? Linc?" She looked as though she thought I was a lunatic, but was kind enough to finally answer with dignity. "Linc never came home last night. I don't know where he is, but he'll be with Judd if he's anywhere."

"Does he stay out all night very often?"

"Nope. He us'lly come t'home. He's a good boy."

"Do you know where he might be?"

"At some dang party, I guess. Maybe at Judd's house. If he's not there, then he'll be at that theater."

"Are you worried about him?"

"I'm worried 'bout him getting picked up by the police. They'll beat his skinny ass, if they do."

"If I see him, I'll tell him you're looking for him."

"He's got to take care of himself now. I'm too old. He's a good kid. He's been studying and reading, and he's real smart."

I explained about Barbara. The woman's lips worked back and forth, her eyes searching the porch floor for something she didn't find. "My Linc is a good boy. He's gonna be very distressed by this. He loves that Barbara. She's been real good to him. She's a real lady. Has a lot of class and don't mind sticking up for the boys. Yes, she is a fine woman. Very kind."

"You know her pretty well?"

"No, can't say I do, but she gave Linc and Judd a janitor job and pays 'em for their work and keeps 'em off the street. She be a good person. And so's her friend."

"Her friend?"

"Rachel. Good woman. Always respectful."

"And Lawrence? Did you meet him?"

She dropped her gaze to the flowers beyond me in the yard. "Well, now, I don't really know him. He'd drop the boys off and leave. Wasn't ever comfortable talking. Some men are like that."

"Quiet?"

"To themselves. Like they're afraid if they talk, you'll get to know too much about them."

I thanked her, gave her my card with the *Daily Orion* phone numbers, and turned to leave.

"Uh, miss?"

I stopped and looked back at her.

"Linc was worried about Phillip. Said he was acting depressed-like. You ask Phillip where they are, 'cause those three are real tight. That Phillip's got a lot on his mind these days. He's a good boy, but I think he does some of his stuff to get attention, you know what I mean? I think he figures that if he gives his folks enough trouble, maybe they'll forget they're mad at each other and jus' be mad at him."

"Thanks. You seem to know quite a bit."

She smiled. "Got plenty of time to think. And, miss? Don't walk in this neighborhood too much, hear? Ain't very safe." She pointed to three pockmarks on the brickwork. "Gunshots."

It was only eight-thirty. I stopped in Capitol Hill at a little place that sells wonderful cinnamon buns to pick up breakfast and a coffee, then drove to the theater. I checked the roof and pounded on the locked doors, but no one answered. Because I had neglected to charge my cell phone, I decided to stop in at the *Daily Orion* to call people.

I found a parking place beneath an elderly silver maple, got out of the car, locked it, and felt a drip on my cheek. The tree was spitting at me. Maples are so surly.

I walked the quick block to the office, enjoying the iris

and early roses in the yards. The sidewalks there are frequently the original sandstone blocks, tilted by the tree roots, so I had to keep an eye on the pavement or risk tripping.

An alley runs behind the building, and Mr. Gerster and Zelda have parking spaces there. They were empty. I would have the building to myself. I was almost surprised, because Mr. Gerster usually comes in even on weekends. I think he feels he can worry more effectively there.

Earlier my plan had been to search through the back issues in the morgue for history on the theater, but the more I thought about Judd and Linc, the less I felt like delving into the dust of the past. The present seemed so much more important now.

I let myself in the front door, locked it behind me, and checked to see if any more mail had come in since I left yesterday afternoon. So much had happened it seemed like a week, so I was surprised to find only a dozen letters that had come late in the afternoon. I took them to my desk, put them in my In pile. We were to have had a rehearsal this afternoon, but I was sure Ogden would want to cancel it. I reached for my phone and punched in Ogden's number.

While I waited for Ogden to answer, my gaze traveled around the room. Every deteriorating inch of the place seemed more lovely than ever before. It was painful to think that in three little weeks I'd be out of here permanently.

Ogden didn't answer. I assumed he was either at the hospital or at the Steadmans' and tried the Steadmans'. I got a busy signal. I rang the hospital and learned that Barbara was still critical, and visitation was limited to family only. I checked for messages on my voice mail. There was only one hang-up.

Finally I gathered up my mail, dropped it in my bag, and

started for the front door. I was halfway across the lobby when Mr. Gerster unlocked the door and entered. Oh, joy!

I smiled and tried to escape without talking to him. He stood before me, his bow tie precise, his suspenders holding his trousers high, and his face lipless. "Why are you working on Saturday, Stella?"

I had no intention of discussing the events of yesterday with him. He has a paternal streak that makes him even more stubborn than I am. "I wasn't, actually. I just stopped in to make some phone calls. My cell phone is out of order."

"I thought you might be working on a story, about that theater you're working for."

"Well, I was sort of thinking about background," I said. I wanted to switch topics real fast. "If Jason gets the job in New York, are you really going to support his leaving?"

"Of course. I think it's a great opportunity for him. I told you that."

"So explain to me again why it is that you can support him, but not me."

His eyes darted around uncomfortably, everywhere but in my direction. Finally he worked up to speech. "Sit down, Stella." That meant he wanted to sit down.

When he was settled in Zelda's chair, safely behind her desk, he launched in. "I have a son, but we've been out of touch, estranged really, for several years. He thinks I'm rigid and impossible, I think he's wild and irresponsible. His mother thought I was too hard on him. I…" He broke off, his icy blue eyes moist and faraway. "I planned always that he would take over the paper. That's what I always worked for, for him. For what he could be when he was grown and responsible. That's what a father works for. His son."

I wanted to shout at him. He had a perfectly wonderful

daughter; didn't she count for anything? I kept still for fear he'd never finish. I wanted to know where this was going.

"You see," he said, continuing in a throaty voice, "the day he left the house, we had argued. He was angry. I was too. We haven't spoken since." His voice trailed off again. I waited, but he seemed to think that explained everything.

I stirred. "I don't see why this means you'll support Jason, but not me."

He looked at me, frankly puzzled. "But a father will do nearly anything for his son."

I felt a little like an idiot, but I had to ask, "So how does this apply to Jason? Are you saying he's your son?"

He looked disconcerted, blinking. "Well, no. That's not what I meant at all. He's sort of like a son, but he's not a son."

"So..?"

"So... I decided not to make the same mistake twice."

"I still don't get it. You could help more than one person at a time. You could help me."

He blinked at me, frowning. "No. I can't. It's too late." He got up and walked away.

I yanked open the door and stepped out, right into Jason's arms. Jason? Could Jason be back already?

Sure enough. There he was, a pretty gorgeous sight, grinning at me like Caesar, my beloved childhood golden retriever. "Hey, there, you're back in a hurry."

Jason grinned. "I figured I'd find you here. I was just going to tell Mr. Gerster about New York."

"Oh?" I tried to keep my curiosity under wraps. "How did it go?"

"Let's go inside; we can talk to Mr. Gerster at the same time."

"Oh, let's not. It's nicer just with you."

"At least come in out of the neighbors' eyes." He pulled

me inside. "New York was okay. Actually, much better than I remember. Sun was out, weather great. You can't beat the city on a warm spring day." He shrugged. "The interviews were fine. I think I answered questions well, such as they were…" He missed a beat, but covered fairly well. "And I didn't want to miss a weekend I could spend with you."

Had he been rejected by New York so soon? That's what I'd wanted, so why did I feel indignant that they had turned him down? I bit my tongue, reminding myself he'd tell me when he was ready. "I love being irresistible."

He smiled, his arms warm around me. "After you called yesterday, I decided to hop a standby and come home. Figured I wouldn't leave you on the loose for a whole weekend." He hesitated. "You don't seem very happy to see me."

"I am—believe me, I am." I wrapped my arms around his neck and settled in for a kiss.

He pulled back after a few minutes, looking puzzled. "Stella, I saw in the papers that the woman you were to keep quiet tried to kill herself."

Mr. Gerster stood in the doorway, the *Denver Post* in his hand. "And why didn't you mention it to me today, Stella?"

I dropped my arms from Jason's neck. "Yes, that's the theater, but—"

Mr. Gerster's eyebrows met in the middle of his forehead. "For the love of Pete, you are not to go anywhere near there, not to get into it, and not to talk to Zelda about it. I won't stand for either of you to be in danger. I'm worried about you and what will become of you."

"Then it will be a real relief when I'm not here anymore, won't it?"

ELEVEN

I MADE QUICK CALLS to Linc and Judd's homes and found they still hadn't shown up. I think Jason would have agreed to go to the moon with me, but instead I dragged him off to see the last person who had seen the boys. Lawrence. I could also get Ogden's address.

We swung by the theater to find the doors were still locked tight. Jason was edgy. "Don't you have a key?"

"No, they didn't think I'd need one, since I'm only a temporary employee, but let's walk around the building and make sure there's no sign of a break-in."

His eyes narrowed to suspicious slits. "*You're* planning to break in there, aren't you?"

"No, not with you along." He didn't think that was funny.

He also didn't like the looks of the back steps to the roof. "Good God, these steps are unsafe!"

"Not quite OSHA standard, but they get you up there." I was feeling very superior to him until I missed the top step again and nearly fell.

"That's it, we're going down."

"Well, they might be up there."

They weren't.

Lawrence and Barbara had a beautiful home on Seventh Avenue in East Capitol Hill. Seventh Avenue is one of those gracious streets with a grassy center island, arching trees, and enough spruce trees so that in all seasons it looks planted and pretty. Their house sat behind a sedate wrought-iron fence with ivy creeping up the white stucco walls toward terra-cotta tile roofing. Delicate flowering plums shaded an incredibly well-trimmed lawn. I went through the gate and rang the doorbell. A vaguely familiar female voice piped out of an unobtrusive speaker, and I identified myself.

The door opened. Rachel greeted us. I introduced Jason, and she explained that Lawrence was on the phone. I was sure she was going to suggest that we come back later, so I oozed in past her and pulled Jason after me. She closed the door in resignation and led the way across the polished parquet entryway flooring. We waded through deep pile carpeting in a museum-quality living room to the library, where Lawrence sat behind a heavily carved desk. The walls were lined with books, all very beautiful and so orderly I immediately doubted he'd ever read them.

I explained to Rachel that I needed the phone numbers and addresses for the cast so I could cancel rehearsal this afternoon. She frowned. "I don't see why Ogden doesn't answer. Did you go by his place?"

"No, Rachel. I have his number but not his address. That's one of the reasons we're here."

She nodded. "All my records are at the theater. I can tell you where Ogden lives, and Cammie and Adrian of course, but Lawrence and Phillip are the only ones who know where those boys live. I wouldn't know where to begin to look for them if they're not home." She gave a light shudder.

"I went round there an hour ago. They haven't been home all night."

I glanced around. Lawrence was still on the phone. "Maybe Phillip could help us out; then I won't have to bother Lawrence."

"Oh, Phillip's downtown at the police station. They wanted to see him this morning."

"Oh, no." I heard Jason's sharp intake of breath. "He's

not by himself, is he? He has a lawyer with him, doesn't he?''

She shook her head. "No. That's what Lawrence is working on right now."

I couldn't believe it. "But he's a youth, a juvenile, he shouldn't be down there by himself."

"He's pretty savvy, you know. And he knows Detective Stokowski. We asked him if he wanted us to wait for him, and he said, 'Whatever,' so since he was comfortable, we came on back here to get a lawyer lined up and all that."

I noticed all the "we" action here, and it was making me a bit uncomfortable. But more than that, I was astounded that they would leave Phillip to deal with the police by himself. It seemed they were assuming some guilt, just as he had predicted. Jason was frowning, looking at his hands.

"Look, Rachel. I really need to talk to Linc and Judd. Maybe if I went up to Phillip's room, I could find something that would give me a clue where they'd be. I figure they'll totally freak out—"

For an instant I'd have sworn she was almost smirking at me. I looked closer. She was the picture of maternal concern, a tiny worry wrinkle on her face. "I don't think they get freaked by much, you know," she said. "They're pretty...worldly. Don't get me wrong, they're great kids, but they've been around the block a few times." She smiled patronizingly. "I don't know what looking at his room will do for you, beyond scaring you to death, but go ahead. Anything you can do for him will help. Lawrence is totally overwhelmed at this point. That's why I'm here. He could barely manage to think straight, so I thought I could put some order in things, but frankly, I don't have much of a relationship with Phillip. I'm not sure who does. So if you can help..." Her voice trailed off as she glanced at Lawrence. "It looks like he'll be on the phone for a few minutes. Just go on upstairs. Phillip's room is the one at the back.''

We waded back through the carpet and climbed the stairs. Of course, I couldn't help peeking into the rooms as we went, just to get an idea of the decor.

Barbara and Lawrence had the master suite on the left side of the hall. It was beautifully done up in a garden motif, a little on the feminine side, but very pretty. Next to that was a small room all decorated in nursery things. "What do you think, Jason? Is she anticipating another baby, or does she simply like cradles and pastel bears?"

Behind me Jason tugged at my arm. "You're not going to look into each room, are you?"

I moved down the hall to the next door. "I want to make sure I've got the right one."

"Stella, cut it out."

I ignored him. "I may never get another chance. This is a great house." I opened the door. The hinges creaked as though they were unaccustomed to opening.

This room smelled of still air and dust. It was done in a tennis racket theme—wallpaper, pictures, rackets suspended from the ceiling, and a shelf of little trophies.

"This room is a shrine. It feels real creepy. Jason, look!" I pointed to the pictures on the wall. "There are *two* boys. The smaller, dark-haired one must be Phillip, but who is the other?"

Jason was reading the trophy labels. "Is Phillip's name Jonathan? These are all inscribed Jonathan."

"I haven't heard of him."

"Must have a brother." He pulled me back to the doorway. "Come on."

I scowled at him. "If you're going to work in New York, you're going to have to develop more nerve, or you'll never get a story." He fell silent, and I moved to the junior-size desk, opened the drawers one by one. In the bottom one I found stationery. Pink onionskin paper with background daisies. Farther back in the drawer were the envelopes. Pink, flowery ones.

I felt cold. "Jason..."

"Stella, let's get out of here, now."

"Wait—this stationery is just like Scared's stationery. I told you about that letter." I took a sheet and an envelope and shoved them into my bag.

"Stella, for God's sake—"

"Look, Jason, there's a blue ballpoint. I had a letter on just this paper from Scared, whose friend seemed to be threatening suicide."

"Oh," he said. "You told Stokowski about it, didn't you?"

"No! It was a distress letter, not a police matter. What would the police do? There was no address, no real name. They couldn't do any more than I did."

"You think Barbara wrote that?"

I shook my head. "No, not Barbara, one of the boys."

Frowning, Jason shook his head. "I don't know—"

"They were writing about Phillip, that's who." Very carefully, using another pen, I raked the ballpoint into the top drawer and pushed it to the back, where it wouldn't be obvious and where I could find it if I needed to. "I think Phillip is a prime candidate for something impulsive like that."

"He sounds like a typical angry kid with a cynical sense of humor."

"You can't tell with teens. Depression looks different in them than in adults. They can look cheerful as hell, then the next thing they'll be completely down. Personally, I think it's a hormone swing half the time, but it's still lethal."

"You've been talking to your social worker friend again."

"I was worried about the letter."

We found Phillip's room at the back of the house, as advertised. It had a sign on the door, No Trespassing. I didn't even hesitate. I shoved open the door.

I'd expected to see posters, pictures, dirty clothes, and empty food containers. I wasn't disappointed.

A computer stood on the desk, a television was propped on the top of a dresser, and a few books were scattered around. I was reading titles when Jason groaned. I turned and saw that he was looking at a dartboard hung on the back of the bedroom door. I moved over closer to see what he was upset about. There was a picture of Barbara in the bull's-eye, with two darts piercing her head.

My stomach lurched, and I felt instantly sick. I wanted to pull the darts out and throw them as far as I could. I even reached for them.

Jason caught my hand. "You can't do that, Stella. You just can't come in here and change stuff, especially if he's a suspect." He glanced around. "There's nothing here that would tell me he's not, you know. This is one troubled kid. I don't know why you're so hooked in with him."

I sighed. "You didn't see him earlier. You've just heard about one side of him. He's a good kid, just bothered by...something. You of all people should understand that; you had a troubled youth."

He shook his head. "I didn't take it out—"

"And you know what it's like to have family abandon you. I don't see what's so different."

"I didn't try to kill anyone."

"Neither did Phillip. In fact, I can't figure out how anyone could. She was always in my line of sight. I could see right through the green gauze of the Venus's-flytrap, so whoever did it had to have some nerve. Must have been damn desperate.''

''Well, it's Stokowski's job. Not yours. He'll nail you if you get mixed up in this, you know. Even if he does have a thing for you.''

I peered at Phillip's desktop, looking for addresses, daisy stationery, and anything else that would tell me where to look for Linc and Judd or—''Thing? Thing? He doesn't have a 'thing' for me.''

''Yes, he does. That's why I'm here. I don't want him making time with you.''

''Jason! He's going with Zelda.''

''I've seen him look at you.''

''I'm flattered, but you're off your nut.'' I left the room and started down the hall. ''Let's find out who this other kid is.''

Rachel was in the kitchen, rattling pans, and Lawrence was off the phone when we got back to the library. His face was lined and gray, and he seemed to have aged in the last twenty-four hours. I introduced Jason and then inquired about Barbara.

He glanced down at his hands, folded on the desktop. ''The doctors say she'll live, but they're not sure what damage she may have sustained.'' He looked at me. ''Because we don't know how long she may have been without oxygen, they don't know how much brain damage she may have. They said it will be a couple of days before they can tell.''

''Is she conscious?''

''They're keeping her unconscious on medications. I guess to let her heal.''

I felt like I was tiptoeing through a lily patch. ''Lawrence, Rachel told me that Phillip is downtown at the police station.''

He sighed. "Detective Stokowski asked him to come down."

As gently as I could, I asked, "Lawrence, I know Phillip is very independent, but don't you think you should be downtown with him?"

He looked helplessly at me. "He said he'd be all right."

"He needs someone there to stand up for him."

"That's what the lawyer said." Lawrence shook his head in defeat. "I never seem to do the right thing for that kid. When he was younger we did fine, but somewhere along the way we lost touch. It's like there's a wall between us, or maybe it's just the distance of years, I don't know. I've never felt so helpless in my life.

"Half the time I want to beat sense into him, the rest of the time I just want to walk away from it all. You can learn how to take care of babies, but teenagers? It's like you never know what's coming. It's so totally unpredictable. One day they're mature, polite, sensible, the next they're out of bounds, out of reach, and out of their minds."

Jason surprised me. He leaned forward in his chair and spoke, a slightly emotional tone in his voice. "Look, it's none of my business, Lawrence, but when I was a kid I had a lot of trouble. I *always* told them to leave me alone, but I really wanted them to be there, to believe in me. There's nothing worse than thinking your parents don't care."

"But I've told him I care."

"I think you have to show him. You need to actually be there."

He sighed. "Yeah, well, I'm going down there, but he'll just tell me he doesn't need me."

"But he does. He's sure he's being blamed for what happened, and it'll take seeing you there even when he says he doesn't need you to convince him you believe in him. My family didn't do that for me—someone else did—but I know things would have been very different if my father had.''

Jason leaned back in his chair. His face was tense, and his eyes were moist. It had taken a tremendous effort for him to say that. I knew suddenly why I would stick by Phillip, and Linc and Judd, too. Someone had stuck by Jason, and it had made the difference. And I'd stick by the boys and hope it made a difference for them.

LAWRENCE GAVE ME a copy of the cast directory and directions to a couple of Linc and Judd's friends' homes and rose to signal that it was time to leave.

"Uh, Lawrence, one quick question before we all get going. Did you drop Linc and Judd off at their homes after you went to the ATM?"

He flinched and tried to cover his reaction by glancing at his watch. "Oh, actually they asked to get out at the ATM machine, said they wanted to walk."

"What time was that?"

"You know, I'm not sure. I think it was about eight-thirty." He blinked rapidly, a sign I associate with people lying about their income, a leftover from my accountant days. He glanced back at me. "Oh, I say. I forgot to give you your advance." He quickly yanked out his wallet and peeled out two hundred-dollar bills.

I folded the bills and put them in my purse as we walked to the front door. "Lawrence, when do you think Barbara can have visitors?"

He shook his head. "I don't know. The doctors only let me in for five minutes at a time. If she's awake, I'll tell her you sent your best wishes."

"Thanks for everything, and tell Phillip we're thinking of him."

I grabbed Jason and hauled him out of there. "Jason," I

said, once we were safely in the car, "have you ever gotten hundred-dollar bills from an ATM machine?"

"Not in Denver. All I ever get are twenties."

"Ninety-nine to one he had those hundreds in his pocket all along. So, why the pretense? And where do you think Lawrence went from eight-thirty to ten o'clock?"

TWELVE

WE WENT TO the addresses Lawrence had given us and drew a blank. The boys hadn't even come to the parties that night. It was as though they'd walked away from the ATM machine and entered a worm hole.

Jason's patience was wearing thin. "Look, why aren't these kids, Phillip, Judd, and Linc, all driving themselves?"

"According to Stokowski, it's part of Linc and Judd's probation—no driving. Phillip has his license suspended for a year for speeding."

He leaned back, thinking. "I hate to be so cynical, Stella, but given their skills, if they wanted to go somewhere they could always liberate a car. I'll bet if we checked, we'd find there was a car stolen and then found again, undamaged but lower on gas." He rubbed his face. "You know, if you're going to check out every teen party in town, you're going to be busy for months. Why do you even care about where they were? What's important is that they weren't at the theater."

I had an uneasy feeling about that.

He signaled, turned onto Colfax, and pulled into a little Greek diner. "I'm hungry. I'm not going another place until we eat."

Jason wolfed his sandwich within seconds. I offered him the large half of mine. "You sure?" he asked. His eyes fixed on the proffered plate.

I put it in front of him. He took an impossibly large bite. When he had finished chewing, he said, "At least Linc and

Judd weren't there. In that sense they're out of the whole mess.''

I looked at Jason, comfortably munching. He thought Linc and Judd weren't involved, so he was supporting what he thought was my active noninvolvement. *That* was why he'd come with me so easily!

"Jason, anyone who wanted to could have come in or out of that theater while we were rehearsing. Once we got Barbara quieted down, no one paid a bit of attention to anything other than business. I didn't even call break at the usual time for fear Barbara would get stirred up again. The only thing that interrupted rehearsal was Meredith complaining. She kept talking about smelling glue or something. But once she realized we weren't going to worry about it, she ignored it.'' I thought for a minute. "Jason, what if it wasn't glue?''

"You said Adrian was always fixing something."

"The cabbage-leaf cover doesn't stay glued down—but what if it wasn't glue, what if it was a solvent? Like ether?''

He stopped chewing. "You think someone gassed Barbara?''

"It would explain why she wouldn't struggle much— she'd slump naturally against the cord. Jason, her own body weight might be enough to strangle her.''

"No....''

"Yeah, it could. All someone had to do was put ether or some other solvent over her face for a few minutes, and she'd be out. In fact, she was drinking tea earlier; what if there was something in the tea? Or maybe she took something to calm down—maybe that's why she was so acquiescent when I ordered her to stand in the flytrap.''

Jason thought about it for a moment, his forehead wrinkled in perplexity. "I haven't seen the stage, but a flytrap seems like an odd place to make her stand. Why didn't you put her up in the office? You said it was built just for her."

I winced. "Maybe I should have. But I figured if she were in the upstairs office, she'd be behind me where I couldn't see her. What she's done before is to scream through the mike and then come bursting down the side aisle. It was so nerve-racking. I was so damn mad! I wanted her where I could see her through the gauze, so I'd know if she even moved. I wanted her as close to the back door as possible, so I could hustle her out if she acted up again."

"Then why not put her right next to the door?"

"That would have been the worst, because everyone enters and exits there. She'd have nabbed each of them as they came off and tried to enter. Pure hell. So I thought the fly-trap was brilliant. Besides, it seemed nicely ironic."

"Nearly fatally ironic."

WE SWUNG BY the theater to see if the boys had come there and found the police tape down and the stage door propped open. "Jason, pull in. I'll bet they're already here."

Four huge black ravens stood in the street at the entrance to the parking lot, taking polite turns pecking at a discarded sandwich. One of them peered at us and cawed to let us know they wouldn't share it.

He slowed. "Hostile guys. Look at the size of those birds."

"Don't knock them. They're our street cleaners."

"Sure wouldn't want one of them overhead."

Jason eyed the scene—the hostile ravens, the parking lot potholes, the paper trash blown against the Cyclone fencing, and the scrawny geraniums in the barrel planter. "You think my car will be safe here?"

"Park by the stage door."

As soon as he'd pulled in and killed the engine, we got

out. He rubbed a small streak of dust from the rear fender, as though he was patting his best friend good-bye.

We checked the steps to the roof. The boys weren't up there.

Inside, only the light in Adrian's workshop was on, casting long shadows into the backstage area. Little snuffling sounds came from Cammie's office. Jason saw I was heading toward them and put on the brakes. "Hold it! I'm bailing, Stella. I'm not up for wet scenes with women I don't even know. I'll just look around a bit." Before I could even answer, he wheeled around and went straight toward Adrian's workshop. It was so much easier to relate to a table saw, no doubt.

I walked carefully past the steps leading to the basement and knocked softly on the wall next to Cammie's office. She looked up, eyes reddened and puffy. Tissues were scattered about on her desk and the floor like wilted azalea blossoms downed by a sudden spring squall.

"How're you doing, Cammie?" I asked softly.

"Not good." She blew her nose loudly into yet another tissue and tossed it in the direction of the wastebasket. I waited for her to continue, but she sat in a morose heap, her glasses on her nose.

"Cammie? Have you seen the boys? I can't seem to find them. They don't know yet."

She looked at me through blurred eyes. "They're not here, and I don't think they're in their little hideout in the basement. Don't worry about them. They'll find you. And they probably already know about her." She sighed. "Barbara always says they've got antennae for trouble." She started to drip tears again, her shoulders shaking in silent sobs.

"I thought you didn't get along with Barbara."

Her head jerked up. "I love Barbara. She's a saint. Everybody loves her. She's held this company together."

I'm always amazed at the way people are canonized as soon as they're dead or safely out of commission. Even the wicked garner redemption in death, and while Barbara wasn't wicked or dead, it hadn't escaped me that her money was alive and well in the coffers of the theater. I had to bite my lip to keep silent.

Cammie's eyes flashed. "She's a fabulous person. I don't know whether the theater can keep going if she...And we need the jobs, Ogden needs his...." She looked up miserably. "You barely know her."

"So tell me about her. She hired all of you; what else does she do?"

"She has kept the little theater alive, the whole tradition, when there's no money for the arts. None of us would be here today if it weren't for her. She's the one that got those boys out of trouble. Hired them, keeps them in school. And Ogden...." Cammie fell silent, staring hard at the tissues at her feet. "I guess you could say she gave him his life back." She drew a trembling breath. "She hired him when no one else would, as a matter of fact."

"Why is that?"

She shook her head.

I didn't know whether that meant she didn't know or wouldn't tell. I was afraid if I pushed it, she'd stop talking altogether. "Did you see Ogden here earlier?"

She nodded, tears coursing down her face.

"Did you talk to him?"

She shook her head. "No. He thinks I begged Barbara to give him the job. He's furious, you wouldn't believe... The last I saw of him, he slammed the door and peeled out of the parking lot."

"You're pretty fond of him, aren't you?"

She nodded miserably. "I've never met anyone like him. I just begin to think I understand him, and then something comes up between us."

"How old are you, Cammie?"

"Twenty-nine."

"Ogden is probably forty. Do you think the age difference bothers him?"

She looked up sharply at me, then her face crumpled. "I thought he really liked the fact that I was young, but the other night, when I was all done up, he got real strange. Since then he's been withdrawn, sort of. Distant."

"Do you remember which night?"

"The night we got the new version of the play. He was already upset about that, and then he came apart when I wore my new nightie. You know that shop, Little Nothings?"

"You bet. They own me, lock, stock, and credit card."

"I got it there. I thought maybe he'd like it. It looks good."

"Everything they sell looks good. Did he say anything?"

"He said it didn't look like me." She shook her head. "Sometimes I get real tired of the artistic temperament, know what I mean? Barbara has an artistic temperament, but while she's hard on people during production, worse this time than before, she makes it all happen. There's a point to her tantrums. Don't you see? Talk to Rachel, she'll tell you. She's been her friend since the beginning."

"Was Barbara always this difficult?"

"Well, she's always wanted things to be right, you know? A perfectionist. I think all that pressure got to her. She couldn't relax anymore." She pushed her glasses up on her nose. "This play was a new direction for her. She called it her renaissance."

The last time I heard anyone say they were having a renaissance, it was a sexual renaissance, and it was a shocker. She had called it a blast, and her husband called it grounds for definite divorce and possible murder. I wondered if Barbara had meant something of that magnitude. "How did Lawrence take this rebirth?"

"Oh, you know. He just says, 'Whatever,' and she does what she wants. Barbara really wanted this play for Phillip. To give him a start in theater."

"Is that what Phillip wanted? A start in theater?"

She looked puzzled at me. "Well, sure. Why wouldn't he? He must have, why else would she do it?"

"When did you first get to see the full script?"

"Oh, the same day as everyone else. She had a hard time writing it."

"What do you mean?"

"Well, she had to rewrite it. She gave us all a copy of the script about six weeks ago, but she came in one day and announced that she needed to make some changes and took them all back. We worked off a brief outline and the first couple scenes right up to when you started."

"Puts the pressure on people, doesn't it? Doesn't give them much time to learn their lines."

"Yes, but it's workable."

"Ogden wasn't very pleased."

She smiled. "No one was. Adrian said it wouldn't work, and even Rachel. She almost never comments, and she said, 'Barbara, this play is too much.' For Rachel, that's saying a lot. Ogden took it better than everyone else, but he's known Barbara a long time. He knew when he took the job that there would be some tough times."

Her eyes focused on some memory she'd called forth. "You know, she really loves that play. She told me it was the cleverest thing she'd ever done and that it would keep us all together."

"What did she mean by that?"

"Oh, she figured it would be a sellout. Another *Mouse-trap*."

Well, in this case, a flytrap. "Did she ever talk to you about her play?"

Cammie glanced away from me, seeming to see for the first time all the tissues she'd thrown around. "I don't quite understand the play yet, but she said it's a message play about drugs. She's pretty adamant about using drugs."

"Phillip seems to think she used them."

"Never. That's the one thing she won't tolerate, drugs. She's moody, but it's the result of all that pressure."

"How can you be so sure?"

She looked off over my shoulder at a spot behind me, her gaze focused on some far-off memory. "Because...because I know that several years ago one of her cast was using and overdosed and died. She took it to heart."

"Who was it?"

She bit her lip until I thought she'd draw blood, then spoke very softly. "My sister. Now, please go away."

I FELT BAD LEAVING Cammie looking even more depressed than when I first went in, but she was clear that she didn't want to talk to me anymore. I didn't much want to talk to me, either. I made a mental note to look that up in the back issues of the *Orion* when I finally got to it.

Before I went to find Jason, I slipped down the basement stairs to find the hideout Cammie referred to. Zelda's sewing room was impressive, with its material, threads, buttons, laces—everything she needed to make costumes. Beyond her room was a vast storeroom that underlay the whole theater. It was crammed with old props, racks of old costumes, sets, all kinds of stuff. They hadn't thrown away anything in the last century.

At the back, through a tortuous path behind a partial wall, I found what must have been an old set for a library, complete with couch, chair, fireplace, lamp, and bookshelves, all arranged in a wonderful private club room. Unfortunately, I also found a coffee can with cigarette butts in it. Thank God someone had installed sprinklers. One spark, and this place could go up in a blaze.

When I got back upstairs, Jason was onstage, inspecting the Venus's-flytrap. "This doesn't look like a real Venus's-flytrap to me. The ones I've seen are little tiny plants."

"You've just been looking at the ones in the grocery store. That's reality. This is fantasy."

"The flytrap part is really good, but the trunk is too thick."

"Well, if you're in the audience you only see a part of the trunk, because the rest of it is behind the second leg, the black curtain. See the anchor rings to hold it?"

He jumped down off the stage and stood in the front row of the theater. "Oh. But I can't see through it."

"The spot has to be on, then you can see just fine. Jason, I'm going to stand where I was last night. Would you go to the stage door, and when I tell you, walk from there behind the scrim—"

"What's that?"

"The very back curtain—and go to the flytrap. Go quickly but real quiet, and don't touch anything. I want to see how long it takes and if I can see you."

Jason reached the stage door.

"Now walk." I listened. "Are you walking?"

No answer.

"Jason, are you there?"

No answer.

"Jason!"

"I'm here in the tree. Didn't you see me?"

"No. I can't see you now. Don't move. I'm going to walk over to see when I can see you." I walked all the way to the stage door without seeing anyone. "Jason, do it again. I want to watch from Cammie's room."

From Cammie's office I couldn't see a thing. From her doorway I could see the stage door only. Anyone entering went beyond the line of sight as soon as they slipped behind the stage curtain. There would be only a window of some seconds of visibility.

Adrian's workshop had been added onto the theater in the last twenty years and was clearly his pride and joy. I felt as though I were intruding in his very private space—as though it were Adrian's workshop, not the theater's workshop. It was a wonderland for a set builder. He had given me a brief tour the first night I worked the play.

It was a large rectangular room with small windows high on the wall to admit northern light, which, Adrian explained, allowed him to see color in natural light, as well as in artificial light from the extensive overhead lighting.

The room had a wide entrance, big enough to move an elephant through, with a short ramp from the stage level to the floor. He had more mechanical tools than my high school shop class, and enough shelving along the walls to hold the stock of a home renovation warehouse.

Along the inside wall stood his workbench, with miniature bins of screws and nails, pens and pencils in a row, and paintbrushes, clean of course, arranged in holders. Everything he might want was right at hand. A telephone and a file cabinet stood at the near end of the workbench. It was picture-perfect—and somehow overdone, as though this were a set rather than a real, producing workshop.

I moved to the most likely place Adrian would stand to see out onstage. From there he could easily see the side door, if he were looking.

"Jason, would you repeat the walk?"

I could see him only in the entry; once he mounted the stage steps, he was beyond my line of vision. And he wasn't visible at all if I was bent over a project on the workbench because of the placement of the file cabinet.

As long as I had a minute, I pulled open the file drawers to see what Adrian kept in there—folders full of receipts, catalogs, play plans, prop drawings, and photos. One file was labeled Current Orders. Inside he had yellow sheets, many with notes in the upper right corner. It would have been easy to rip off a corner with the note "Too much" on it and stuff it in Barbara's pocket.

The door slammed. Adrian appeared, his hair ruffled, his eyes tired. And in a very soft voice, each word carefully enunciated, he asked, "What are you doing in my files?"

THIRTEEN

FURIOUS, ADRIAN STEPPED forward and repeated, "What do you think you are doing in my drawers?"

"Looking for Linc and Judd."

"In my file cabinet? Don't you think they're a little large for the drawers?"

"I thought they might be lying low here."

"In my drawers?"

"Well, God only knows what you've got in your drawers, Adrian."

I pointed to the stack of pink-and-white invoices in the in-basket. "I saw the invoices and thought they looked just like the paper in Barbara's pocket. When the files were open—"

"They were locked. I always keep them locked."

"They weren't locked, they were open—so I assumed you wouldn't mind, especially since you're so close to Barbara. After all, I'd think you'd be as interested as I am in finding out what is going on here. Don't you see—"

A tiny muscle along his jawbone jumped; he was flexing his jaw. "Nothing is going on, as you so eloquently put it."

I eased back, only to find I was trapped against the workbench. "Something is wrong, and I promised Phillip I'd try to help him."

"You think I'm stealing from Barbara?"

"Are you?"

"You were grubbing around in there trying to prove it, weren't you?"

"Are you?"

He exhaled in a snort. "Hell, no! There's no need. She gives us whatever we ask for, within reason."

"Then why were you saving some of those receipts out in a separate file hidden at the back of the drawer?"

His eyes narrowed. "You little snoop—"

"You think someone's siphoning money, don't you? You've been saving those up, haven't you?"

"You've got no business—"

"Do you also think that same someone tried to kill her?"

"No!" He shook his head. "No! What are you saying?"

"I'm saying that it looks to me like you've been saving some of the invoices because you think someone's embezzling. Maybe not much, but a little at a time. It's true, isn't it?"

His mouth clamped shut.

"Did you show them to Barbara? Was she upset?"

He refused to answer.

"That's why she was so angry with Lawrence, isn't it? She thinks he's been taking a little off the top, and that's why she's ragging him over my pay, isn't it?"

He was silent, but his gaze wavered and dropped to the floor. Confirmation enough for me. I started to speak, then held my tongue. Adrian's face had grown haggard, his mouth working as though he could barely keep from talking. He was looking mighty guilty. I'm familiar with the look and the feeling.

I let him struggle for a moment, then asked, "Adrian, when did you show her the file?"

He ran a hand through his hair, shoving it off his forehead, revealing a gently receding hairline. "I met with her yesterday morning." He looked up. "I'm afraid it pushed her over the edge."

"I think it upset someone else a lot more."

A look of disbelief crossed his face. "Nobody here would harm her."

"Well, the police seem to think someone did, Adrian."

His breath came faster, and something in his expression turned bleak. "But I...I thought she just...collapsed under stress."

"And accidentally put her head through a gold cord that accidentally cut off the blood supply to her brain? I don't think so, Adrian. Furthermore, the police have called Phillip downtown to talk to him."

"But Phillip isn't—" He broke off.

"That's right. Phillip wouldn't have access to the invoices, would he? Who would, Adrian? Rachel and Lawrence, right? And of those two, who? Lawrence?"

Adrian glanced quickly around the shop. "Lawrence is a good guy, and he tries, but he just doesn't have the starch."

"That's a nice way of saying he's a spineless wimp."

He smiled. "Barbara has always been the driving force."

I remembered the picture of the second child in the musty bedroom at the Steadmans'. "Adrian, tell me about Jonathan; what happened to him? Where does he fit in the picture?"

He rubbed his chin, again a graceful gesture that reminded me of the stage; but beneath that, I felt, was a more genuine man. "Barbara was talented, but her career never blossomed, so she naturally had hopes for her sons. Jonathan was a child prodigy. So cute, so talented. He took to things right away. Couldn't have been more promising....."

"And...?"

He rose from the stool and began to absently straighten items on the workbench. "Jonathan and Phillip were iceskating with Lawrence in Georgetown. Jonathan went too close to the sluice where the ice was thin and fell through. They couldn't get him out."

I thought about it for a minute. I thought I remembered hearing about the accident. "When was that?"

"Eight years ago. I don't think Barbara or Lawrence ever quite got over it. Maybe that's why Phillip has had the trouble he has. Barbara shut herself away for a good six months after his death. Lawrence filled in as best he could, but he doesn't.... he can't.... he just doesn't have the strength or whatever that he needs with a kid like Phillip."

He drew in a deep breath. "You only saw Barbara at her worst. She hasn't been like that before. Oh, maybe she got a little protective and pushy with Phillip, but ever since she lost Jonathan, she's been devoted to helping Phillip succeed. You don't know what it means to her....." His voice trailed off.

I finally urged him on. "Tell me."

Adrian stooped, gathered up several bottles from the floor beneath the workbench, and started over to the shelves along the wall, talking as he arranged them.

"Phillip's good, he's even got more talent than Jonathan had. In fact, he's much brighter than Jonathan ever was, maybe because things were so tough for him. Even before Jonathan drowned, Phillip had to excel in order to get any notice at all, so he got to be a champion at the worst high jinks, just to get attention, I think. He told me Barbara only saw Jonathan on the stage, never him. And more than once she'd slip and call him Jon."

Phillip's behavior, his reaction to his parents, his hopelessness, and his belief that he couldn't please them were more understandable. How awful to be called by your dead brother's name. How much worse to have him die in such an awful way, especially since he must have resented Jonathan's successes. And then I had a chilling thought: What if before the accident Phillip in his eight-year-old way had wished his brother dead? I thought of how little kids so readily believe they cause disaster. Jonathan's death would be so much more traumatic. I shuddered inwardly. It was a wonder Phillip wasn't more messed up.

Adrian finished arranging the bottles and wiped his hands on a rag.

"Wait, Adrian, what were those?"

He looked puzzled, glancing first at me, then at the bottles. "Solvent, paint thinner—why?"

"Ether?"

He glanced down quickly. "Yes, ether."

"You just wiped them off when you put them back."

"I always do."

"Well, how convenient."

Jason, who had been hovering nervously around the corner, just out of sight but close enough to eavesdrop, came in at that point. "Hey, Adrian. How'd you keep the Venus's-flytrap from flipping over when someone's on it?"

He smiled. "Real simple. I sank anchor rings in the floor and put clamps on the tree trunk, so it's actually anchored tight. It'll hold up to three hundred pounds or more."

"Why is it made to anchor offstage?"

I glanced at Jason. I wished I'd thought of that.

Adrian grinned. "Have you ever worked with twenty-five little kids around? You anchor everything every time. In fact, it was Phillip who climbed on it offstage the very first time and flipped it over on himself. Damn near killed him. Barbara had a fit, so I put in anchors offstage as well. Now I tie everything down all the time. It's sort of a joke around here." He seemed relaxed now, less suspicious.

"Adrian, you were in a perfect place to see the stage door, the stage, and the wings."

His eyes narrowed. "True. But I didn't stand there. When I wasn't onstage in rehearsal, I was working on stage effects. Trying to come up with a better smoke effect."

I really wanted to believe him.

"Stella, you don't get it." Adrian eased himself onto a stool as though his back were sore. He looked squarely at me, his gaze boring into mine. "I loved her. My whole life was Barbara."

There wasn't anything to say to that, so I kept quiet.

He went on. His timing was superb. "Barb meant so well. She was truly an angel to us all. Without her, we'd have had nothing at all like this, but she made it all possible. The whole life. She basically rescued Ogden. She supported Lawrence, gave him purpose. Allowed me to act and to do my woodworking."

"Smothering?"

He hesitated. "She didn't mean to...."

It sounded to me as if she were controlling everyone. I shivered lightly. He caught it. Very observant for someone who was overwhelmed with loss and grief for the love of his life.

"It must be hard living with an angel." I had to work to keep from sounding sarcastic. He caught that too, I think.

He bowed his head. "Sometimes. When you owe someone everything, it's hard to refuse them, but it's not impossible." He raised his head. "I found it possible to differ with her. I think everyone here has. Ask Rachel. She and Rachel are as close as twins, yet they don't always agree." He smiled. "You see, we all love her. She really is an exceptional woman. Maybe we just made allowances because she was so special."

Pardon me while I gagged on the saccharine. "Adrian, where are Linc and Judd?"

He glanced away. "I'm not sure." A half-lie if there ever was one.

I decided to pour on the pressure. I picked up the phone

on Adrian's workbench and punched in Lawrence Stead-man's numbers. Rachel answered.

"Rachel, it's me, Stella. May I speak to Phillip?"

"He's still at the police station. Lawrence said they're holding him."

Adrian overheard. His face suddenly aged. It might have been put on for my benefit, but I thought he was genuinely upset. It was suddenly much more important to talk to Linc and Judd.

"Adrian, let's get real here. Phillip could be up to his ass in trouble, and because of their background, I think all three boys are in some jeopardy. The only thing that might save Linc and Judd some grief is that they weren't here. In fact, they may not even know about this yet."

"They know." He hesitated, then finally capitulated. "They're at my place. They spent the night there."

"I see. How are they taking it?"

"Like they take everything, real cool." He scuffed at the floor with his foot. "Where they've grown up, they've had to learn to hide their feelings just to survive, so you won't get much expression out of them, unless they want you to see it."

"You told them about Barbara?"

He shifted his weight uncomfortably. "I didn't have to. They were here when we found her."

FOURTEEN

ADRIAN LIVED IN the Baker neighborhood, near First Avenue and Cherokee, in a small two-story brick house that looked as if it had been built just after the turn of the century. The house, freshly painted white with spruce green trim and flanked by roses, was set on one side of two lots, so there was a shady side yard with a hammock strung between two large maple trees. Linc lay stretched out in it.

"Just what do you think you'll do here, Stella?" Jason was irritated, and beneath that, worried.

"Mainly I want to find out what they know about this and how they're doing. If there's anything they saw or know that could help Phillip...."

"If there is, it may put them in the hot seat. You think they'll tell you?"

"I think they're more likely to tell me than the police."

Jason parked across the street, and we approached quietly. The lawn was an automatic sprinkling system kind of lawn, thick and lush. I was nearly next to him when Linc heard me and started as though he'd been deep in thought.

"Hey, there, Linc. What's up?"

"Nothing, man," he said, looking momentarily confused. "Who's the dude?"

I introduced Jason. "Jason works at the paper with me. How're you guys doing?"

Linc frowned. "Sucks, man. This shit is *bad.* Can't believe it."

I nodded and pulled up a stool to sit on. Jason stood behind me uneasily. I reminded myself that they were probably thinking, as Adrian supposedly had, that Barbara had hurt herself. Since neither was likely to respond well if I just asked what did they know, I tried to think of a way to frame it more circumspectly. "Ever have this kind of thing happen before?"

"Never knew anyone try to off themselves," he said, and his brow wrinkled slightly, giving him a sad but puzzled look. "Dudes where I live don't need to kill themselves. They got plenty willin' to do that for them."

"Pretty hard thing."

He nodded briefly.

"I was worried you guys didn't know about Barbara, but Adrian said you were there last night."

"Yeah, waitin' for Phillip."

I wanted to ask why they didn't just tell Lawrence they didn't need a ride home, but I figured he'd clam up if I did. His face was crinkled in concern, and another idea struck me. "You worried about Phillip?"

"Not really." Of course he was; the shift in his gaze and the defensiveness in his voice gave him away.

"He's going to be real upset over this. You guys are pretty fond of Barbara, aren't you?"

"Yeah. She's all right." He carefully kept his gaze on a bird searching in the grass for its dinner.

If they had walked from the ATM machine shortly before nine o'clock, they must have been soaked to the skin by the time they got back to the theater. "Must have been kind of wet up there on the roof....."

He glanced at me, then away. I'd made a mistake. Of course, they had their place in the basement. "You guys have extra clothes there, in the basement?"

His eyebrows flickered, and a phantom smile lit the corner of his lips. I worked to keep a straight face. No doubt they'd made use of the costumes in the basement. There were rows of things they could have chosen from.

"Linc, when you were in the basement, did you hear anything?"

"What d'ya mean?"

"Well, like thumps or odd sounds that made you notice or that might have been, oh, different."

He looked blank. "No. Didn't notice. Just the usual footsteps, people onstage walking around. We're not directly under the stage, you know. We're under the back and Cammie's office."

"Yeah, just thought I'd ask. You heard the police, though."

He smirked. "I can hear police a mile away. They walk that way."

"Have you talked to Phillip today?"

"Couldn't reach him."

"The police asked him to talk to them."

He frowned. "He went?" I nodded. "Stokowski?" I nodded again. "Sheeit," he said. It covered a lot of things.

"How'd you get here?"

He yawned, gaining time. "Adrian's a good guy. He's said we can always count on him, so we came here last night."

"You get here before Adrian?"

He nodded angelically; his eye contact was too good. "Maybe...nine-twenty." Two to one that was a lie.

"And Adrian? He must have got here at...?"

"Right at ten."

The police had barely come by ten. Adrian hadn't left the theater until eleven. Linc was lying through his pearly whites.

"And Adrian, what did he tell you about Barbara?"

He looked over at me; his cool gaze dropped a bit, he

licked his lips. "He said she hung herself from the Venus's-flytrap." He swung his feet to the ground and stood up to stretch.

"Phillip was pretty angry with her last night."

"They got into it, but Barbara was okay, you know. Phillip wouldn't have hurt her, not for anything."

"He said he'd kill her."

He shrugged. "Just talk, man. He didn't mean it."

"So when you guys saw the cops, what'd you think?"

"Oh, man." His voice shook. This had the ring of truth. "I knew somethin' had gone down. I...." He realized he'd slipped up. He fell silent, blinking rapidly.

"When you came inside, what'd you think?"

"We were up on the roof by then. All those cars screeched up. Man, we just hit the bricks. Outta there."

"Well, when you saw Lawrence, he was...." I let it dangle, wanting him to finish it for me.

"He was walking in the door."

Walking in the door? The timing was off. I kept my voice steady so he wouldn't clam up. "And that would have been what time, do you think?"

He raised his brows. "Just before ten."

"Do you wear a watch?"

He held out his wrist. "Luminous dial." He looked at me, face wrinkled. "Why's Stokowski talking to Phillip?"

"He thinks someone tried to kill Barbara."

He sat down abruptly. "No shit!"

I LEFT JASON with Linc and went into Adrian's house through the back door. I stepped into the kitchen and took a moment to get my bearings.

Adrian's house was beautifully renovated on the inside. He had modernized the kitchen without losing the essence of the original country charm. The cupboard doors were white wood and glass and tidy enough to look super. I was a little concerned that I'd leave eyeball prints on them. It was almost too clean to be true. And filled with the smell of new paint.

The kitchen opened onto a combined dining room and living room. It had a gas fireplace, antique tiles, and an antique mahogany mantel. The furniture was all covered with drop cloths, and painting equipment was stacked in the corner. Adrian was repainting the walls in a soft cream color.

Judd was in the living room, engrossed in the television. As soon as he noticed me, he flicked the channel. I wasn't sure what he had been watching, but I had a good idea from the heavy breathing, moans, and groans that it wasn't Sunday school material.

"So, Judd, what's up?"

He flicked the remote, dousing the picture, and shook his head. "Just hangin'."

I shuddered at the choice of words and cast about for something neutral to say. "Looks like Adrian's painting the place."

"Yeah."

He looked around, appearing relieved to talk about something not involved with him. "He started that a week ago. Took down a bunch of pictures and threw them away. Said it was time to let go."

"Let go? What'd he mean?"

"I think it was an old girlfriend." He grinned. "Blond."

"Linc said you know about Barbara."

"Bummer, huh?" He met my gaze briefly, then found comfort in staring at the floor.

I sat in the chair to his left. "Linc told me you guys saw Lawrence leave the theater just before the cops came last night."

Judd sat very still, thinking so hard and fast I could practically hear the blood rushing through his brain cells.

He finally looked at me, his gaze troubled. "Are the cops blaming Phillip?"

I needed to go carefully. If I believed Linc, Judd still thought Barbara had hurt herself. "No. But they're talking to him. He needs your help."

"There's no way the cops can pin this one on Phillip, she did it to herself." It was one of those statements that's really a question.

"Judd, I'm worried about Phillip, and I promised to help him. You can help by telling me exactly what you saw. I know you were there."

He looked hard at me, as if he were weighing lies against the truth. He sighed and began to talk. "We were waiting for Phillip to finish, then we were all going to go to this party up north. Westminster. Phillip came out once, told us he'd be done pretty soon, we were just hanging. Smoking." He glanced at me for my reaction. I kept it flat. "It was about quarter to ten when Lawrence rolled up and went inside. He came back out in maybe five minutes, looking upset. Got in his car, drove away. Cops came about ten minutes later. As soon as I heard the sirens, we split."

"Didn't wait around to see what was happening?"

He shook his head, gaze on the floor.

"Did Lawrence run?"

He frowned. "He was just walking fast."

"So he peeled out of the drive?"

Judd looked at me, shaking his head. "He was going fast, but he didn't peel any rubber. That old boat he drives can't peel. And he wouldn't, anyway."

"Forgot." I was thinking furiously. They'd both said Lawrence came back to the theater, went in, and then came out upset. He could have come in, discovered Barbara, shoved the keys in her pocket, and left. Could he have actually come in, killed her, and then shoved the keys in her pocket? If so, what was important about the keys? "How long did Lawrence stay?"

Judd leaned his head back on the couch and closed his eyes. "Not long. In maybe two, three minutes and right back out."

"Did anybody see you when you were inside?"

He shook his head, his brow furrowed from worry. "Most of the time we were in the workshop. For a while we were in the basement with Zelda."

One thing I could check on at least.

Judd sat forward. "Oh no, I forgot. We weren't with Zelda. She wasn't there, so we went up to Cammie's office. Cammie wasn't there either. I guess she was up in the lights on the catwalk."

"Did you see her up there?"

He shrugged his shoulders. "No, but where else would she be?"

"Judd, what time do you think it was when you came up from the basement and went out on the roof?"

He was quiet for several beats, then he spoke softly. "Maybe nine-thirty."

"You and Linc were together the whole time?"

"Oh, sure."

I looked at him. He looked at me and smiled innocently, carefully rearranged his arms and legs, then shuffled again. His body language said he was working hard at something. The greatest story ever told, most likely. Somewhere there he'd told a lie or two, and I couldn't put my finger on it.

I drew in a breath. "How did you know what time it was?"

He gave me a withering glance. "I wear a watch. It glows in the dark and beeps the hour."

"You're sure it was the ten o'clock beep and not the nine o'clock beep when you saw Lawrence?"

Nothing moved on him, except he seemed to pale and his eyelids danced briefly. "I'm sure." But he had hesitated. It was an unrehearsed lie—opposed to his practiced lies, I guessed.

"Judd, you and Linc are lying to me. I think you both went back to the theater to wait for Phillip so you could all slip out and go partying, all right. That's why Phillip kept going outside, he was looking for you two. But...I'll bet big money that the two of you got there before nine and you saw Lawrence come in and out again around nine, not around ten. And when you came upstairs, you found Barbara and thought she was dead and you guys hit the bricks and never looked back. Right?"

He stared at me, pale and stricken, his head shaking slowly and very unconvincingly. "No. You're wrong. We didn't see Lawrence there, not until around quarter to ten."

I shook my head.

He faltered, his gaze dropped to the floor. "We didn't hurt her. We thought she was dead." He looked up, troubled, pleading. "Phillip didn't do it, either. I know it. You want someone to stick it on, get Rachel."

"Why Rachel?"

He hunkered down, scowling, his hands clenched. He was angry. Not, I thought, so much at me as at his helplessness in the face of the blame he was certain would come to him. "Why not? Or Cammie. She's got as much reason as I do, or more. I'll tell you why, 'cause we're easy to hang it on."

"You're not helping him by lying all over the place. What do you think the police will think?"

"I'm not talking to the cops. Those badasses are going to pin it on one of us, you'll see. They can't wait to put Phillip inside."

"Why is that?"

He looked up, sullen, a sort of hopelessness in his expression. "We've been in trouble before. They been waitin' for something to pin on us."

"You've given them some reason."

"We never hurt anybody. Just cars. Most of the time just took them for a ride around. You know what's one of the worst things about being poor? You don't have nothing to do and nowhere to go, and nobody sees you. They lay their old eyes on you, and they don't even see you. It's like you're invisible.

"The only time they see you is in court. Then they see you bigger than life. Tell everybody just what a badass you are and how you don't amount to anything. How your grades are shit. Man, they don't half lie. And then, just to get you out of doing someone else's crime, your attorney's gotta tell it like you're some social cripple who slimed up out of the gutter with no one to love you and nothing to eat and wear. They lie too. Whole system lies. Nobody just says, Hey, man, the kids are bored and they're real good at opening cars and driving and so they drove. That's it."

"And because of that...?"

"And 'cause of that, they're gonna stick old Phillip where the sun doesn't shine and lock him inside for the rest of his countin' days. And if they don't stick him, they'll stick me or Linc. 'Cause we're invisible. We don't even count anyway."

He threw himself back on the couch, seemingly defeated by his own words and worn out from the emotion. His lips were twisted in what I figured was his effort to keep from leaking tears.

FIFTEEN

WHILE I TALKED TO Linc and Judd, Jason called Adrian and asked him to come home, talk to the boys, and get them to call their families. As soon as he arrived, we climbed into Jason's car, but instead of starting it, he sat jingling the car keys, thinking.

"We need to leave for the Steadmans'," I prompted.

"In a minute. We need to talk first." Jason was troubled, almost angry with me. "Stella, you've been told by both Stokowski and Gerster to stay out of this. I know you don't pay any attention to Gerster—"

"Remember? I'm on a terminal contract now."

"—but you should at least listen to Stokowski. I know he likes you, but he won't let that stand in his way."

"He barely likes me, and I'm not messing in anything. I'm doing two simple things. I'm getting background for a story for the paper, and I'm trying to make sure the boys and Phillip feel they have someone in their corner. Without that, they're going to feel completely alienated. You know what that feels like.

"And, if you remember," I continued, "I'm filling in for the almost famous and about to leave for New York City reporter, Jason Paul." I grinned, trying hard to make a joke, but he didn't grin back. Instead he gripped the steering wheel and stared straight ahead.

"Look, Jason, I shouldn't have to explain to you why I feel I have to do this. I can't abandon these kids; they don't have anyone else on their side. I know you're upset, but I don't think you want me to quit either."

At first I thought his stubborn profile and his set jaw meant he didn't like it, and probably didn't believe it, but wasn't sure how to argue back. Then I began to get a sense that there was more to it. He was struggling with something else, something more personal to him. I waited.

He didn't look at me. His voice was soft, almost sad. "I know why you're doing it. You feel sorry for them, especially Phillip. Any bleeding heart, any sad kid, and you're there standing up for him."

He turned to me, the sun glinting across his face, lighting his lovely brown eyes, except now they were pained. "Is that why you like me? Because you think I'm a loser? Is that why you're so upset with my New York call?"

His accusation hurt. "Jason! No, it isn't. Absolutely not. I'm not the least bit jealous of your New York call." I studied my hands, realized they were clutching each other so tight my knuckles were white. "I might be just a tad jealous."

It was true I had a bad feeling about it, but that was because the whole New York call didn't make sense to me, and because it meant a change in our relationship. Right now, though, I didn't want to get into it with him. I just wanted to get over to the Steadmans' and see about Phillip. Jason was important, but Phillip's situation was crucial.

As gently as I could, I said, "Jason, can we talk about this later? I'm really worried about Phillip. He's in trouble, and he truly doesn't have much support."

"Taking the side of the underdog?"

"No, supporting the innocent."

"When I said Phillip needed someone standing up for him, I was talking to Lawrence. He needs his family, his father especially, to believe in him. It's nice you do, but it's Lawrence that counts." He looked into my eyes. "Besides, Stella, if you're right, it could be damn dangerous. You're going around stirring everyone up by asking questions, and you may say all you want about getting background for a story, but if there's a killer out there, he or she isn't going to believe it. I love you. I don't want you in danger. I don't want to love a dead woman. I need a live one who will love and believe in me.''

"Jason, I love you, and I do believe in you."

He seemed to search my eyes as though looking for signs I was speaking from pity alone, then dropped his gaze to his lap. He still didn't start the car. "Stella, I have to tell you something." Then he fell silent.

I waited.

He had trouble starting, and when he did, his expression was sad. I have seldom felt so alarmed. "What is it?"

"Stella, I'm not going back to New York." His voice was flat and too calm, as if he were working hard to steady it. "I was in the can, and I overheard two of the guys talking. They were saying the job was wired for a favorite son, the son of a board member. I was called to interview so they could satisfy the need to 'search' for the position without having to worry about real competition for the favorite."

In the deadly quiet that followed, I heard leaves rustling in the breeze. A long way away I heard a siren. Closer I heard a mother calling her child. My eyes stung.

I felt like crying for him. His disappointment, the pain in his face, were so vivid I felt it in my heart. I was instantly furious at them for being so cruel, so heartless, as to raise his hopes that high for their own selfish ends. I wanted to scream at them. I didn't know what to say to Jason.

From the first I'd been uneasy about the job. I'd had that spell; the call had come through so...oddly. How had New York heard of a reporter in Denver who had only a few credits? There were so many who wrote so well and so often in both Denver dailies, and Jason had had only two or three pieces picked up by them. Of course he was good, but it was way too coincidental. Of course, I wasn't going to say most of those things.

What I wanted was to hold him close and tell him it was all right, but that wasn't going to help either. He wanted my sympathy, but more than that, he wanted to feel good about himself again. I figured reasoning first and sympathy second would be the best approach. At least, I hoped it was.

"Jason, you knew it was a long shot when you agreed to interview. And like *you* said, they were counting on you not presenting any competition. But think of this, they must have been very impressed with you, or they certainly wouldn't have continued the interviewing. They'd have talked to you for a day at most and then sent you packing, and instead, they interviewed you for a week. You must have been unbelievably good to keep them so interested in you."

He thought about it. "Yeah, maybe so." He looked at me and grinned kind of lopsided. "Thanks."

"Even if the other guy got the job, they've got your name, they've talked to you, and they'll remember you. It can't hurt. Maybe if that person doesn't work out, they'll call you back."

He thought about it. "I'm not getting my hopes up."

But I could tell he was. The line between support and false encouragement can be mighty thin. I hoped I hadn't stepped over it.

He started the car and pulled away. "I'm not giving up. I'm being realistic. And I'm not getting my hopes up too high."

"Jason, I know how much you want it. I hope it all works out, I truly do.....'' That was a lie, of course. I wanted to turn the clock back. I wanted him here in Denver at the *Orion* with me with everything great, as it had been before

I resigned and he got his call, but there was no point in talking about it now.

"Jason, changing the subject. What did you think about the boys?"

He stopped at the stoplight a bit abruptly and turned to me, irritated. "Well, God forbid we linger too long on my problems. You want to know if I think these two hardened little criminals could kill someone? The answer is yes. And why do I say that? Because some of the nicest people I've met, in my sordid past, were criminals. And I believe that under the right circumstances nice people can kill. And you know that."

He was pretty steamed, but I ignored it. "So you think they did it?"

He shook his head, exasperated. "I think it's unlikely— but if they decided to, they'd get in and out without being seen—"

"They're pretty good on their feet."

He grimaced. "Look, they're like cat burglars, but why would they hurt her? What possible motive could they have?"

"Suppose Barbara threatened them?"

"With what? What could she do? Actually, she was one of the few who liked them, remember?"

"That isn't true. Rachel likes them."

"Hah! She keeps as far away from Linc and Judd as she can."

"She doesn't."

"She may not hate them, but she does only what she has to, trust me. I can read that woman's body language. I've been on the receiving end of the professional nicey-nice before, remember?"

"So if you were in their place, what would you do now?"

He crossed the intersection and turned onto Sixth Avenue,

his irritation melting. He isn't good at maintaining rage, or even anger, thank goodness. Besides, I could tell that somewhere inside he liked the boys. He accelerated, passing a huge dark red suburban utility vehicle full of little boys in baseball uniforms. "I'd run like hell."

"And if you were Phillip?"

"Run even faster."

THE STEADMANS' NEIGHBORHOOD was quiet, staid, turning its back on the trouble at their house. The trees were stately, the grass well trimmed, the houses painted with respectability. I wondered how often the Steadmans had barbecued with these neighbors, or if they even knew them. I felt as though they were not quite anchored in the reality of this solidly respectable neighborhood. Or maybe anyone's respectable neighborhood. Who were their friends?

Rachel answered the door again, her cheeks flushed. "Oh, Stella. It turns out they didn't hold Phillip, thank goodness. Lawrence misunderstood. He's so upset. He's on the phone now with an attorney, so I guess we don't need you." She tried to urge us out the door, but I stood my ground, holding on to Jason, who was more than willing to turn around and leave.

I inched forward into her face until she moved back uncomfortably. "Well, I really need to talk to Phillip for a sec. Thank goodness he's all right."

"He's lying down right now—" I shoved Jason toward Rachel and took off for the stairs. Rachel murmured after me, "—but maybe you can make him feel better." When I looked back from the top of the stairs, she was smiling happily at Jason and had her hand possessively on his arm, guiding him toward the living room.

Upstairs Phillip was lying on his back on his bed, staring

at the ceiling, his right arm flung over his forehead. He made
no move when I pushed open the door.

"Phillip? How are you doing?"

"Okay."

I sat on the end of his bed. Immediately my gaze went
to the back of the door. The darts in his mother's picture
had been pulled out and now pinned a red rose to the dartboard just beneath her picture. In spite of his brave words,
there were dried tear streaks on his face. I cast about for
something profound to say and came up short. "What did
the police want?"

He gave me the idiot stare I deserved for a stupid question.

"You tired? Want me to go?"

He thought about that one, but as I started to get up he
answered, "No."

"You mind talking about it?"

No answer.

"Linc and Judd are pretty worried about you."

No response.

"They told me they returned to the theater last night
around nine. They were in the basement for a while, and
when they came upstairs, they saw Barbara. They thought
she was dead, and they hid up on the roof. Then they left
when they heard the police sirens. When you went to the
roof last night, you were looking for them, weren't you?"

Shrug. He rolled over, glared briefly at me, then sat up,
his long legs over the edge of the bed on the floor. His feet
looked like they were size 17EEE. He leaned forward, his
elbows on his knees, hands fisted on his cheeks. His hair
fell forward so I couldn't see his eyes, and he seemed to
like it that way.

"They said your dad was there."

"They're lying. He wasn't."

"How do you know?"

"Didn't see him."

"Did you see Linc and Judd there?"

No answer.

It's damn frustrating trying to talk to a sullen teen. I wanted to shake the words out of him and tell him to shape up, all of which would have accomplished nothing at all. "Phillip, help out here. You're holding back."

No answer. Not even the customary shrug. I glanced around the room and caught sight of the books on his bookshelves. *No Exit, The Plague,* Lord Byron's collected poems, *Notes from the Underground, Crime and Punishment, On the Road.* I couldn't tell whether he was into a nihilistic or a heroic role, or if this was the dark side of his soul.

"Who are you protecting, Phillip? Your dad? Or Linc and Judd?" He flinched, but he didn't talk.

My gaze fell on his desk. One of Barbara's albums lay open to a picture from years ago. Barbara was linking arms with Ogden, smiling into his face. She was very lovely in those days; even Ogden was handsome. His hair hadn't receded into the distinctive widow's peak yet, and his cheeks were fuller. He had the same rangy good looks that Phillip would have in a few years. "Your mom and Ogden have been friends a long time."

Phillip looked up at me, then rose and slammed the album shut. "He's a shit," he said and threw himself down on the bed again.

I tried to engage him a while longer and finally gave up. Downstairs I found all three—Lawrence, Rachel, and Jason—in the library. Lawrence was sitting at his desk, head in hands; Jason was frowning into the distance; and even Rachel was looking at her watch. I raised my eyebrows at Jason mutely, asking him what was going on. He nodded at Lawrence.

Lawrence roused himself, scrubbed at his face as though he were wiping away some dreadful sight, and sighed. "I just can't believe this is happening. I don't know where to start, I don't know what to do."

His gaze focused on me. "I need to thank you, Stella. If you hadn't said something to me, I would never have thought to go downtown and get Phillip. He'd probably still be there, being grilled by those guys. He doesn't seem to be able to defend himself. I don't know what's the matter with him. He always stood up for himself before."

As I started to say thanks, Rachel interrupted by rising briskly to her feet. "Lawrence, I think we need to go. We're due at the hospital. Sister Mary Rose Margaret wanted to meet with us."

Lawrence looked at her, surprised. "Sister...?"

"—for a little counseling session. I thought it would help."

"Rachel, I'm not even a member of a church, much less Catholic."

"Actually, she isn't either. She's in one of those evangelical groups that reach out to people in need. So it doesn't matter that you're not a church person."

Horror was written on Lawrence's face.

Rachel faltered. "We don't have to do the counseling, but she offered, and I thought...." The earlier flush drained from her cheeks, leaving her pale and forlorn. "I thought...there's so little comfort now...." Her chin quivered.

Lawrence looked at her stricken face and melted. If he hadn't had starch in his shirt, there wouldn't have been anything holding him up. He rose slowly to his feet, his shoulders sagging. "Oh dear, Rachel, sorry. Whatever. Thanks."

He looked at me apologetically, searching for something to say. "I forget Barbara and Rachel are old friends and...kind of alike, you know. Both so determined, so...Rachel, I didn't mean to...You've been so helpful....." He gave up and moved out from behind the desk, pausing briefly at the window to look out at the sunshine on the lawn.

I figured he was babbling because he was embarrassed that he'd caused Rachel even a moment's discomfort. This man was practically apologizing for breathing. Living with someone perpetually apologizing would grow very tiresome, very quickly. I began to see how Barbara came to be so irritable. If he apologized one more time, I'd want to yell at him.

Jason rose, and I followed reluctantly.

Our little procession, headed by Lawrence, was crossing the living room when he stopped abruptly. Phillip stood at the bottom of the stairs. "Phillip, you want to go with us to see your mother?"

"All of you?"

"Rachel and I. Uh, there's a, a counselor there who wants to talk to us. Maybe you'd like to come to that, too."

Phillip shrugged. "Going to talk about the family skeletons? Maybe dredge up the saint again?"

The little color Lawrence had had in his cheeks faded.

Phillip was nearly as pale as Lawrence. He tore his gaze away from Lawrence in what appeared to be some satisfaction at the pain he had obviously caused. "The saint is my cherished older brother, Jonathan. The one that was supposed to be here instead of me." Phillip came into the living room and threw himself onto the couch, sprawling across the pristine cushions. "He would have made everything right, wouldn't he...*Dad?*"

He emphasized the word *Dad,* and I remembered he usually called his parents by their names. Lawrence turned toward him, staring and unable to reply.

Phillip waited, and when Lawrence didn't reply, he continued in bitter tones. "Jonathan was the golden boy. He was the good kid. You've all heard of Cain and Abel? He was Abel. See?" He pulled his hair back from his face, revealing a faint pink scar near his hairline in the center of his forehead. "The mark of Cain, isn't it, Dad?"

He let his hair flip back in place. "Maybe you can tell the good therapist about how we were playing on the ice on the lake in Georgetown. And how Jonathan fell through. You and Barbara were devastated, of course. Barbara always said she didn't know how I survived. She also meant, *why* did I survive? Well, you know what I say. The good die young."

It was unbelievably painful. I couldn't keep quiet. "Phillip...."

He raised his head, his eyes dull and empty. "You know about weird things Stella. Tell me, how do you compete with the dead?"

It was an awful moment. Lawrence's lips moved in mute, futile little twitches. I had visions of him keeling over with a stroke on the spot.

Jason pulled me to the door. Phillip came behind, opened the door, and stood aside to let us go.

I put a hand on his arm. There was nothing, and yet so much, to say. I wished I could do something, anything to comfort him. "Phillip...Phillip, what are you trying to do? Talk yourself into even more trouble?"

His face was waxen and carefully controlled. "You think it can be any worse than it is? Please go, Stella."

Jason pulled on my arm. "Come on, Stella. There isn't anything you can do here."

"But...." I looked at Phillip. He was clearly so miserable and so hopeless. I thought again of those nihilistic books on his shelves, and I didn't want to leave him like this. It would be better to elicit some kind of promise from him that he'd contact me. "Phillip, call me. See your mom, then call me."

He shrugged.

140 ━━━━━━━━━━━━━━━━━━━━━━━━━━━━━━

he shelves, and Fluffy can do tame tricks too. I've had he better get some kind of response from this, that he'd expected. "Fluffy, come on. Rattle your cage, throttle out—"

SIXTEEN

JASON WAS SHAKEN and silent after the Steadmans and I began to be a bit concerned about him as well as Phillip. I told him about Lips and Fluffy's egg and the need to keep the prospective parents well fed. I think he was as relieved as I was to have something else to think about. It was so much easier to deal with buying dinner for anoles than with Phillip's state of mind.

There was something charming about the sleepy rats, the lazy tarantulas, and the snotty iguanas. The hatchling parrots were my favorite, so ugly and so adorable. We stood in the demi-light of the Colorado Seed and Pet Shop on Broadway, thankful to have the distraction of the price of crickets.

Usually when things get too incredibly sad and stressful, I'm a comfort eater—a really sad movie is a guaranteed three-pound gain—but given Fluffy and Lips's impending parenthood, it seemed much more beneficent to martyr myself and splurge on them.

"*Nine* cents a head? The price of crickets has gone up again!?!" I glared at the plastic bag seething with two dozen expensive crickets. "Nine cents apiece! They're only two-thirds grown, not even singing yet. How can you charge that much?"

Fred, the shop owner, a wonderfully patient man, smiled. "There's a shortage of medium-size crickets."

I thought of Fluffy, his beady little eyes and his little ribs heaving with excitement over fresh crickets. "Are the full-grown ones cheaper?"

"Same price." He smiled and added, "Full-grown crickets chirp, you know."

"How big are they?" Behind me Jason slapped his forehead and shoved a five-dollar bill at me. I refused it. I have my pride. I don't accept charity for my dependants.

The large crickets were at least twice the size of the mediums. A bargain. "Make it two dozen large ones."

Fred carefully dumped the medium crickets back into the medium box, and moved to the large crickets. He shook the paper towel tube into the bag, and crickets tumbled to the bottom of it. Then he pulled the bag taut, gently pinning them, and counted. Two too many.

"You want the extra two?"

If I can't top off my gas tank, he can't top off my cricket bag. I shook my head. He reached in, picked up two big ones, and dropped them back into the box.

"That will be $2.16, plus seven percent tax, for a total $2.31," he said.

"There shouldn't be any tax. There's no tax on food in Colorado."

He smiled.

I dug in the bottom of my considerable purse. "Some people eat insects." I counted out the money and handed it over.

He shook his head and rang up the sale. "So how come you're splurging on crickets instead of wax worms?"

"Fluffy and Lips have an egg," I announced.

Fred smiled. "They usually don't hatch."

"What if it does? What do I feed a baby lizard?"

"Wingless fruit flies."

Jason rolled his eyes. "Oh, my God!"

When we left, I was carrying a week's worth of lizard dinners and Jason was muttering something about the difference between frugal and just plain cheap.

We drove back to the town house and dusted the crickets with calcium powder, then emptied them into the terrarium with Fluffy and Lips. I secured the terrarium lid. At nine cents apiece, I wasn't going to let them stroll around the house.

Fluffy eyed them critically, then blinked at me. One of the larger crickets crawled over him. He closed his eyes. He wasn't all that happy. He prefers small, tender crickets. Lips ducked under the log. I leaned down close to the terrarium and said sternly but softly, so Jason wouldn't hear, "Beggars can't be choosers. We all have to put up with hardships once in a while, guys. Buck up."

Fluffy waited a few minutes more to make sure I understood that he really didn't like mature crickets, then he nailed one. Miniature Jurassic Park.

By evening Lips had struggled with a truly ferocious cricket before getting it down and seemed to have a mild case of hiccups. The remaining crickets had congregated on the hot rock, and were chirping together for entertainment. Fluffy was sleeping with one hand over his head.

Jason was very unhappy. "I didn't know those things made all that noise." He turned up the stereo. The crickets chirped louder. "I think they like jazz."

In the end, we went to Jason's place.

WHILE JASON FIXED a salad and grilled hamburgers, I called the hospital and learned that Barbara was improving slowly; the unit clerk sounded more hopeful than before. She said visitation was still limited to family and then asked if I wanted to speak to either Lawrence or Phillip. So I knew they had both arrived there, at least.

I also called police headquarters to tell Stokowski that I thought his questioning of Phillip had been devastating. I reached only his voice mail and left a message understating my feelings. It probably would make Stokowski furious, but if I hadn't said anything, I'd have been thinking about it all night. I knew Jason needed my attention that night.

As I poured Chilean red wine to celebrate Lips and Fluffy's egg and Jason's return, the phone rang. Jason lifted the receiver, said hello, and instantly straightened up. He listened for a while, then explained that he'd left New York, figuring he'd hear from them next week sometime. He did not say he'd heard the job was wired.

From the tone of his voice, I knew what they were saying. His cheeks grew pink, and when he hung up, he was smiling and his eyes sparkled. "I got the job. Stella, they want me. They had a special meeting this morning, decided I was the one they need. No further interviewing. I'm in. They want me! Me! Jason Paul. Not some favorite son, but me."

I smiled, said congratulations, and tried my damnedest to be joyful for him. "When do they want you?"

"As soon as I can get there. Monday would be best."

"Monday! That soon? What are you going to tell Mr. Gerster?"

"Oh, my God." He picked up the receiver and punched in the numbers. He told Mr. Gerster in detail, explained why he had come home, then said they wanted him on Monday but offered to give two weeks' notice. It was obvious to me he wanted to leave immediately, and it must have been to Mr. Gerster too. I expected Gerster to protest and at least insist on the two weeks' notice, but nope. Inexplicably, he agreed to let Jason go without notice. Why?

I think he even congratulated Jason. In fact, I was pretty sure from Jason's end of the conversation that Mr. Gerster assured him I'd be able to pick up the pieces, and the paper would carry on. I had only two and a half weeks left of May. How in the world would Gerster replace the two of us in that time? I could only shake my head. Why on earth had Gerster agreed to all this? It was as if he'd expected all along that Jason would be gone. Unhappy, but accepting. I didn't get it. Jason was his favorite above everyone, maybe even over Zelda. It made absolutely no sense.

Jason cradled the receiver and stood for a minute, reveling in his success. He was ecstatic. He grabbed me, whirled me around, and then held me so tight I could barely breathe. "Stella, it's going to be great. And now that you don't have a job here after the end of May, you can join me. I'll find us a place, and you can come at the end of May, or the first of June, if you need an extra day to pack."

He pulled me over to the couch and down onto his lap. "You'll love New York. You won't believe how beautiful it is in spring. I think I'll look for a place in SoHo, or the Village."

"Jason—"

"Maybe a loft—"

"Jason, listen to me. You're getting ahead of things."

"I've forgotten something, haven't I?"

"Yes, you have."

"I know. Will you marry me? I'd like to—"

"No."

"Noooo?"

"No. Jason, listen to me, you're taking me for granted."

"I wasn't taking you for granted. I *asked* you to marry me."

"You didn't ask me what I thought, whether I planned to come, what I would do. You didn't think about my career." I was so upset, mad, furious, sad, sick, I couldn't seem to say it the way I wanted to. I wanted to be cool and sophisticated and simply slice him to shreds; instead I could barely keep my voice from cracking over the lump in my throat. "Jason, I'm not going to live off you, with no income, no self-...no self. I'm just not going to do it."

He looked staggered. "Why not?"

"What did I just say? Didn't you listen?"

He looked around the room, dazed. "I guess I was thinking about New York and how great it is that I got the job."

"It is great. And I'm happy for you."

"No, you're not. You're jealous. You're the one who's been competing all this time." He grinned and tried to wrap his arms around me. "Come here. I love you. I want you with me. You'll get a job there. It's that simple."

"It's not simple, Jason. You don't even know if you'll like the job."

"Stella, don't you see? This is my chance to prove myself. Really prove myself to my father, to everyone."

"You don't even know...." I flashed on Mr. Gerster and his story about his son and stopped midsentence. I didn't say it, thank God. I bit back the temptation to tell him he was the favorite son, and he didn't even suspect. "You don't need to prove yourself to me, Jason. *Not to anyone.* You already have. I think what you're tasting is ambition."

"What's wrong with ambition?"

"Nothing, I guess. Depending on what it does to you."

"Well, isn't that the feminine way? You're going to tell me ambition isn't okay? It's uncouth or something? You know what I think? I think you're scared. I think you're afraid to commit yourself to me, you still don't really trust me, and you don't believe in me."

There was a kernel of truth in those words—tiny, but enough so that I hesitated one telling second. Finally I said, "Jason, I can't just up and leave like that. You have just taken for granted that I'd be willing to go with you. You haven't really asked me. And the truth is, I do believe in you. I think you'll make a success of whatever you decide to do. I've seen you do it. But we need time.''

"You're not willing to follow me?"

"Jason, let me put it this way. If our situations were reversed, would *you* follow *me?*"

His reddened cheeks and averted gaze gave me my answer.

SEVENTEEN

SUNDAY MORNING came too fast. One way and another Jason and I found an awkward truce and managed to spend our last hours together enjoying each other on one level, although grieving on another. I saw Jason off on the plane with a lump in my throat and a very visible tear in my eye. I was miserable and more lonely than I wanted to admit. I felt as though I was in some kind of altered state, unable to believe all this had really happened.

At home Fluffy sat on my neck and tried to cheer me up, but tiny little lizard feet are chilly and not exactly cuddly.

Meredith called around noon to confirm our usual Sunday pizza. "You sound so forlorn."

"I'll tell you tonight. I'm not ready to talk about it."

She caught her breath. "Nothing else has gone wrong at the theater, has it? Are the Steadmans all right?"

"No, they're not all right, but they're all still alive, and that's something."

IT SEEMED FITTING to spend the rest of the afternoon at the *Daily Orion*, reading back issues for history on the theater and Barbara. The *Orion*'s morgue is almost another world. Dusty and moldering, it's a huge basement room taking up nearly the length of the building, stuffed with papers, initially in good order, now simply stacked in piles around the edges of the room.

I started at the far end in the orderly area of storage and found I was only a few years off. By moving sequentially through the piles around the edge of the room, I finally found the first mention of Barbara Steadman. Her wedding announcement. From that I could move back, looking for her maiden name to the first mentions of her in Denver.

Twenty-two years ago Barbara had inherited her family's fortune when her parents and grandmother perished in a terrible house fire. As I read the accounts, I vaguely remembered hearing my parents talk about it, although at the age of eleven I'd been more interested in trying out for cheerleading than local disasters.

Barbara had come home late and found the family home in flames. The story indicated that she had attempted to enter the home but had been held back by neighbors. Apparently distraught, Barbara had initially insisted the fire was arson, but subsequent investigation laid the cause to faulty electrical wiring. The deaths of her parents and grandmother resulted from toxic gases due to the smoldering fire.

A period of six months went by with no mention of Barbara until a small notice appeared, mentioning that she had bought and planned to launch a community theater. Six months after that, Barbara was in full social swing.

For the next three years there were accounts of flamboyant parties to launch different productions and pictures showing her with different men, most frequently with Adrian Foster, our current older male lead, and Ogden Bane, our current play director. I was struck by the fact that these people were still here, working in this theater after all these years—seventeen, actually. A very long time in the theater world.

There was one picture in which she, Adrian, Ogden, and a young starlet, Lettie Starling, were posed by a fountain, all looking slightly worse for the wear. The caption indicated that they were announcing the latest play, written by Ogden, then a very promising writer-director, titled *Paradise*.

Lawrence appeared in stories two years later, having come to Denver with a traveling theater company and then stayed on, acting in Barbara's theater. Six months after his first mention, they were married. Their wedding was a social splash, including a horse and carriage ride around Central City before it became a gambling mecca.

Her wedding didn't seem to slow her down. Parties, theater notices, reviews and raves about her productions and acting. There were frequent pictures of Barbara and Lawrence and Ogden, with various very young girls, most often Lettie Starling. I even found a few of Rachel, who as a young woman had been quite pretty in a quiet, contained way. But beyond hints of raucous behavior at parties, nothing. The *Daily Orion,* though, had been a proper, mannerly paper. No real scandals were reported. And there was no mention of a young woman dying of drug-related causes.

I came upstairs from the spider's den about an hour and a half later, feeling as though I was coated with webs, dust, and little crawly things.

Meredith was little comfort that night at the Pig N Whistle. She looked lovely, with her glossy chestnut hair and large brown eyes. She had on a simple, sea green, ankle-length dress that fell from her shoulders, unhindered by cellulite. It made my orange-and-gold-and-navy trousers and top look a little bright, but under it all was a sapphire blue lace and satin confection that my credit card would remember for several installments. Fluffy was ecstatic. He loves the Pig N Whistle.

I, of course, had ordered, so the pizza would have more than three shrimps and a spinach leaf on it. Meredith believes in minimal ingestion. Even in grief—especially in grief—I insist on substantial digestion.

Meredith was doe-eyed and languid. "I like that Ogden, but I'm not getting anywhere with him," she said.

"Good. You need to stay focused on your goal. Finding the Deeper You."

"What if I don't like her when I find her?" She looked at me and laughed. "I'm just trying to get a smile out of you. I don't see why on earth you didn't tell Jason you'd go with him."

"It's this simple. If Jason and I are a couple, then my opinion is needed. The fact that he jumped into it with no consideration for me and no consultation with me means we aren't a couple. It's that clear. That's what I'm sad about."

"Oh."

The pizza arrived steaming, laden with everything except black olives, which I've taken a dislike to after a recent accidental ripe olive overdose.

She busied herself with a sliver of the pizza, removing everything with an iota of fat on it. Her discard heap represented a cardiac attack. I simply ate all mine, figuring that someone had to make up for her.

She finished first. It's easy if you eat only one two-inch sliver. "But you are helping Phillip, aren't you?"

I paused to fish an anchovy out of her slag heap. "What do you mean?"

"Please don't act naive with me. I'm the one who knows you best, better than your own mother. You're doing something, aren't you?"

I wiped my fingers and mouth delicately. "I'm merely working on a little story about the theater and getting background, that's all."

She nodded. "That's probably enough. Now, what do you want me to do?"

That stopped me. Meredith has never volunteered to become involved in any of my difficulties. She gets particularly nervous whenever things are sticky, such as now with Phillip and Stokowski.

"All right, find out what Ogden owed Barbara."

"That's easy. He owed her because she hired him. Rachel told me no one else would hire him."

"Why not?"

"He had a drinking problem."

"There must be more to it than that. He got what amounts to being blacklisted. A lot of people have drinking problems, and they aren't blacklisted, so there must be more to it. He must have done something else. So what was it?"

She was very quiet for a moment, then asked, "Why do you want to know? What are you going to do with the information?"

"I think it might be important."

"You're picking on him because I like him. Is this another of your ways of trying to discourage me?"

Of course it was, but it was more than that. "You said you weren't romantically interested in him. Sounds to me as though you are."

I kept thinking about the pictures I'd seen in the paper, Adrian and the starlets. Lettie Starling had looked really young. "There's more to Ogden than just the broad exterior persona that we see."

She put down her pizza and wrinkled her nose prettily. "What do you mean?"

"Well, we all have exterior personas—that portion of ourselves that we show to the public. And some people show more of themselves, and some less. Barbara, Adrian, Lawrence, Ogden, Phillip, even Cammie, all have huge exterior personas. They're all almost bigger than life. They seem to feel things more vividly. They're so much more dramatic that I forget this is only their exterior self and there's a whole interior self, too. And interiors are very private."

She looked at me skeptically. "What are their interiors?"

I smiled. "Those are the dungeons of the soul. And that's what I want to find out about."

"I don't know, Stella. It sounds kinky to me."

THE NEXT DAY, Monday, I'd awakened convinced that yesterday I had missed something when I was looking through the old Orion issues. I hadn't found out what Ogden had done to be banished from Denver, and I hadn't found any notice of Cammie's sister. I was sure there would be mention of both of those items somewhere. Perhaps I'd stopped too soon.

By seven-thirty A.M., I was at the desk in the Orion morgue, a cup of coffee at my side, a nostalgic radio station playing, and a stack of old papers in front of me. I hadn't slept all that well, and I was cranky, so I figured it was much safer to hide out in the morgue. It's hard to argue with dead issues.

My finger traced down the inside page of a slim issue from July 17, sixteen years ago, when it caught on a name— Ogden Bane. Arrested and charged with contributing to the delinquency of a minor. And that was the year he left Denver. Contributing to the delinquency of a minor was usually a euphemism for sharing alcohol. Normally it was not enough to make the papers, or to drive a person out of town, so what else could he have done that wasn't there?

And how might it fit into the play?

Was the snake representative of evil? Drugs? Or a person, maybe Ogden? If so, why on earth would he come back to Denver to direct a play that would only embarrass him personally as well as professionally?

My eyes burned with fatigue from the poor light. As I replaced the papers, I heard footsteps on the stairs. Zelda appeared, wearing a disgusted expression on her face.

"There you are. We've been looking all over for you.

What are you doing down here? Nobody can find you. If I hadn't figured it out, you'd still be missing.''

"I'm not missing, Zelda. I'm researching a story."

She pursed her red, red lips. "I'd say you were hiding out. Like you didn't want to face me."

"What?''

"I'm no fool. I know you're 'helping' Stokowski, so what are you doing to me?"

"Zelda, I'm not doing anything with Lee. What are you talking about?"

"I'm talking about all the time he spent with you at Joe's Burro Bar, 'investigating.' And all the calls—"

"Zelda," I said, shaking my head. Zelda's jealousy disturbed me. I thought about the time I'd spent with Stokowski in the grill. I had to admit there was an attraction there, on both sides, but that was it. Zelda was jealous because she could sense it and because she was dissatisfied with Lee's attention. "Look, Zelda, I like Lee, as a friend. Nothing more. He is not in love with me, nor I with him. You don't have a thing to be jealous about. I wouldn't ever go behind your back."

Her expression slowly softened until it was replaced with resignation. Deflated, she replied, "I suppose." She sighed and pushed a spit curl back from her cheek. "I'm sorry. It's just that I like to be the only flower he's smelling, and when I see him look at you, or at Meredith for that matter, I get the idea he still sees a whole field full of daisies."

"So why don't you talk to him about it?"

"I don't want to look like a fool to him."

"But you don't mind looking like one with me?"

She grimaced and smoothed her skirt, awkward in unaccustomed embarrassment. "Jealousy is ugly, isn't it?"

"Zelda, honey, Lee is Lee. He's never going to be a warm, fuzzy, passionate guy who only needs you to make his life whole. He's single-minded. When he gets a case he doesn't stop to think about anything else. This is probably the way he'll always be. It doesn't mean he doesn't care for you." I took a deep breath. "Maybe you need a different kind of guy."

I held my breath. As soon as I had said it, I realized it was blunt, even cruel. How I wished I could retrieve it!

She just sat there, thinking and blinking. After about four minutes that seemed like an hour, she gathered herself up and went to the stairs. She had one foot on the bottom step when she turned and said, "I guess I'd just about kill for him."

I waited till she was upstairs, then picked up my coffee cup and radio and climbed up the stairs to my desk in the corner of the newsroom.

I lifted the top five letters from the stack and riffled through them. One dropped to the desktop, a note-size pink envelope with a unicorn sticker in the corner in place of a return address. I opened it and shook out the letter.

Dear Stella,
My boyfriend is a Sagittarius and I'm a Taurus. He's always doing something weird, almost unexpected. His latest thing is scuba diving, and we live in Denver. Denver is a desert!

I liked his adventures at first, but now I wonder if we make a good pair, because I'm always trying to change him. I'd really like for him to settle down, and he says I'm just bull-headed. That part might be true, too.

Is this a doomed relationship?

Troubled Taurus

I glanced at my drawer with the chocolate collection and my rounded hips and then penned a quick reply.

Dear Troubled,
Some relationships are difficult, and yours will be one of those if you are constantly trying to change your partner. Sagittarians tend to like change, the unusual and the unexpected. Taurus tends to be rooted in common sense and slow to change. The two of you will need to enjoy being two individuals instead of trying to be one. Tough, but not impossible.

Good luck,
Stella the Stargazer

I opened the next letter. It was on ripple paper written with a purple ballpoint pen.

Dear Stella,
I'm thirty-five years old, a Pisces, and I live with my mother, who is an Aries. Mother bought us matching miniskirt outfits for my birthday and wants us to have matching hairdos. We are about the same size and sound alike. When I told her I wanted to move out she went into hysterics and said she'd die if I left. Is this normal? What should I do? I would like to start dating soon.

Puzzled Pisces

I wrote a simple reply.

Dear Puzzled,
It's time you moved out and got a life of your own. As long as you choose to stay with her and bow to her fear of being alone, you are telling her she's right.

You're even saying she isn't good enough or strong enough to find her own friends and be liked for herself.

And by not moving out, you are telling her you also aren't strong enough to find your own way. This kind of double dependency is not good for either of you. Move out. Start dating yesterday. Aries can be unreasonably pushy, while Pisces tends to submit and carry a grudge. Recognize these hazards.

Stella

I put down my pen. It was so much easier to see resolutions for other people's problems. Why couldn't I get a handle on my own? What I needed was a Stella the Stargazer to write to. I buried my head in my hands. I decided to write myself a letter. It was easier than I'd thought it would be.

Dear Stella,
I'm a Virgo, and my boyfriend is a Capricorn—likes high places, success, and is determined to watch out for himself first. I can see all his faults at a glance, and while I admire them, I want him to want me more than anything. To give up his job in New York for me. Without my asking. Or at least offer to. At the very least, ask me what I thought about it all before he accepted. What should I do? Is this a doomed relationship?

Jane Austen Smith

I looked at the letter and wrote a quick reply in pencil.

Dear Jane,
How like a Virgo; you've spotted all his faults but overlooked your own with grace and ease. You would

do well to love him as much as you want him to love you. Sitting on your perfectionistic pompoms won't get you a loving relationship, nor a lasting one. If you aren't ready to go to NYC with him, why should he be ready to stay in Denver?

Stella

I looked at it, stricken.

"Stella?"

I nearly fell off my chair, and turned to find Mr. Gerster standing a safe six feet away. I'd been thinking so hard, I hadn't heard him approach. "Yes?"

"I've been thinking about you leaving and Jason now gone, and I was wondering if you'd consider training Andy tomorrow?"

"Train Andy?" It was too much. Angry, burning tears actually gathered in my eyes. I was enraged. Train my replacement? "I don't think I can do that."

He tugged nervously at his bow tie. "But I need to have him trained before you leave."

The ring of the phone was far away, filtered by my raging humiliation and fury. Eyes burning, I lifted the receiver to my ear. Mr. Gerster backed wordlessly away, surprise written across his face.

"Stella, it's me, Phillip. Can I talk to you? Privately?"

EIGHTEEN

IT WAS A RELIEF to get out of the office. I picked Phillip up at the corner of Sixth and Steele and proceeded straight to the closest burger heaven. Hamburger therapy works well. Feed kids in a car, and they'll talk. Especially if it's moving. I don't know if it's that their mouths get moving, so they are more comfortable talking, or if there's something about a full stomach and a moving vehicle, but whatever it is, it worked on Phillip.

We went south on Colorado Boulevard and wandered through southeast Denver, then west on 470 to Wadsworth and back up the Sixth Avenue Freeway. By the time we got to Wadsworth and Sixth, Phillip had admitted to a teenage hell made worse by Barbara's interminable interference. "It wouldn't be so bad, but Dad keeps trying to make excuses for me. He tells Barbara that I'm real smart, but the way he says it makes me sound so freaking stupid I might as well be a complete idiot."

"Sounds like he thinks you're smart, though."

"You don't get it." He was quiet for a while. "Maybe it doesn't matter what he thinks. Nobody listens to him anyway. Barbara doesn't." He looked out the side window, awkwardly covering a catch in his voice. "Why can't they just be normal?"

"What would normal be, Phillip?"

"Normal is when they love you without trying to make you into something outstanding. Why can't I just be ordinary? I *am* ordinary." He looked steadily at me, scowling. "I wish I'd died instead of Jonathan. Then I could be the saint. The perfect kid, and he could live with being the family disappointment.''

There was something incredibly appealing about Phillip trying so hard to be tough and sophisticated. One of these days he might pull through and make a wonderful, sensitive man, but right now he was a boy, sixteen and barely able to keep afloat.

I was uncomfortable, not sure I was handling this in an effective way, but never one to miss an opportunity to put in my two cents, I plowed on and muttered some pretty feeble attempts to bolster him. I've lived twice as long as he has, and all I could do was offer genuine sympathy, feeling helpless, maybe because he was asking questions to which I myself had no answers.

''What about Linc and Judd, Phillip? They're your friends, they believe in you. They like you for who you are.''

''They're about as important as I am.'' He tapped his foot against the floor of the car. ''You know what we are? We're freaks.''

''What do you mean?''

''There are geeks, freaks, druggers, and the in group,'' he said. He was more comfortable talking about this. I guessed that he'd often talked about it to Linc and Judd. ''You can figure out the in group. That doesn't take any brains. The jocks are in the in group, of course. Geeks are the ones who study and get good grades. Half the time they don't even know they're out of it. They like computers and wear their jeans under their armpits. The druggers barely notice what they wear, and their eyes are zeros.''

''There's more to life than being popular.''

''I'm not talking popular. I'm talking real. Freaks aren't real. We're basically invisible. When they do see us, they think we're weird. Might as well be gone.''

"All right, Phillip. What are you really talking about?"

He stared out the side window for several minutes, then spoke in a low, husky voice. "I wish I were dead."

We were on the Sixth Avenue overpass, with cars whizzing alongside, and it took all of my self-control to keep a bland face and tone of voice. "I don't think it would be much better. Think about it, Phillip. Would you really like to be six under? That's really out of it, you know. That's the ultimate. A dirt nap."

"A DIRT NAP? You called death a dirt nap? What were you thinking?" Meredith was shouting at me. It takes a lot to get Meredith to shout, but once done....

I held the telephone out at arm's length. "I wasn't thinking," I replied. "It just flew out of my mouth."

"Like so many things. And then what happened? Did he step out into traffic and hurt himself? You must have put him over the edge."

"Actually, he was real quiet for a bit, then he laughed. I thought it was a healthy sign—the laughter, I mean. I let him off at Linc's house and made sure Linc was there and would keep an eye on him. Then I dug up Lawrence at the theater."

"Dug up? Stella, are you hearing yourself?"

"Stop it, Meredith. I told Lawrence that Phillip was really upset and that he needed to keep track of him."

"Did you tell him that Phillip sneaks out of the house all the time through his window?"

"All he said was, 'Whatever.' He's absolutely overwhelmed by everything. Then he claimed he had come back to the theater and talked to Phillip during the time he was offstage, so Phillip couldn't have attempted to kill her. But the way he said it made everything worse. Meredith, he sounded as though he was dummying up the alibi because he believes Phillip is guilty.''

"Maybe he does. Maybe Phillip is.''

"Stop. By the way, I haven't reached Ogden yet, but Lawrence said we'd have rehearsal tonight. Did you find out what Ogden owed Barbara?''

"I haven't been able to reach him either.''

LAWRENCE HAD ALSO told me there was a rehearsal that night and was surprised I hadn't heard from Ogden. Neither Zelda nor Cammie had talked to him either.

Cammie snuffled over the telephone. "I haven't heard anything from Ogden since yesterday. I thought we'd go out last night, but he didn't call, and I couldn't reach him.'' She blew her nose, then continued. "If you ask me, if Lawrence had ever said anything other than 'Whatever,' maybe none of this would have happened. Barbara would be okay, and Phillip wouldn't be in the trouble he's in.''

"You think Phillip did this?''

"Well, he could have. Sometimes I think Lawrence set it all up so Phillip would drive his mother over the edge and Lawrence would be free.''

"Really!'' Finger-pointing isn't as dull as I thought.

"Lawrence abdicated his role as husband and father. He stood around with his thumb up his nose and acceded to Barbara, letting her rule like a tyrant, railing at Phillip....It's not so far-fetched.''

Lawrence backstage. Lawrence angry. Lawrence being nagged constantly. It could play, except for one thing; Lawrence wasn't in the theater. He left at eight-thirty, and he didn't come back until around ten. "What time was it when you saw him that night?''

"I didn't say he did it. I said he set it up.''

"You don't seem very fond of Lawrence."

"I'm not. He's been pretty rotten to Ogden, he's a spineless wimp, and if you ask me, he's been pretty friendly with Rachel."

"Was he a friend of your sister?"

"He hated her. He was responsible for her losing her leading role."

"Cammie, what was your sister's name?"

"Lettie Starling. She used Mom's maiden name for her last name. She thought the name Dinkum wouldn't play. She was so depressed after Lawrence fired her from the lead, she...it was awful."

"Why did he do that?"

"They were putting on *Cat on a Hot Tin Roof*. He convinced Barbara that Lettie was too young to play Maggie, that it would corrupt her. Lettie never got over that. Lawrence said she was strung out, but that was a lie."

I remembered the spotlight exploding when Meredith was in the middle of her lines. "Cammie, do you remember what time the light outage was?"

"What? Oh, I don't know, I think...about nine-fifteen, why?"

"You were in your office when it happened, weren't you?"

Hesitation. "Yeah—at least, I think so. Why?"

Her office was a long, narrow affair with her desk midway along the wall. She wouldn't have seen Santa in his birthday suit. "How long after the spot went out was it before you went up to fix it?"

"Maybe five or ten minutes." But her voice wasn't as sure as before. "I don't know, Stella. This whole play is a Macbeth. Jinxed. We ought to cancel the show before somebody actually dies."

I CALLED LAWRENCE to tell him that everyone was set for rehearsal tonight. He was surprised to hear I hadn't reached Ogden yet. "When did you hear from him?"

"I talked to him, oh, last night around dinnertime, after we got back from visiting Barbara. She's coming along real well, by the way. They're pretty sure she'll make it now."

"Great. Was Ogden at home when you talked to him?"

"At home and possibly celebrating something. You know, Stella, everyone except you seems to think Phillip had something to do with Barbara's accident—"

"It wasn't an accident, Lawrence."

"Whatever. But I want you to know I saw Phillip at the theater that night. He was outside, going up on the roof."

Why was he telling me this? "What time was that, Lawrence?"

"Uh, about nine-thirty. Maybe a little before then."

Was he lying? Was he admitting he was there? Trying to cover for Phillip? It didn't make sense. It especially made no sense that he would tell me. "Oh? Have you talked to Detective Stokowski about all this?"

"A few minutes ago."

Lawrence was putting himself in jeopardy by admitting that he saw Phillip offstage that night. If he was telling the truth, though, it meant he was there. And that meant he had as much opportunity as anyone else, and perhaps a lot more motive. He wouldn't be the first henpecked husband who decided enough was enough. Looked reasonable to me.

I called Stokowski. He answered on the second ring.

"Lee, Lawrence told me a few minutes ago that he was with Phillip during the time he was offstage, so Phillip has an alibi."

"He's just trying to cover for the kid."

"Maybe he wants *you* to think that because *he* doesn't have a good alibi. It's very simple; you lay blame on someone, by acting as though you're lying for them. That way they look even more guilty, and you look like a sacrificing saint."

"You're going overboard here. Lawrence has a solid alibi. You're not getting into the case, are you?"

"No." I was emphatic. "But Phillip is getting scapegoated here. I, however, am merely writing a background story on the theater for the paper. I'm filling in for Jason."

"I heard. Zelda said you're really leaving the *Orion*. She said Mr. Gerster is real down, too. She thinks he'll close shop."

I could feel my blood pressure rising. Stokowski was doing nothing more than trying to distract me. "Like hell he will. He's going to put Andy the gofer in charge. Makes me feel valuable. You haven't seen Ogden lately, have you?"

"Not since Saturday morning. There's a nice safe job for you. Why don't you go find him?"

"I think somebody better."

IT WAS CLOSE TO one o'clock when I pulled up in front of Ogden's apartment building on South Pennsylvania in the west Washington Park area. He lived in one of the characterless three-and four-story brick buildings that replaced the quaint turn-of-the-century homes during the renovation frenzy of the sixties and seventies. His was a four-story, beige brick, six-unit building just north of Alameda.

I rang the bell for admittance, with no response. I was knocking on the manager's door when Cammie pulled up. She waved and called out, "Wait!"

"Do you have a key?" I shouted.

She shook her head.

The manager finally answered and grudgingly agreed to check on Ogden. We hustled up to the third floor, where the manager fitted the key into the end door on the left side of the hallway. The door opened inward with a prophetic groan.

Ogden's apartment had all the signs of a furnished rental: worn gold carpeting, beige walls, brown tweed couch, and chairs that looked soft but were hard as a rock and itchy to sit on. The pictures on the wall were determinedly pastoral and looked as though they were bolted there for the ages. The place was more impersonal than Motel 6. The only evidence of real habitation was a board-and-brick bookcase under the picture window, a flock of snapshots, framed, standing on the top shelf...and a foot sticking out from the couch.

"Oh, no!" Cammie yelped.

Ogden was sprawled half on and half off the couch, his right arm stretched toward the telephone as though he'd been trying to call for help.

"Oh, my God!" the manager said and gulped. He turned a nasty shade of gray, said he'd call an ambulance, and disappeared down the stairs.

Cammie flew to Ogden's side, knelt, and reached for his head. At the last minute she hesitated and glanced up at me, her eyes filling again, her chin trembling. "I think he's dead."

There was no obvious blood, no vomit. No terrible death smell of loosened sphincters. I knelt on the other side of him and touched his face. It was cool, damp, still pliable. "Check his pulse," I said, as though I was some expert.

He was breathing in short, ragged gasps and shallow pants. He felt cold, almost clammy. I felt a fluttery pulse in his wrist.

Shock? He was unbelievably pale, staring now and unresponsive, his lips gray, mouth sagging open. I ran to his bedroom, grabbed the bedspread off his bed, and took it back to tuck around him. Then I called Stokowski and left him a message.

"Hold his head, we'll slide him to the floor," I ordered. He groaned when his hips bumped, but Cammie managed not to drop his head. His left arm flopped out, and I saw a steel bracelet. A medi-alert. Diabetic. "Did you know he was diabetic?"

Cammie nodded. "Of course. Everyone knows." She began to croon to him, holding his hand and stroking his head.

I returned to his bedroom to a pile of mail I'd spotted on a little desk. Carefully, I peered at the envelopes. He had a car insurance notice, a telephone bill—opened but not yet paid, no long-distance calls noted—and a car payment bill. It was almost like looking at my own mail.

I checked his closet and drawers and found a few feminine articles of clothing that looked like they'd fit Cammie, but not the quantity I associate with regular staying over. I wondered what stage their relationship was in.

The bathroom revealed no interesting drugs or salves. He appeared to take meticulous care of his teeth; at least, he had enough equipment to open a small dental hygiene clinic, and happily there were no antifungal ointments or VD remedies. Nor were there any feminine necessities. I guessed the relationship was barely there.

The kitchen sink held several pieces of unwashed flatware, a couple glasses, one with orange juice residue, and a plate with the remains of a large piece of what appeared to be cake and ice cream. I checked the trash and found a mound of chicken bones and plastic containers, discards of a roasted chicken dinner from Boston Chicken, and a Sara Lee cake box. And right with it was a disposable syringe and an empty insulin vial.

In the refrigerator were a quart of milk, a shriveled apple, half a loaf of whole-wheat bread, a six-pack of Heinekens, and his diabetes gear—syringes, vials of insulin, one unsealed, and a blood testing kit. All together in the vegetable bin. Handy.

"Cammie, has he had spells like this before?"

"Nothing like this. Once in a while he'll say he needs to eat something, but he carries those juice cartons and sips those if he feels he needs something in a hurry. He's really careful about it. Tests his blood twice, three times a day." She stroked his forehead and murmured to him.

The fire department rescue truck arrived, the ambulance and the police shortly thereafter. I told them about the insulin, and the paramedics seemed to think he was most likely in diabetic shock.

Cammie was nearly hysterical. "Can't you tell me whether he's going to be all right?"

The older paramedic finally had a minute to pay attention to us. "I can tell you this. A little longer, and he would have been dead."

NINETEEN

LATER THAT NIGHT the hospital confirmed that Ogden had been in a diabetic coma, having apparently neglected his insulin. Stokowski was there when I arrived, hoping to talk to Ogden.

"You're considering the possibility that someone adulterated his insulin, aren't you? A little added sugar water could do it. The officer got the vial from the trash as well as the opened one in the fridge, didn't he?"

"You're messing in this, aren't you?"

"I'm concerned for him. I'm the one who found him, remember? You told me to go looking for him."

"I did. And now I'm telling you to back off. The vial is in the lab right now. It's conceivable that the whole thing is an accident."

"He was an experienced diabetic. Why don't we ask him about his insulin?"

Ogden's face was still an unhealthy shade of pale, and his eyes were ringed with fatigue. He could have played the part of a ghost without any makeup. "I'm fine. Really I am," he said, but he didn't lift his head or make any attempt to sit up. His hand was cold and bony to the touch.

"Ogden," I asked, "did you notice anything unusual about the insulin? Anything a bit different?"

He shook his head briefly. "I overate, didn't use enough insulin. Don't remember anything else."

Stokowski moved up to the bedside. "Ogden, was the insulin open when you used it?"

"I opened it yesterday."

"We're testing it to see if it was altered at all. Did you think it might be?"

"No. They think I may just be out of adjustment because of the stress."

"How long are you going to be here?" I asked.

"Out tomorrow, I think." He smiled weakly. "Lousy insurance."

"We'll miss you at rehearsal. Anything you especially want me to do?"

He shook his head. That small conversation seemed to leave him drained.

"Ogden, does anyone else have a key to your apartment?"

"No."

Stokowski spoke up. "In the last three days, was anyone in your apartment besides you?"

He was silent for a few seconds, eyes at half-mast. "Adrian, Cammie, Rachel...."

The nurse entered the room, signaling for us to leave. I had one last question. "Ogden, on Friday night did you see Lawrence at any time after eight-thirty? Could he have returned earlier and left again?"

His eyes were closed, but I thought I saw minute movements beneath his eyelids, as though he was searching his memory for something—or making it up. "No, I didn't see him." His voice was nearly a whisper.

I was halfway across the room when I heard him say, "He came in at the end, around ten."

I went back and leaned in real close. "I don't believe you were even at the theater, Ogden."

His eyes flew open.

"Where were you?"

No answer.

Stokowski was rigid, a cautionary hand on my arm.

"Ogden, tell me. Who did Barbara aim that play at?"

His eyes were furious. "Nobody."

I didn't believe it for a minute.

STOKOWSKI PRACTICALLY dragged me from the room.
"What are you doing, and what was all that about?"

"Lee, Adrian said that Barbara claimed to have written
that play on several levels. Her words, 'several levels.' I
think she really meant several targets. The play has made
people anxious. For instance, Phillip thinks his mother
wanted him to have died instead of Jonathan. He got that
idea from the Venus's-flytrap ending in the play, where he
has to throw himself into it. I believe the rest of the cast
are interpreting the play personally as well."

"This is pure conjecture. Unless you have something else
to base this on—"

"What about two attempted murders? Don't they count
for anything?"

He paused, the expression on his face grim. "Look at it
this way, Stella. Barbara has always loved publicity. Recently her theater has had declining audiences, her productions have been undistinguished, and her career is in the
doldrums. But with her quote 'accident,' she is back in the
news. Ogden is diabetic, overeats and drinks, mismeasures
his insulin, and crashes. Both are fully explained, and there's
nothing that says they are anything but accidents."

"The only accidental thing about Barbara's 'accident'
was that she lived."

"What time do you normally take a break?"

"At nine-fifteen."

"So if you had taken a normal break, she'd have been
found after very little time and would have been resuscitated
with little consequence."

"You're really wrong on this one, Lee. Trust me, someone is systematically trying to kill off this cast, and I think it has everything to do with the story behind the play.''

I LEFT STOKOWSKI and headed home to check on Fluffy and Lips and finish Mom's tuna casserole for dinner. Not even tuna casserole can keep me from worrying. When I'd talked to Lee, I was so sure I was right and so angry that he wouldn't do anything. The anger had made me brave at the time, that and the fact that he was there. But alone, I felt anxious and more than a little worried about everyone's safety, especially my own.

I spent time catching a couple of flies for my guys. I've found that flies don't seem to be able to see clear glass jars, so I can put a jar over them as they crawl on the windowpane. Then I slip a card under the jar to keep them in, shake them, to disorient them and drop them in the terrarium. Don't even have to touch them.

Like a gentleman, Fluffy waited for Lips to get the first one. Lips usually snatches flies as though she were starving, but she turned away from them and buried her head under the log. She was brown and moody again.

Troubled, I looked for the egg. After several minutes of hunting, I found half an empty shell on the terrarium floor. I moaned. I should have known those giant crickets were a bad idea. Damn things! They must have found the egg and eaten it. The only thing that kept me from smashing each one of them was the certain knowledge that Fluffy and Lips would eat them, slowly and one at a time. If the crickets had any sensibility at all, they'd suffer. And I wanted them to suffer.

No wonder Lips wouldn't relate. Even Fluffy seemed a bit down. He caught and ate the flies but then closed his eyes. He didn't even want to go on his leash with me that night.

I tried to reach Jason to relate my reptilian tragedy, but he was out, so I left a lengthy message telling him how I found only the remnants of the egg and how Lips was depressed and Fluffy morose. By the time I told him how bad I felt, I was morose myself and practically crying. I hadn't realized how much that egg had come to mean to me too. Even though I had known it would be impossible to hatch, that simple little egg had held out a wonderful promise.

The other thing I realized was that Jason was one of the very few people in the world I could talk to about such things without being laughed at. And now he, too, was gone.

I HAD A CHOICE. I could pray that Lee was right and leave things alone, wait and see what happened. Or I could do something. Doing something won, because to do nothing leaves me free to worry even more. As depressed as I was, rereading the play turned out to be relatively uplifting, primarily because it gave me something else to concentrate on.

I came to a couple decisions. The most important was that, regardless of Stokowski's opinions, I believed firmly that both Barbara and Ogden were victims of attempted murder. I also believed that whoever had done those two would try again, but with both Ogden and Barbara safe in the hospital, there was a window of opportunity before the killer tried and succeeded.

I decided that I would follow the exact same rehearsal schedule that we had had the night Barbara was nearly killed. I wanted to check the time frame for the attack on Barbara, which I figured took place in a twenty-to-thirty-minute window from nine o'clock to nine-twenty or nine-thirty, assuming the boys were telling the truth when they said they found Barbara at nine-thirty. This would also give me a chance to really analyze the play for all the ''levels'' Barbara thought she'd put in there.

I settled down halfway back in the theater, checked the time, and started the play. This was the first dress rehearsal, and the first time to see everyone in costume. Phillip and the singing mushrooms opened the play. They were terrific. Zelda's costuming was marvelous. Frankly, the rest of the play could be cut, and this scene could stand on its own as sheer entertainment. Linc and Judd obviously loved their parts and were very talented.

As the play progressed I could see how Barbara had shaped it to play as an antidrug morality tale suitable for children and an allegory about the dangers of temptation for adults. It was that and more. For the first time the play began to come alive, and it was interesting, not intrinsically, but because I sensed something new was happening.

Adrian, playing the part of Slither, the snake, was great. His costume and makeup were outstanding. When he stood beneath the number-one spot, I was stunned. His eyes became sunken dark orbs, his cheekbones stood out in relief, and his jaw seemed stubborn, like Ogden's. Was that deliberate? I made a note in the margin of the script to ask if Barbara was responsible for designing the costumes and makeup also.

The greatest shock of all was the appearance of Meredith as Eve in a blond wig. I was mesmerized. Not because she was good with her lines; she wasn't. But because she looked so like the pictures of Lettie Starling in the back issues of the *Daily Orion*.

Of course, it could all be Zelda's interpretation, since she was in charge of costumes and makeup, but if Barbara had designed it...then who really was the snake? Adrian? Ogden? Or by some stretch, could it be Lawrence?

Barbara was not a subtle woman, nor was she an accomplished playwright. She had no history as a writer, and there was no indication that she was particularly imaginative; in fact, the opposite was true. She was very skillful at imitating, at acting. Of course, there had to be personal history in the play. The question was, how much and whose history.

After the first two acts, I called a break so Zelda and Cammie could work with Meredith on the Venus's-flytrap scene. Phillip and the mushrooms wasted no time getting outside for a smoke, so I tackled Adrian, who was onstage, reattaching a loosened edge of the cabbage-leaf bench. He glanced up as I approached, then squinted at the tack and tapped it in.

"Adrian, how much did Barbara tell you about this play as she wrote it?"

He checked the rest of the covering for other loose bits, then finally responded. "A little. Like I told you before, she meant it to have multiple meanings."

"Why do you think she did that?"

"She wanted it to appeal to different audiences. She has always been dramatic." His voice was gentle, mellow. A golden smile lit his eyes. "She can't give up the limelight. She loves attention."

"You care a great deal for her," I said.

"Yeah, I always have. She's not the most talented actress in the world, but she has a driving spirit, and she can be so funny when she's up." He shook his head. "But when she's down, she's horrid."

"Sounds like a nursery rhyme."

He laughed lightly. "She's a complicated woman and not easy to be around. I think the only things she really cares about in the world are her career and her boys. That includes Linc and Judd, for some reason."

"And her career now means the play?"

"She's set her goal to become a famous playwright, so she will have something live on after she dies."

"Nearly came sooner than she planned. Did she design the costumes and makeup, too, or is that Zelda's creation?"

"She did the whole thing. Top to bottom."

"When did she finish the costume directions?"

"I saw the whole script the same day you did."

"You mean ten days ago?"

He smiled. "Yeah."

"Where did she get the idea for this play?"

"From me. She said I told her to quit making up fantastic situations and just write about something she knew." He rose, dusting off his hands. "She wanted to write something that would use the boys, of course, but she had a terrible time coming up with the idea. I don't know how many things she went through.

"Now, she lived a lot in her lifetime. She wasn't one to let things go by without trying them. Phillip gets his rebellion honestly; it's not something out of the blue, much as Lawrence would like people to believe that.

"Barbara was a wild thing when she was young, and she could have written any number of things from her own life. Don't know why she chose the Garden of Eden. Doesn't make much sense to me, but she was sure pleased with it. Said it was the deepest thing she'd ever written."

"It was the only thing she'd written, wasn't it?"

"Yes."

"And she didn't ever tell you what all her 'levels' were?"

"No. I haven't really thought about it, although—" He stopped, his glance rising to the box office window. I looked, too, and saw Lawrence standing there, watching us. Adrian waved, and Lawrence turned away without acknowledging it. Adrian's expression hardened. It occurred to me that Lawrence could have been exceedingly jealous of Barbara, but so could Adrian.

He looked back at me and shook his head. "I suppose

she could have meant a lot of things by it." He stood up stiffly and stretched. "I need a cigarette before rehearsal starts again."

I scurried up the stage steps and followed him into his workshop, where he replaced his hammer and tacks and began to straighten his workbench.

"Adrian, why do you suppose Barbara wanted Ogden to direct the play? I know she insisted on it."

He took a minute to answer, arranging little jars of tacks and nails on the shelf. "I think she purely wanted to help him out. She likes him. He's talented. She likes to rescue wounded birds."

"She said he owed her. What did she mean?"

He brushed sawdust off the workbench, picked up a broom, and started sweeping. I figured it was a metaphor for what he really wanted to do, sweep me out of his workroom. Freud lives. I didn't move, so he had to stop. I could hear the irritation in his voice when he answered. "Look, you're asking questions about stuff that doesn't matter. Now I'm going for a smoke. This stuff is old history, it's not relevant."

"Someone thinks it relevant. Someone has nearly succeeded in killing two people. The next time, someone may die. I think the play is the catalyst, and someone here wants to keep it from being produced."

Two pink spots appeared on his cheeks. "Ogden is diabetic, he has trouble with it all the time. There's no reason to think this incident was any different than one of his ordinary episodes. He probably ate and drank too much." Adrian waved his arm angrily, knocking a stack of papers onto the floor. "I didn't have anything to do with it, and if you're right, digging up old stuff will only make it worse."

I gathered up the papers and held them out to him. "Have

you found the receipt with the missing corner, Adrian? Have you mentioned that to the police?''

"Mentioned what?''

I turned. It was Stokowski, sturdy, rumpled, and irritable. "I'll take those papers. Mentioned what to me, Stella?''

TWENTY

STOKOWSKI SPENT twenty minutes or so with Adrian, then came down the stage steps toward me. Zelda spotted him, called out, and then walked with him down the side aisle. They talked briefly, and he patted her on the shoulder and pointed to me. Her smile faded, and she stalked away.

Stokowski walked with the heavy purposefulness that defined him. His jacket seemed to be fitting looser, and there was a lean, hungry look in his expression that made his jaw look even more stubborn. He settled into the seat next to me. I started rehearsal again.

"You look like you're losing weight, Lee," I whispered.

"Zelda said I was too heavy and put me on a diet. I guess she's right, but it sure makes for dull food." He cocked his head, assuring himself that Zelda was down in front and occupied with rehearsal, then he pulled a candy bar from his jacket pocket. "Here," he said and thrust it at me. "Open it and take half."

"So it's my sin if she asks?"

He nodded. "Have to break out once in a while." The chocolate disappeared into his mouth, and he settled comfortably into the seat. "Zelda said you're following Friday night's schedule. You just took a break at the regular intermission, right? This was the point at which you told Barbara to be quiet or you'd throw her out?"

"She stopped rehearsal in the middle of scene one, act two, the first scene after intermission."

He looked at his watch. "And then she said she didn't have her keys, and you told her to stand by the Venus's-flytrap." I nodded, my spirits sagging. "Then what?" he asked.

"Then I started rehearsal again....Lee, we are in rehearsal now. I can't talk to you and concentrate on them."

"This is important."

Zelda sulkily agreed to take over for a few minutes, and Lee and I went to the rear of the theater, where I could keep a vague eye on things and still talk to him.

"How was it that Ogden had you take over the latter half of rehearsal?"

I explained that it wasn't the first time he'd asked me to take the second part of rehearsal. It allowed him to make whatever adjustments he wanted—lighting, scenery, or whatever. Sometimes I suspected he had used the time to smoke outside, because he'd come in exuding tobacco smoke smell.

"And that night he'd had me take over about ten minutes after Lawrence left. He said he had to pick up something from the drugstore before it closed. I assumed it was an excuse because rehearsal wasn't going well—Meredith was fluffing her lines and everyone was off timing, trying to help her one way or another—but I found the King Soopers receipt in his trash. He was at the checkout counter at five past nine."

"You simply have a passion for going through people's trash?"

"Cammie said he was diabetic, I was trying to verify it. The paramedics were already there."

He looked at me skeptically. "All right, the night Barbara was injured, during rehearsal, where was Phillip?"

"Phillip was onstage for this and the next scene and then off. That's when he went outside."

"You saw him go?"

Of course, I hadn't. I assumed he had gone. "No."

"So he could have gone behind the scrim, and you wouldn't have noticed."

"But—" I had been ready to say that Adrian would have, but he might not have, since he was coaching Meredith through their scene. "Cammie...no, she was up replacing the light."

"So that was about quarter to nine?"

"About then, I'm not sure. Maybe closer to nine."

He made a little note on his pad. "Now think very carefully," he said. "When did you see Barbara moving last?"

"I don't know. The whole trouble is," I said slowly, "I could sort of see her in silhouette the whole time, but I was so mad at her, I didn't really want to look at her. So as long as she was quiet, I ignored her."

Lee looked puzzled. "Look at the flytrap now. It's exactly where it was that night, half visible. It's only fully onstage for the last scene, when Phillip is supposed to leap into it. There's a little stub of a branch that juts out just below the big branch. It's part of the old tree trunk and was designed so a kid could sit there when it was used as a tree in the production of *Swiss Family Robinson*. Adrian just converted the tree trunk to a Venus's-flytrap stalk for this play."

He still looked puzzled. "Was the lighting exactly the same as now?"

"The same, except for maybe twenty minutes when Cammie had to change the spot. Look," I said. "I'll show you." I got up, went up onstage, behind the scrim to the flytrap, and leaned against the trunk, between the gauze leaves. The leaves were easily four inches from my arm. My rear was snug against the tree trunk. Anyone trying to get a paw into my right pocket would have broken a finger. Barbara probably fit more easily—she was smaller than I am—but it still would have been very tight.

I stayed there for a minute, then got up and moved offstage into the wings. The sudden darkness blinded me. I turned, caught my foot on something hard and heavy, and tripped. I plunged forward, arms flailing. My forehead whacked an iron bar, but by luck I managed to grab the side of the ladder to the catwalk as I went down. That broke my fall, or I could have had a nasty accident—not fatal, but very unpleasant.

Of course, the ruckus interrupted rehearsal, and Phillip came loping over to me. He gave me a hand up and asked, "What happened?"

I brushed myself off and, embarrassed, tried to laugh the whole thing away. By this time my eyes were adjusted to the dark, and I could see that I'd stumbled over a carelessly placed curtain weight. "Nothing, just clumsy. I tripped over a sandbag."

"It shouldn't be there," Phillip said. He peered at my forehead. "You're going to have a goose egg."

"I'm okay, Phillip."

He reluctantly backed off, then picked up the sandbag and dropped it against the wall with the others. "You sure you're all right?"

"Yes, I'm sure. Go on back to rehearsal."

When I got back to my seat, Lee was finishing a note on his pad. "What was that all about?" He peered at my face. "You've got a lump on your forehead."

I shrugged. "I just tripped over a sandbag weight. I guess I'm getting clumsy."

He studied my face. "You sure that's all it was?"

"Of course."

"I don't like it." He flipped the end of his pencil against the pad, thinking, then seemed to come to some conclusion. "Okay, I see what you mean about the flytrap."

"I know I glanced at Barbara occasionally, because around nine-thirty or so I noticed her head lolling forward on her chest and figured she was asleep. In fact, I didn't call a break then for fear she'd wake up and start in again.''

He made a brief note. ''And how hard is it to make a spotlight blow?''

I closed my eyes. ''Not at all hard. Someone could drop a bit of ice water on it when it's really hot, breaks the glass. In fact, they shatter sometimes, like it did then.''

''So someone could blow the light, then race downstairs without being seen by Rachel in the office, slip down the aisle—''

''Nope, not down the aisle, because Cammie would be coming up the aisle and they'd be seen.''

''So, out the front door and in the side door—''

''That would work.''

''—behind the scrim to the flytrap, where Barbara would see her attacker—so why did he let her live?''

''Barbara wouldn't have seen him. He'd have come from behind, slapped an ether-soaked rag over her face to subdue her, then slipped the cord around her neck and leaned her forward so her own weight would cut off the blood to her brain. Then he'd calmly go back out behind the scrim and out the stage door or back to his place, the workshop, stage, whatever.''

''I'm certainly glad you're not working on this case, Stella. Here's a question for you. It wasn't a foolproof method, so why would anyone risk that much and yet leave so much to chance?''

I shook my head. Either the killer did not know how to kill, or he didn't care whether she died or not.

''Going back to the night of the murder, I understand you told Barbara to go home, and she said she couldn't because she didn't have her keys, but they were in her pocket when you got her down.''

''Correct, in her left pocket.'' I thought about it for a

minute. "She was right-handed. If *she* had put her keys in her pocket, she would have put them in her right-hand pocket. But her right side was snug up against the flytrap, so someone else wanting to slip them into her pocket would have *had* to put them into her left-hand one. She was balanced very carefully, leaning against the trunk. If someone moved her, she would have fallen and made enough ruckus to attract attention."

Lee rubbed his chin, thinking. "Phillip or either of the boys could have taken the keys and then slipped them back in her pocket....."

"What for? Phillip's been using his bedroom window for a door for months, why would he worry about a key? And Linc and Judd have been janitoring the theater and have their own key. And they haven't needed keys to drive cars for years. Now, consider this. The keys were taken to make sure she would stay here. The extra car was at home—she could have gone there, got the second car—but if she has no keys...she will stay here." I waited for him to pick up on it. He didn't.

"Look, Lee, Barbara and Lawrence were having serious marital troubles. She didn't trust him. Adrian told me he had shown her invoices that morning that he suspected were padded. She was very upset about it. She not only suspected he was skimming, I'm sure from the way she insisted on knowing where he was going, what he was doing all the time, she suspected he was having an affair as well. Even that night, she was grilling him on where he was going. I think he took the keys to make sure she would stay here."

Lee considered it.

"Furthermore," I said, "I overheard Barbara tell Ogden he owed her. I think she was twisting his arm to get him to follow Lawrence for her. You ask Ogden."

I waited while he finished making notes, then continued.

"Lawrence was seen coming in before ten and hustling right back out. He could have come in, found her, and, thinking she was dead, replaced the keys." I knew the boys had come in and seen her and thought she was dead, but I wasn't going to tell him unless he asked me. It would only heap blame on them. They had no reason to hurt her and no reason to want her confined to the theater. But Lawrence did. "Are you sure Lawrence has a decent alibi?"

"Stella, I'm the one doing the investigation here. You're not."

"And you're the one who says everything that has happened is accidental. You came in here asking questions."

He started to say something, but stopped. Lawrence was tromping heavily up the aisle toward us. Sighing, he leaned over Stokowski and in a very loud whisper said, "Detective Stokowski, I need to tell you something; could we talk?" He didn't seem to mind that I was there.

Stokowski looked at his watch, then at the stage, then at me. "How much longer does this go?" he asked, meaning the rehearsal.

"There are two more scenes and another act with three scenes. About an hour," I replied.

"This won't take long," Lawrence said. "I just need to tell you that I'm the one who tried to hurt Barbara. I just couldn't go on thinking that you'd blame Phillip, so I have to tell you, I did it."

Stokowski looked impassively at him, noted something on his pad, adding the time, then asked, "And what time was that?"

"Uh, nine-thirty, no, ten o'clock, uh, really quarter to ten."

"You don't seem very certain."

"I'm not. I was very upset, and I didn't look at my watch."

Everyone else had; I don't know why he hadn't. This sounded like the phoniest confession I'd ever heard. And that includes Billy Joe Altman's confession in fifth grade. Billy Joe was a very sneaky kid who stole the milk money and then confessed in a disbelievable way, because he figured that no one would believe a guilty kid would own up, so they'd automatically dismiss the idea that he was guilty. Unfortunately he forgot that he had a hole in his pocket, and the money fell out as he walked back to his desk. It might have worked otherwise.

I glanced at Stokowski's face, trying to read his thoughts. He was as impassive as a stone monolith. He rose. "We should go to the station; I think we've got some talking to do."

Lawrence ambled down the aisle, and I grabbed Lee's arm. "Lee, that could be a phonied-up confession simply to look innocent when he's really guilty. You can't believe—"

"Stella, stay out of this. If you meddle in it, I promise I'll arrest you right on the spot, and you won't even get Thursday visitation."

TWENTY-ONE

THE REST OF rehearsal was a blur in my mind, and mercifully short. My heart frankly ached for Phillip.

Rehearsal was barely over when Cammie left to go to Ogden's side at the hospital. No one wanted to hang around; even Phillip left in record time. Zelda made sure Adrian would take the boys home, then slammed out in a pique, leaving me to lock up. Rachel must have left earlier, because the box office was dark, and I found I was alone in the theater.

It was the perfect opportunity to go through the business office, peruse the books, if I could find them and they weren't locked up, and Lawrence's desk. It was spooky, but I couldn't have asked for a better chance.

The box office door was locked, but not by the deadbolt, only by the loose doorknob lock, which was so shallow that a plastic grocery store card slipped it open.

The first thing that struck me was a large ledger lying open on Lawrence's desk, as though he had been going over it and forgot to put it back when he decided to "confess" to Stokowski. I pored over it.

The records were simple, almost idiotically so, and seemingly in order. But of course they would be. The salaries were generous and included even rental of an apartment for Ogden. I checked the date of the rental. A month before he actually came, Rachel had made the deposit, which included first and last month's rent. He certainly had a sweet deal. I wondered what else he'd bargained for.

Expenses for materials looked high, but not exorbitant.

But of course over time someone could amass a significant amount. Presumably the theater had always run in the red, constantly getting infusions of cash from Barbara. I ranged back over three years without seeing any obvious fiddle, but it would take a far more detailed examination of the records than I could do then. In fact, it would take matching the invoices to the receipts to really nail down discrepancies. It was my professional opinion that there was in fact a small, long-standing fiddle going on. And I figured it was probably Rachel who was benefiting from it.

Except for that and the fact that the theater was bleeding red ink, everything seemed in order. It also seemed as if it were Barbara's private charity; the theater certainly was not making any money. But while embezzlement might be a motive for an attack on Barbara, it didn't explain the one on Ogden—unless Stokowski was right, and Ogden's episode was truly accidental. Or unless Ogden had somehow found out about the fiddle, and thus had to be eliminated.

I left the ledger open as I found it and started through Lawrence's desk. It was amazing.

Most people at least accumulate a few bits of correspondence, but not Lawrence. His desk was absolutely barren of records, letters, hints or evidence of any activity, business, or monkey business. His desk was so clean it was almost as though he had cleared it out—or expected it to be searched. Had he recently cleaned it out? I made a mental note to ask Rachel the next time I saw her. Would I find more evidence of work in his office at home? I'd noticed the alarm system on his home the first time I was there. It was a good one. How on earth could I get in there unnoticed?

The only things of interest I found were an electronic football game, an action adventure paperback, enough pencils to write a history of China, an empty Hostess Cupcake wrapper, and three small Snickers bars.

I ate one of the Snickers bars, pocketed one, and left the last. I was brought up never to take the last cookie on the plate.

I attacked the file cabinet, which was locked. I tried my best to open it, with zero success.

Finally, I went over the part of Rachel's desk that wasn't locked. She at least accumulated things. She had a stack of telephone messages she'd kept, a Rolodex full of names, addresses, and phone numbers, and correspondence in open files on her desk, but nothing of much interest. There was no appointment book I could find and no second set of records or even canceled checks. Finally, out of sheer cussedness, I looked under her desk pad, through her trash, and under her desk drawer. Nothing.

I went back to Lawrence's desk and peeked under his desk-pad calendar. A yellow invoice with one corner torn off. How convenient. Two to one, the corner in Barbara's pocket would match it. I lifted the telephone and punched in Stokowski's office number. I knew I'd only get a voice message, but I figured I'd leave a message. He'd get it sometime that night or the next morning; either would be fine.

All of that finished, I set the lock on the door, cut the lights, and pulled the door shut. It was unbelievably dark at the top of the stairs. I felt for a light switch, found it, and flipped it on. The light in the office came on—I could see it leaking out under the door—but the one out here didn't.

I felt for a second switch, found it, and flipped it on. Nothing.

I felt like a fool. Of course it wouldn't come on. I should have figured it would be out. Anyone who would blow a spotlight would have removed the overhead light so they couldn't be seen by anyone in the balcony office. Whoever tried to kill Barbara had put a fair amount of thinking into this.

If I broke into the office and left the door open so I could see, it would be obvious someone had been there. On the other hand, if I calmed down and stumbled carefully downstairs, I could leave everything as it had been. There really wasn't any choice.

Gradually, as I calmed and my eyes adjusted to the extreme darkness, I could see a gray gloom pooled in the lobby below. While I couldn't see my feet or the stairs, the light seeping in around the outlines of the doors enabled me to just barely make out the stairs toward the bottom and the lobby floor.

I felt my way down the stairs and along the back of the lobby, running my hand along the wall for balance and direction. Nowhere did I find a light switch.

There were break bars on the front doors by law—I could always exit that way. If I really needed to, I could get out. The silent alarm, though, would rouse the police, possibly require me to stay there, and would cause all kinds of hassle. If I went to the side exit, I could easily disarm the alarm, leave, and reset it.

Surely there was a light switch in the auditorium. Unfortunately, I could not find it.

The only thing darker than that auditorium would have been a coal mine in a power outage. I was wrapped in dark, blanketed with it. I could smell it, along with the scent of the dusty velvet seats and paint. I could even hear the occasional car passing in the street outside, but I couldn't see a thing. I fumbled along the wall with my hand, searching for a switch plate. Nothing.

Slowly I felt my way down the side aisle. I'd been up and down it dozens of times, and although I knew it was a straight shot to the stage steps, it was as scary as if I'd never been there at all. It was made worse by the sensation of going down, as though I was descending into hell.

A couple of honking cars passed in the street outside, the sounds muffled, faraway. I inched forward. It seemed like I'd gone a block. I stopped. Had I heard something? A footfall, or just the building settling?

In the midst of the still, hot theater I shivered. Irrationally, I shrank against the wall for protection from some unformed fear. My heart thudded in my chest. Several seconds went by before I corralled my senseless panic and settled down to proceed rationally.

It was inky dark, without even a glimmer of light. I couldn't tell how far I'd gone, couldn't even tell what direction I was going, except that I was feeling along the wall with my hand.

How close was I to the stage steps? I felt ahead with my toe. My foot banged into the first riser. The sound echoed in the still of the theater.

A chill swept over my arms again, and I was breathing in short, sharp little breaths, panting like a woman in labor.

I calmed myself, took stock of where I was. I reminded myself there would be more light in the workshop. The shop had windows—shaded, but they would still let in a bit of light around the edges of the shade. Even that dim light would be a relief. I moved forward, listening carefully, my ears ringing in the silence.

Carefully, I stepped up each of the five steps to the stage. I didn't realize how tense I was until I brushed against the stage curtain and felt my heart leap.

My eyes were straining. I felt along the rough plaster of the wall, moving with a little shuffling step until I reached the frame of the workshop door.

The sharp scent of pine wood, glue, and paint came on a

light stir of air from the shop. The doorway was some five feet wide, and beyond it the wall ran another ten feet to the side entrance. Halfway across the doorway I heard a scritching sound, tiny mouse feet. I stopped. My hair prickled.

I listened again. Please don't let it be mice, but please don't let it be a large rat either. Eleven feet, and I'd be at the entry. I took another couple steps. I heard another scuff on the floor in the shop. Bigger.

Rats? I hate rats. I know they're endemic in any city, especially along waterways, creeks, and in old buildings. Most of the time I blot out the thought. Rats. The stuff of nightmares. I reminded myself I was a lot bigger than they were, and it was only a few feet to the door.

My heart was racing, breath coming in little gasps. I heard the sound again, behind me now, in the shop.

I leaped forward. Blindly. Groped the air ahead of me, lurching for the door. My hand brushed the heavy velvet of the stage curtain. How could that be?

Where was I? How had I got turned around?

I forgot to follow the wall.

I turned, my arms out, searching, fumbling desperately.

I remembered the stairwell to the basement was nearby. I stepped carefully, pushing one foot ahead, feeling for the edge of the stairwell. It should be ahead by ten feet, but I wasn't sure how far I'd gone.

I turned again, feeling for the wall, sidestepped. Nothing.

Then I heard a footstep. I stopped.

Not a rodent. A two-legged footstep. A human. Behind me. Relief swept over me. A human, warm and strong, who would find a light switch. I opened my mouth to call out. And stopped.

Why would anyone be creeping around in the theater without the lights on? Unless they were sneaking around. Unless...they knew I was here and were hiding, to get me.

I listened for a second footstep. Nothing.

My skin prickled. The sound of material rubbing against itself. I whirled away, stumbling to the side, not quite in time. The blow came hard and sharp, glancing off my right shoulder. Pain shot through my arm, numbing as it went.

I fell against the rough plaster of the wall, rolled along it, felt the woodwork of the doorjamb, and grasped for the doorknob.

A hand grabbed me, spun me against the wall, pinning me.

"Who are you, and what do you think you're doing here?"

"Adrian?"

"Stella?"

"Adrian, let go of me." He loosened his grip.

Fear and panic washed over me, leaving my knees shaking and a light sweat on my forehead. Then it swept into anger and suspicion. "Why are you here? In the dark?"

His voice was rough, hoarse. "Why are *you* here?"

I wanted light so I could follow the expressions on his face; even if he was a consummate actor, I'd feel better watching him. "Let's get some light first. Then we can talk."

"Oh, yeah." He flicked on a flashlight.

"No, I want real lights."

He flicked on the lights and doused his flashlight. He looked tired, worn, and maybe a bit confused. When he spoke, his voice was guarded, as though he was still very suspicious of me. "I tried to reach Phillip, couldn't, and couldn't get Lawrence either, so I came here. Sometimes Phillip stays here at night, and I thought I could reach him."

"Why do you want to?"

"Probably for the same reason you're concerned about him. I think he's being made the fall guy in this. I came in just as the light in Rachel's office went out, so I didn't see who was coming down the stairs. Since Rachel knows this place inside out, I figured it wasn't her, or she'd have turned on the lights.''

"Who did you think it was?''

He didn't answer right away. "It doesn't matter.''

Most likely he suspected the boys were up to no good but didn't want to finger them. But why was he here in the first place? A chill ran over my arms.

Adrian had not only been in a position to see what went on, he could have taken advantage of the light outage to kill Barbara. He could have faked the whole love-of-Barbara scene he'd just put on for me earlier. He hadn't seen the play until a few days ago. He would have been as shocked as anyone. Barbara had cast him as the snake in the play; had she written that part to reflect what she saw as his character? Did she on some level believe he had something to do with Lettie's death?

He was watching me closely. "You been doing quite a bit of research on our little theater here, haven't you, Stella?''

"I'm writing a spotlight article for the next issue of the *Orion*. I figured it would be good publicity for the play. But I've learned quite a bit about the early days.''

His voice was quiet. "Oh, really?''

He hadn't said one thing to threaten me, yet I was suddenly very aware that no one knew I was here.

I eased toward the stage door. "Most of the article will come out in the paper this Thursday. The conclusion of the article is in the *Orion*'s safe.''

I wanted to draw from Adrian as much as I could about Lettie, especially the things he would know that would never have been in the press. "I saw a lot about Lettie Starling in those early articles.''

"It was a tragic business. Simple and very sad. She was a beautiful, talented girl."

"If she had everything going for her, why the drugs?"

"Why does anyone do drugs? She was a mixed-up kid with no idea of the magnitude of her talent or what it meant."

"Were you in love with her?"

He ran a hand through his hair—stalling for time? I wondered. "I think so. I think nearly every man who knew her fell in love with her, except perhaps Lawrence, who had eyes only for Barbara. Lettie was a kind of child-woman, and the most sensual creature I've ever known. I don't know why she used drugs. I know she had times when she was terribly depressed, and I've always figured that she simply got careless, risked a little too much one night. She was like that. She liked to push the envelope."

"Where did she get her stuff?"

He shrugged. "Who knows where anyone gets it? A lot of people were trying out cocaine in those days, it was the drug of the hip and swinging."

I moved diagonally to the wall, as though I wanted to lean against it, but quite a bit closer to the door. I was about three feet from it. I inched toward it again. "I got the impression that she and Ogden were very close toward the end."

His expression hardened, and his breathing seemed to have changed. "Too close."

"She was very young, wasn't she? Younger than Phillip is now, I believe. Cammie said something about her having been in love with someone here. I had the impression it was you."

His eyes narrowed; his gaze shifted to some spot over my left shoulder, as though he were traveling back to earlier, painful memories. "Not me, I'm sorry to say. She was a child, with a child's passionate feelings. I was too old for her, I know that now, but at the time I was so madly in love with her, I'd have done nearly anything for her.''

"Including getting her drugs?"

He reacted as if I'd struck him. "Never. I didn't realize the extent of her use until later, but I'd never get her drugs."

"But you know who did."

"I suspect so."

"Who was that?"

"I don't know for sure, so I'm not going to say, but I will say that she was in love with Ogden, not me. No one ever said anything, and her death was recorded as accidental overdose, but I always believed she thought Ogden had deserted her and took an overdose because of that."

He frowned, his hair falling across his forehead. I couldn't tell whether this was an act or a gentle inquiring mind. He straightened. "I get the idea you think Lettie's death has something to do with the attack on Barbara."

"I think there's a connection, Adrian. I think the play stirred up the past, and I think that's why Barbara was attacked."

Frowning, he looked down at his feet and scuffed at a wood chip on the floor. Normally a harmless gesture, it was now menacing; I could feel his anger growing. "You're only going to make everything worse." His voice was flat and very distinct. "The truth can—" He broke off.

"The truth can what, Adrian? Kill?"

He glared at me. "The truth can be real unpleasant."

TWENTY-TWO

I LEFT THE THEATER, my knees a bit weak, my palms slick with sweat, and my fingers shaky. Adrian had at no time threatened or raised his voice. In fact, all he'd done was mouth platitudes, but the whole thing had unnerved me. I could barely unlock my car door and get my key into the ignition. Over the roar of the engine, I heard someone calling my name.

Glancing up, I saw on the rooftop two people waving their arms wildly. "Stella, wait!"

It took two heartbeats to register that it was Linc and Judd. I realized I was still a little out of it. Linc got to me first, too out of breath to talk. Judd was right behind.

"What's happening?"

"We came through the lot, saw your car, and were waiting for you."

"Why?"

"Thought we'd talk to you."

This didn't make sense. "Don't you guys ever go home?"

They looked at each other, then back at me. Linc spoke slowly. "The cops were looking for us. They came to Adrian's, and they've been to our houses."

"They probably just want to talk to you."

"Yeah, right. Have to catch us first."

"You could get into real trouble for this."

"We know you're trying to help Phillip, and we thought...." Judd kicked at a rock on the tarmac. "Maybe we'd help out. Like you are."

"And how would that be?"

"We can do stuff. We can follow you and make sure you're safe while you're investigating."

Linc nodded. "Yeah, you're…Phillip's…person. See, you're one of the few people who sees us. If you're not around, we'll really be invisible."

Judd chimed in. "We could be like the Guardian Angels."

"You mean the group that prowls Colfax, the citizens' police force?"

They grinned. "Yeah. We know a lot about cops and crooks."

"How old are you guys?"

Linc pulled himself up. "I'm fifteen. He's almost sixteen."

It sounded very good. Too good. Not quite true. "You mean, if I'm not here, Phillip and you might get stuck for all this."

Linc grinned, and Judd scuffed his foot. "Yeah. 'Bout right."

I looked at them: too smart, streetwise, and definitely calculating. Always on the edge or just outside the law, but somehow endearing. Was that how Stokowski saw me? I shook myself. Of course not. "What are you planning right now?"

Again they hesitated, and Linc spoke first. "Dinner."

JUDD AND LINC finally agreed to go home. I dropped them off at their doors, waited to see them inside, and then went straight to the Steadmans'. It was eleven at night, but lights were still on. I knocked on the door, almost expecting Rachel to open it.

Phillip answered.

"Hi, Phillip," I said. "We need to talk."

I followed him into the kitchen, where he was in the process of finishing off a pizza. He threw himself into a chair, motioned for me to sit down, and offered me a piece. I took a sliver. I love pizza, but this made my fourth in as many days. For some reason, it didn't look all that appetizing.

I noticed a duffel bag on the floor by the back door. "Going somewhere?"

He stared at the floor. "I can't stand being in the same house with Dad."

"Because—?" I waited, but he didn't say anything. He grew red around the eyes, as though the emotion he was trying to choke back was threatening to come out anyway. I thought about trying to reassure him, then held my tongue. Silence seemed a better method.

Finally, after what seemed like a lifetime, he responded, his voice cracking. "He wants a divorce. They fight a lot. Mom's the kind who goes ballistic over anything. Dad used to try to reason with her, but he gave up and stopped talking. He'd just say 'Whatever' and shake his head. She'd cool off and then they'd go on in peace for a while, until the next blowup."

His voice cracked again, and he took a few breaths to recover. "Last week. They were onstage, blocking, and she started yelling about money and where was he all the time, and he said he was through. He wanted a divorce. She really went ballistic then."

"When was this, Phillip?"

"Sunday before this last one, after rehearsal. Mom was furious because Zelda refused to be assistant director, and they had hired you to be her watchdog. She said she didn't need a baby-sitter. Said you were his girlfriend, and on and on."

"Barbara thought I was involved with your dad?"

"She's accused him of having a girlfriend for months now. He always says it isn't so, but there are times when he's not around, and he won't say where he's been."

"You saw your dad come back the night your mom was found, right?"

He nodded, not meeting my gaze.

"What time was it?"

His voice dropped. "Just before you found her. We were all onstage, and I saw him by Mom. He was touching her. I thought it was strange the way she wasn't looking at him. She seemed to be asleep, so I didn't think too much of it. It was so great just having her quiet....."

I recognized that guilt; it was old familiar territory for me. The terrible voice in the brain that asked, What if I'd just done differently, behaved differently, thought to ask, do, say something—could I have made it right?.... "Phillip." I touched his hand gently. "I'm sorry."

His voice sank to a hoarse whisper. "Neither of them wanted me. They each said the other had to take me."

I wished he were six so I could hold him tight and make him feel safe and loved. Seldom have I felt so bad for anyone as I did just then for this gangling, awkward, despairing kid. I caught myself feeling so helpless to make his life whole, I practically swallowed up his despair as mine. No big help to him.

"Phillip, both of your parents love you. When they said the other had to take you, it was a way of trying to keep the other one engaged. An emotional lasso. People do that without thinking. They're furious and want to hurt the other, but at the same time they want to keep them....Does that make sense?"

"No."

"Well, let's talk about them individually. Your dad cares very much for you, he simply has a very hard time saying it." At least he didn't protest. "And your mom also didn't tell you, but all that energy she put into the play and high-lighting your role, that was for you. Because she loved you."

He shook his head. "Everybody comes here now talking about how generous she was, fixing up the building, making a community theater—hell, Cammie talked about how great it was that she put in a sprinkler system. She didn't put it in for our safety. It's to keep her precious costumes from burning up. All of it is for her to be center stage."

"But, Phillip—"

"She doesn't even see me as a separate person, I'm a...an extension of her, another way for her to star. Everything is always about her. There isn't a day when she isn't the center of attention. It isn't for me. I don't want it. Jon didn't want it when he was alive, he just went along like he always did. He was exactly like Dad—smile, say nothing, and let her rip."

He rubbed his hands over his face, scrubbing hard at it, then dropped them, loosely fisted, on the tabletop. "I've thought about this a lot, 'cause at first I thought she was doing it for me, too. But it was as though she's stuck in a rut. If she doesn't get attention, she isn't alive, so she has to keep getting it. I'm just out there so she can get even more attention, now she's the biggest, grandest stage mother of all time. I'm like a face-lift for her."

There was a lot of truth in what he said. "Phillip, she did the best she could for you. If it wasn't enough, or it wasn't right, or it was also self-serving, at least she tried. People don't always have the capacity to love in a way that helps us, but that doesn't mean they don't care."

He stared at his hands, too large for his body right now, and muttered, "I guess some people don't fit their kids."

IT TOOK A WHILE, but I was able to convince Phillip to stay home, at least for now. We were still talking when Lawrence came in. He looked washed out, disheveled, and defeated.

Phillip jumped up, overturning his chair. "You—"

Lawrence raised his hands, like a drowning man calling for help. "Phillip, wait—"

I stood. "Phillip, tell your dad why you're so upset with him."

If you count progress in the tiniest of steps, they made progress. Phillip told his dad he'd overheard him arguing with Barbara, and he knew she accused him of having a lover. Lawrence bowed his head, his shoulders sagging. When Phillip finished, he sighed and said, "I'm sorry you heard all that."

I finally said that Phillip had told me he heard them each say they didn't want him. Lawrence looked stunned, shook his head, and finally mumbled, "I'm sorry."

It wasn't enough. I wanted to reach across the desk, grab him by the ears, and shake him until he either developed some spine or said something to Phillip to make him feel loved. Lawrence met my gaze, then rubbed his face. He seemed to understand more was needed.

"Look, Phillip, your mom and I said a lot of terrible things to each other. At the time we were really angry, and I'm afraid we meant to hurt each other. But neither of us meant to hurt you. We both love you. Your mother loves you dearly. And so do I."

For Lawrence, this was a huge step. I wasn't sure Phillip understood just how big.

Phillip's head was down, his hair forward so we couldn't see his face. "She doesn't show it."

"Neither do I much, I guess. Neither one of us has been very good at feelings, son. But that doesn't mean we don't care." Lawrence looked bleakly at me, then at Phillip. "You might as well know. Your mother was right. I have had an affair. It was stupid and very hurtful, and I'm not even sure why I did it. I promised her I would break it off, and I did. The night she was attacked, I was at the woman's house, breaking off our relationship. The truth is, I love you and your mother very much, but I'm not good at telling you. I...hope it isn't too late.''

TWENTY-THREE

LAWRENCE WAS a dejected man, and I felt like I was beating a wounded animal, but I had to ask. "Did you also tell Stokowski that you are the one who put the keys back in Barbara's pocket?"

He nodded miserably. "I thought she was asleep, and I didn't want to wake her and start the whole argument over again. I was going to put them in her purse or drop them in Adrian's workshop, but when I saw her on the flytrap, it was perfect. I figured I'd return in about fifteen minutes, and if she kicked up a fuss, I'd help her find her keys in her pocket. Honest to God, I thought I'd die when I came back and she'd been taken to the hospital. If I'd realized…I might have been able to…." He convinced me. I thought he was being honest.

Lawrence also admitted he had confessed to divert Stokowski from Phillip, which merely annoyed Stokowski and initially infuriated Phillip, although he later realized that Lawrence was misguidedly trying to protect him.

Phillip quite cynically quoted Lawrence to himself, saying that words came easy in their family, the behaviors would be what counted. It occurred to me that the worst part of adolescence was that one minute the kid was six years old and the next he was sixty, and you never knew which you were going to deal with.

By the time I finally left, father and son had reached a minor truce, and I had come to the conclusion that in spite of his doubtless many sins, Lawrence had not made the attack on Barbara.

As I lay on my bed, struggling to sleep, I tried to refit the pieces of the puzzle as I knew them. Lawrence and both boys had left the theater about eight-thirty-five; Lawrence had dropped the boys at the ATM machine, then gone to his lover's house, returning to the theater about nine-forty-five.

Ogden had left about eight-forty-five, gone to the King Soopers, picked up insulin, and then gone where? The next night he uses his new insulin, and by the next day he's close to death because, if I'm right, his insulin has been tampered with. The question was, had it been done by Rachel or Cammie or Adrian, or had he himself done it to cover his own tracks? After all, there had been no trouble until Ogden returned to Denver.

If we stuck to the time frame, Barbara was subdued right between nine and nine-thirty. If Ogden came back after picking up his insulin, he could easily have set Barbara up and slipped back out of the theater.

Of course, there still were Cammie, Rachel, and Adrian.

Cammie was at the theater the whole night. She was Lettie Starling's sister. Could she? She could blame Barbara and Ogden for Lettie's death, but why, when Barbara apparently had been against drugs all along and was clearly worth more to Cammie alive than dead? She had no way to effectively drain cash from the theater. Cammie was in love with Ogden.

Adrian was there the whole time, too. Saint Adrian, as Phillip had called him, had looked with striking dislike up at the office window where Lawrence was standing. He professed to love Barbara, so why would he try to kill her? He had known Ogden a long time ago, too. He might have ancient history with Ogden, but if anything, he was more likely than any of them to have seen who had tried to kill her.

Rachel was in the theater the whole time working on the books, which were so simple a gorilla could keep them and still have time for a day job. Rachel was my prime suspect for siphoning money out of the theater, and she was reputed to be in love with Lawrence. She could have planned to eliminate Barbara, taking her husband and her cash and the theater for herself. And this was it! She could have overheard Barbara and Lawrence arguing onstage when Lawrence asked for the divorce. That could be the starting point. She thinks Lawrence is in love with her finally. He's asking Barbara for a divorce; she says she'll never give him a penny, and Rachel decides to kill her.

Then, if she learned that Lawrence had a mistress and it wasn't her, she would be in a perfect position to implicate him in the money scheme. As for Ogden, he might have seen her when he came back and so had to be eliminated. It was tangled, but it played.

I'd figured if it wasn't money at the bottom of all this, it must be love. Now it seemed it was both. How on earth could I prove it?

THE NEXT MORNING was a moody Tuesday. I was tired from the night before but woke with the six o'clock sunshine full in my face. The air was already a warm, thick humid blanket. It felt like there would be a storm by noon.

The eastern skies were clear and blue, but clouds were piling up over the mountains, ready to roll over Denver. Even as late as the third week in May, we seemed to be having threats of Canadian cold. The pansies in the yardlette would do fine, even if it snowed lightly, but the petunias I'd shoved into the ground two days ago were frankly cold and discouraged looking.

I fixed a bag lunch—an anchovy sandwich with an apple

for dessert—and had the last of the vegetable soup for breakfast. I gave Mom a quick call. She was barely calm.

"Janie, dear, I think you should know. Not that I want to worry you, the crisis is over. You didn't miss out on much, and I'm sure we'd have found you eventually if your father had died. You know how every morning I set his high-blood-pressure pill and the dog's thyroid pill on the kitchen counter?

"Well, your father was in a hurry this morning, and he took the dog's thyroid pill instead of his. Do you know what the doctor said? He said he figured your dad's tail would wag all day."

She paused while I laughed. "You think it's funny. He spent half an hour on the phone with poison control. I'm fixing tuna casserole tonight, what would you like for dessert?"

"Steak and salad."

I had barely hung up when the phone rang. It was Zelda. "Stella, remember you promised you'd cover the desk for me while I'm up on the rack."

She was referring to her annual physical exam. "I remember. Anything I should know?"

"Perhaps that is what I should ask you."

"Zelda, I am not fooling around with Lee." She let me know she was not convinced.

I got to the newspaper offices a bit early, gathered my correspondence, and settled in. There was a note on the desk from Mr. Gerster saying he wouldn't be in until ten o'clock. That was fine with me. I could get all my correspondence finished up, the column completed, and a story or two for the next issue.

The only excitement was Andy the gofer coming in ten minutes early and making extra-strong coffee. At nine-forty-five the phone rang and nearly startled me out of my chair.

A brisk voice came over the line asking for Mr. Gerster. I offered to take a message.

"This is Josh Mackey from Apex Media. I left a message for him several weeks ago about syndication of the Stella the Stargazer column and wondered if he'd changed his mind. We'd very much like to talk with him and with the columnist."

"Perhaps I can help—I'm Stella the Stargazer."

"Really? Great! As I told Gerster, we'd like to talk to you about syndicating your column. Do you have an agent, or are you representing yourself?"

"I'll probably represent myself."

My hand was shaking when I hung up after we'd settled on a time. Mr. Gerster had had a call several weeks ago. I leafed back through Zelda's phone message record book. There it was, a whole month earlier. He'd never told me. In fact, he'd implied that no one ever inquired; well, actually, I'd assumed no one had—I hadn't asked outright. Betrayed. Why would he do such a thing?

I leafed back farther and found there had also been calls from New York regarding Jason more than a month ago, and he hadn't passed them on to Jason until two weeks ago. Why? And even more, why did he finally decide to?

Gerster arrived while I was still in shock. He stopped, picked up mail, nodded hello. It wasn't until he was standing directly in front of me that I realized he was talking to me.

"I said, were there any messages for me?"

I looked at him. "Messages?" I said stupidly. "Only one from Apex Media, wanting to know if you'd reconsidered your refusal to talk syndication of my column." I handed him the pink slip.

His lips, already thin, disappeared into his face. His

glance rested on the open message record book. He took the slip. "I see."

"I guess I do too," I said. He went on back through the corridor to his office as though nothing were different.

But I didn't. It was one thing for him to simply decide I wasn't ready, but to have denied, lied about, getting queries on syndication was too much. I couldn't understand why he would do it. And to Jason as well. Why had he screened out those calls? And why lie about them? It was such a petty thing. I kept expecting to feel some mobilizing surge of rage, but instead all I got was an empty feeling, hollow, as though there just wasn't a feeling to cover this situation. No reaction. Void. Is that what betrayal felt like?

And what would I say to Jason?

Suddenly, I wanted only to talk to him. He at least was in a warm, wonderful place with a job opening up for him, people who saw his potential and wanted to help him.

And of course I'd been as cranky and jealous as I could be, and it would be totally understandable if he had no time at all for me. I considered calling him, decided against it. I hadn't figured out what I'd say about Gerster, or if I should just keep it to myself. Jason liked and admired Mr. Gerster. What possible good would it do to smash that? By telling him about Gerster's betrayal, I'd only be diminishing one more person in Jason's life...and he'd had enough people turn out to be less than they should be.

Would Jason's father be pleased with him now that he was working in New York for a big paper? Would that make him proud and loving? I thought it wouldn't. I suspected there would always be something to criticize and something greater to strive for. Jason would have to recognize his own worth. And maybe I would too. Maybe that was why I needed to negotiate syndication on my own.

I was still mulling all this over when the phone rang

again. It was Jason. He was worried about me, telling me again, insufferably, how I should stay away from the theater and stay out of trouble. I decided on the spot not to tell him yet about Mr. Gerster's messages. His voice was like two loving arms wrapping around me, warm and reassuring. I was so busy enjoying the feeling, I almost missed what he said and had to ask him to repeat it.

"I said, I miss you and I love you. The weather here is warm, the air clean, the job fascinating, and the people wonderful. I haven't found a place to live yet—one of the guys is out of town on assignment for a month, and I'm bunking in there until I get a place." He gave me the number there and said again he missed me, I was his best friend. In the middle of telling him how much I missed him, I noticed Zelda standing in the doorway. Embarrassed, I finished the call and hung up, promising to call later. My eyes burned, and a lump lodged in my throat. I took my stuff and headed for my desk.

In the time it took me to get there, I made a decision. I was going to New York. I had asked Jason if he would follow me if the situation was reversed, but in truth, maybe this time I needed to follow him. It wasn't as though I had nothing to bring to the relationship. Now that I had the possibility of syndication, I wasn't totally dependent.

I picked up the phone and punched in the numbers for my travel agent. I hadn't used her since my lucrative days as a CPA, but she remembered me. "I want a one-way to New York City on June 2." She convinced me that I could buy a round-trip ticket for much less and make the return date a long way away.

Zelda had come into the room and was standing by my side. She had been listening in. Her eyes were round, solemn. "You're going one-way to New York? You're going to go? Good for you. Um, can I talk to you a minute?'' Her face was unusually serious.

"Zelda, it's a surprise for Jason, so keep it to yourself, okay?" She nodded. I suddenly remembered her exam and felt a huge thump in my chest. "Oh, Zelda, was your exam all right?"

"Oh, sure. That's not what I want to talk about. I want to apologize to you, for a bunch of stuff. I listened in on your conversation with Jason. I didn't mean to, I just came in and...overheard it. I've been so jealous of you with Stokowski, I've been a real hellion. I shouldn't have said the things I did, and I shouldn't have accused you of fooling around with him."

She pulled Jason's desk chair around and sat in it. "I wish Lee and I were as good friends as you and Jason are. Jason would do about anything for you, you know. If you asked him, he'd come back. I know that's what you want."

"That's why I can't ask him. This is a wonderful chance for him, and I can't stand in his way. I'd never be able to look at myself in the mirror."

Zelda looked at her feet, her brow wrinkled. I knew she was truly struggling with something, because otherwise she'd have remembered she didn't want to crease her skin. "Stella, I've got to tell you something. Mr. Gerster hasn't been straight with you, or with Jason. There were calls from someone about syndication of your column, and there were calls from New York for Jason, too. A long time ago, like a month."

"I know. One came in today, and I found the earlier messages in the book. I just don't understand why."

She shook her head. "I don't know. I don't understand either, but what you said about not standing in Jason's way made me wish I'd told you earlier. Mr. Gerster really likes you and Jason a lot. He's always been so protective of you.

I think he can't stand to lose you. I guess a person can lose just so many people, then you don't want to let go anymore, at any cost.''

"That might be true, Zelda, but right now I'm so flaming angry I don't want to be understanding of him. It was wrong, and he shouldn't have done it.''

"I don't know....He's always been a real good man, and he's always had good reasons, even if he is, you know, out of touch. I think there's something else going on with him. But that's not what I need to say. I need to say, I'm sorry. I learned something about jealousy, though. I'm going to work on Cammie. She's been in love with that jerk Ogden, and I figure I can help her out.''

"I don't think you should mess in this, Zelda.''

"It's not up to us to decide whether they're good for each other. I can help her look good. All she needs is a bit of fluff in her hair, shape up her eyebrows, and ditch those glasses and those awful shoes, and she'd look like an angel.''

"Zelda, this is a bad idea—''

Meredith breezed into the newsroom. "What's a bad idea?''

"I'm telling Stella how I'm going to make over Cammie.''

"Meredith, don't get into this.''

"Ohhh! What a good idea.''

"Meredith, I have to talk to you about something important. And this is not a good idea. It's terrible. You're just feeling guilty because you made her jealous, and making her look like a Barbie doll isn't going to make up for it.''

"Of course it is.''

TWENTY-FOUR

"ZELDA," I SAID. "If you feel so bad about not telling me earlier, I've got a way you can make up for it."

She looked stricken. It's one thing to say you want to make up for something, it's another when someone takes you up on it. She had clearly planned lip service only. "Oh?"

"Find out where Lawrence says he was during the rehearsal and where Ogden went."

"How am I going to do that?"

"I'll bet anything Cammie knows, so while the two of you are 'improving' her, you can drag that little bit of information out of her."

"I can tell you where Lawrence went," Meredith said. "I heard him tell one of the officers to check out this address. Twenty-three Pearl Street."

Zelda looked grim. "I'll just bet it isn't any churchyard, if you know what I mean." She raised an eyebrow and bustled back to her desk in the front office.

I sat Meredith down for a minute. She looked sidewise at me. "Are you going to lecture me on unsuitable men?" I shook my head. "Then it must be about one of your spells. You have that look. Like doom warmed over."

I explained how I'd seen disaster when I first picked up the manuscript with Jason's message from New York on top.

She thought for a minute. "You've never understood these things before, and you've never been able to control them. Why is it bothering you now?"

"I'm more worried, I guess, because you're involved in the play and Jason is involved in the message, and I don't know which one the spell concerned."

"Well, I'll be careful, but I think it's all because you're in love with Jason, and yet you don't want to commit yourself. You probably haven't even admitted it to yourself. One of these days you're going to have to decide whether you're going to follow your heart or not."

"Meredith, that's right-brain, impulsive...stuff."

"There's a place for right-brain impulses, or we wouldn't still have it in our genetic reservoir." She closed her eyes. "You know, you don't really appreciate your gift."

"It's not a gift, Meredith. It's a burden. All it really is, is hyper-ability to sniff out disaster without any ability to know where it's coming from or who it's going to happen to. It leaves me sick with worry. I wake up in the middle of the night thinking doom has come."

"That, my dear, is hormones."

I DIDN'T FEEL much better for having talked about it to Meredith, but I had got her to promise to be very careful. Then I shoved the last of my correspondence into my purse and left to see if I could find Lawrence's alibi and verify it.

It was noon, and the sun was still shining, but clouds had piled up over the mountains and were spilling over the foothills onto the western edge of Denver. It looked to me as though we were in for a late-afternoon storm. Denver's version of the monsoon season starts in May.

Twenty-three Pearl Street was one of a row of sedate brick bungalows and modest two-story turn-of-the-century houses, partially shaded by large silver maple trees on the parking strip. The othe side of the street was a mix of Victorians and apartment buildings much like the one Ogden lived in. The yards were all well trimmed; most had a few flowers showing, and there had apparently been a sale on geraniums, because they all seemed to have at least one in a pot on the porch. Number twenty-three was a one-story red brick bungalow with an oak swing on the front porch and a picturesque olive tree draped over one corner. Lacy curtains hung in the front window along with a small, antique framed stained-glass window.

I knocked. No one answered.

I lifted an envelope out of the mailbox. It was addressed to Alicia Farrar. At least I knew her name now.

I walked around the side to the back of the house, half expecting to be greeted by a slavering sharp-toothed guard dog, but all I found was a tidy yard, well planted and pleasantly shaded by a large silver maple in the back. I checked the usual places for a hidden key and found nothing. No signs of children—no tricycles, no toys, no sandbox.

I peeked in the back window and saw a homey kitchen, dishes drying in the drainer. In the side windows I saw a pleasant dining room, a large spider plant, and a table with fresh flowers on it. Roses. Long-stemmed red roses. Very expensive, the kind usually sent by lovers.

Then I went next door and knocked there. An older gray-haired woman with very sharp eyes opened the door rather too quickly. I had the distinct impression she'd been watching me the whole time.

"Hello, I'm looking for Ms. Farrar. When is she likely to be home?"

"Now, who are you?"

"I'm a reporter from the *Daily Orion*. Her address came up on my random survey, and I'm hoping to interview her." It was as close to the truth as I could invent in that short time.

"How do I know you're who you say you are?"

I thought about it for a minute, then pulled out several of

my letters, addressed to Stella the Stargazer, and held them out in front of her.

"Oh, you're Stella the Stargazer? I almost wrote to you the other day. I have this niece who thinks she's in love, and I think the young man is completely unsuitable. I've been reading your column, and you seem to be an expert on unsuitable men."

"You've no idea."

"Now, come right on in and let me tell you about it all."

It took all the patience and skill I possessed to get information from her. I managed it only by promising to write the poor niece a letter. But I got the name, description, and life story of the lovely woman, Alicia Farrar, who lived next door and had a gentleman caller, as she called him.

And yes, he'd been there last Friday night. She happened to notice because she was watering her yard at quarter to nine when he came, and then she happened to be looking for her cat when he left, at quarter to ten.

Barbara had been insisting that Ogden had to do something because he "owed her." It could well be that she wanted him to follow Lawrence because she suspected he had something on the side. "Did you happen to notice any strange parked cars in your street that night?"

She drew herself up. "I certainly did. This person drove up at nine-fifteen and parked right in front of my house and just sat there, smoking in his car, until nine-thirty-five. And I got his license number." A very observant woman.

"Are you certain of the time?"

"I certainly am. I know it was nine-thirty-five because I called the police at nine-thirty-five to report him. I figured he was out there casing the place. You can't be too careful these days, you know. People everywhere going crazy. Godless, ignorant, and thieving people. Sign of the times. That's why I have cats. Have to take care of the poor things, and they'll take care of you.''

I noticed she had a large tea bag tied to her wrist. She caught me staring at it and waved it in my face. ''Tea bag. I'm using it for a patch. I'm trying to quit. Too much tea, and you get spider tumors and your teeth turn brown.....''

I FELT AS IF I were almost back at square one. How did the two common threads, the play and Lettie Starling, tie all these people together into a murderous knot?

I knew where Lawrence had been—and Ogden, if the license plates numbers matched, and I was sure they would.

Lawrence appeared to have a solid alibi. He would have returned to the theater just before ten, as Linc and Judd had said. He could have done just as he said—taken the keys to make sure Barbara stayed at the theater, returned, slipped the keys into Barbara's pocket. Then, thinking she was dead, he panicked and left. He was guilty of something, at least adultery, but not murder.

And it seemed reasonable to assume Barbara had sent Ogden after him. But Ogden hadn't left right away, so he must have had a very clear idea of where to find Lawrence. Had he followed him before?

I was curious about why he would return to Denver to produce a play that might be a real dog. He was in a slump, sure, but directing a loser wasn't the best way to resurrect his career. So why had he agreed to it? Ogden might also have the answer to a couple of big questions about Lettie.

And finally, I figured that keeping the play in active rehearsal would keep up the pressure. If nothing else, the continued pressure might make something hit the fan.

I ignored that old saying: That which hits the fan doesn't spread evenly.

TWENTY-FIVE

OGDEN'S APARTMENT was a scant five minutes away. His car was parked behind the building, and its license plate numbers matched those of the car that sat outside Lawrence's lovely's house. I parked next to it in a reserved slot and rang the security bell at the back entrance. When Ogden answered, I said, "Delivery for Mr. Bane." The buzzer sounded and let me in. So much for security in that building.

Ogden answered my knock looking unshaven, baggy-eyed, and shaky. His eyes, more sunken than before, narrowed almost to disappearing when he saw me. "What do you want?"

I put my foot in the door so he couldn't shut it in my face, but that meant he slammed it on my toes. "Cut it out, Ogden. That hurts."

Muttering, he opened the door, then shuffled back to the couch, where it was evident from the blankets and coffee cups that he'd been spending time.

His apartment was just as bleak as it was the last time I was there. The only personal touches in the whole room were his pictures. They were always of Ogden; the only thing that changed was the accompanying young woman. Even that didn't change all that much; usually it was Lettie.

I decided to remain standing and stay rather close to the door, just in case he got aggressive. "When did you get out of the hospital?"

"Noon," he said and dropped onto the couch, pulling a

sheet over his legs. "You know, I just told Cammie to leave, and I'd like for you to as well."

"I will," I promised. "I only need a little help from you. How are you feeling?"

"I'll live, if that's what you want to know."

"I really wanted to know if you were planning to be at rehearsal tonight."

He leaned his head back on the couch, eyes closed and long-suffering. "No. Tomorrow, though."

"Ogden, have you had these episodes before?"

"No. Well, maybe once or twice." He rubbed his neck. "Look, I drank too much. I like to drink when I'm sad. And glad. And mad. Like now." He looked belligerently at me. "Well, isn't that what you wanted to hear?"

I hate talking to hostile alcoholics, sober, reformed, or otherwise. "Look, I'm not here to judge whether you're a swell guy who's persecuted by the public or a nasty asshole who's earned every tragedy he's had. You nearly died, and if you didn't screw up your insulin yourself, then someone did it to you, and they might try again."

"No one did a thing to me." He rubbed a hand over his face, as if scrubbing it back to life. "I'm okay. I don't plan to hurt myself, and I'm not going to drown myself in a bottle again."

"I thought maybe you'd had a dose of guilt after following Lawrence to Alicia Farrar's again."

He blinked too often. I knew he was surprised that I knew. I also knew he was going to lie. I hate that. So predictable. He stared at me, defiantly. "Who? I don't know anyone by that name."

"Don't, Ogden. Lawrence told me about her. I know you were there watching him. And her neighbor phoned in a complaint about you and left your license number. It's a matter of time before the police put it all together."

He closed his eyes, and I could see the muscles of his jaw moving as he clenched and unclenched his jaw. He had a nasty temper. When he spoke, his voice was low and cold. "Barbara asked me to follow him. He had promised to break off with this person, and she wanted to check up on him. That's all."

"You had followed him before, hadn't you?" The expression on his face confirmed it. "Why did you agree to come back and direct her play even though you knew it could be a real bow-wow?"

"I didn't know that for sure. I got the script the same day you did. Before that, all I had was the first act and a character list, just like everyone else."

"It must have been a shock."

"To everyone."

"How did Barbara convince you to come back without even a script?"

"She offered cash, living expenses, an apartment, a letter of recommendation, and a chance to prove I could do the everyday directing of a play. You may think directors command a big salary, but I can tell you there are thousands of directors, all adequate and most seriously underpaid. Anybody wanting a director has their pick of plenty of respectable, dependable people."

He kicked off the blanket. "And I'm not considered dependable. Barbara offered me a chance to prove myself again. Even if it was a…an amateur effort."

"It must have brought back memories, returning here." He didn't answer. He was gazing at a picture of Lettie. "Lettie must have been very lovely."

"She was."

"And was Adrian in love with her too?"

"The only one who wasn't was Lawrence. He was always

straitlaced, and at that time so in love with Barbara he couldn't see anyone else. But, yeah, Lettie was wonderful.''

"She was in love with you?"

His expression was incredibly sad. I think for the first time I saw him without his protective shield of cynicism. "We were going to get married." He stopped to clear his throat. "She was supposed to join me....."

"She was very young."

He shot a furious look at me. "Yes, she was young. Damned young!" He drew in a furious breath. "That's another part of my sordid past. She was too young, and while I hadn't known it when I started going with her, when I found out, I didn't stop seeing her. I couldn't. I was in love."

"Were you eloping?"

"We planned to. Her parents were against me, thought I was too old for her, so we'd planned to slip away, and then I had to leave. She was going to join me the next day, but she didn't come, and didn't come. And then I learned she was dead from an overdose...the very day we were to get married."

"Why did you leave town when you did?"

His feet crashed to the floor. "My God!" His face paled; little beads of sweat stood out on his forehead, twin red spots colored his cheeks. "Why are you raking all this up? I've lived with this for...years!"

"And you did nothing?"

"Oh, no. I did plenty. I drank, I pitied myself, I ranted and raved and took Barbara's money to stay out of town. Lettie's parents wanted to charge me with statutory rape, contributing to the delinquency, and assisting suicide, everything they could think of."

He rose and walked to the window. "I think they would have, and they'd probably have succeeded in making at least some of the charges stick, but Barbara intervened. Even Cammie helped. She knew about Lettie's drug use, you see. She'd tried to help her get off them, even lied for her sometimes. Between the two of them, they got the parents calmed down. And I stayed away.''

"Lettie was using cocaine. Where did she get it and the money for it?''

He reached for a packet of cigarettes, drew one out, and lit it, shaking the match out, then flicking it onto the little coffee table in front of him. Stalling.

He inhaled, paused, then blew a great cloud of smoke out his nose. "I gave her money. She said it was for clothes, food, gas. When I found out, I stopped giving her cash and convinced her to quit. Although it was real hard for her, she quit the coke. Then I realized she'd merely moved on to pills, maybe because they were cheaper. Uppers, downers, it didn't seem to matter. I think she must have stolen a prescription pad, because she always managed to come up with them.'' He picked up one of the pictures, looked at it, and set it down again.

"You knew what the play was about before you came, didn't you?''

"No, but as soon as Barbara said she was writing a modern allegory about Eden, I suspected it would be about Lettie. I decided I didn't have anything to lose anymore.''

"Are you sure? The play shows the snake killing Lettie.''

He turned to me, almost shaking with anger. "You don't understand. I loved her. I tried to get her off drugs.''

"Ogden, I'm not trying to irritate you, I'm trying to get to the bottom of all this. Someone with a lot to lose was threatened by the play and tried to kill her, I think to stop the play.''

"That's ridiculous. There's no guarantee it would stop

the play; in fact, there's every reason to think it would still go on after a little while.''

"Not if there were subsequent 'accidents.'" He seemed to be thinking about that. I continued. "Now, whoever did that must have known Phillip would be a prime suspect and taken advantage of it.''

"Don't look at me. I didn't do anything to Barbara. In fact, I don't see how anyone could, except Barbara herself. You were right there in the audience the whole time, and Barbara was visible behind the gauze of the flytrap.''

"Well, that's the truly brilliant part. It was supposed to be a killing in plain sight. Or the illusion of plain sight. And it worked very simply. The person only had to slip along behind the scrim, come up behind her, and slip an ether-soaked rag over her face. The killer only risked being seen if someone was right in front of the flytrap, but the rehearsal at that point was stage front, and from any other position he would be hidden. And only Barbara's silhouette was visible through the gauze.''

"Barbara was a strong woman, Stella. She'd fight.''

"That's right. So here is another point of intersection with Lettie's story. Drugs. I think Barbara had been using drugs, and by the time she settled on the flytrap she was groggy. So anyone using an ether-soaked cloth could easily subdue her. Then, when she slipped into unconsciousness, her body sagged forward, and the weight of it against the cord would finish her off.''

"But she didn't die.''

"She would have if she hadn't been wearing that bat-winged blouse with the bulky turtleneck. It was the only thing that saved her.''

His face momentarily sagged. "Damn, that would work.'' He glanced away, suddenly vulnerable.

I might have felt sympathy for him, but Phillip was being

set up to take the fall, and nobody was doing a thing about it.

"Ogden, you could have set up Barbara before you left."

"Then why would I have bothered following Lawrence? I'm no rose, Stella, but I'm not a killer." His lips curled in a sneer. "And why would I blackmail old Larry? He's a pussycat."

"Maybe to keep your job. He didn't want to hire you in the first place, and as soon as Barbara was out of the way, he'd fire you."

He leaned forward, scrubbing out his cigarette in an ashtray that already had three crushed butts in it. "I don't need to blackmail him. I don't like him, and he hates me, but I've got a contract with a lovely golden parachute, so if he fires me, I'm in hog heaven. Much better off than having to direct the play. I made that a clear part of the deal." He got up from the couch, noticeably wobbly, and walked to the kitchenette. A cupboard door opened and closed.

I stepped over to the pictures. There was one with Lettie, Barbara, very pregnant, and Rachel, both looking like near children themselves. Rachel was slender, with an elfin face and large eyes. No glasses, no sensible shoes. "Hey, Ogden, is this our Rachel?"

He poked his head out of the kitchenette. "Yeah, that's Rachel." He disappeared back into the kitchen, and I heard him running water; then he came to the doorway again, carrying a glass of ice water. "There's an example of still waters running deep. Looks a little different now, doesn't she?"

"What do you mean by that?"

"Nothing," he said with a nasty smile. "But I honestly didn't try to kill our Barbara. I'm actually quite fond of her."

He leaned casually against the door frame into the

kitchen. "I knew her better than a lot of people. I knew what it did to her when Lawrence told her he wanted a divorce."

"You were there?"

"I was in the box office with Rachel. Lawrence caught Barbara on the stage. Evidently he forgot that the stage is wired, or perhaps he didn't care, but I don't think he meant for us to hear. Barbara was devastated. Took it like she'd stuck her finger in an electric socket. I think he was surprised."

"And where was Phillip?"

He pursed his lips. "I don't know. I don't think he knew."

"He knew."

"Well, maybe it turns out everyone except you knew then. Hell, I don't know."

"Right now the police are focusing on Phillip as the murderer, and someone is letting him take the fall. Doesn't that bother you? He's your son, isn't he?"

His glass dropped to the floor and shattered, water and shards of glass spraying the air. "No! Damn you. You're crazy—" He rose, stepped over the mess, and advanced toward me. "You're making this up—" He stopped, wincing.

It was my bet that he'd cut his foot, but whatever stopped him, I was glad. I backed to the door, grabbed the doorknob in my hand. "There are plenty of accounts of you and Barbara in back issues of the *Orion,* and one from the *Post* long after she was married to Lawrence that I saw in Phillip's room, on his desk. I think that's part of the trouble he's having right now. I'm sure he wonders if you are his father."

Ogden shook his head, his expression alternating between bewilderment and fury. "I'm not Phillip's father, although

I'd be proud to be. I'm sterile. Have been since I had mumps at nineteen.''

"Oh, please, that's just too convenient. It's about as true as 'Trust me' and 'The check is in the mail.'''

"Well, you can check my medical records if you have to," he retorted, reddening. "Now get out!"

"What are you going to tell Phillip?"

He frowned. "Not a damn thing." He was breathing hard and favoring his foot. "You're going to get someone killed at this rate." He threw his head back, looking out from under half-closed eyelids. "In fact, you're putting yourself in a hell of a lot of danger."

TWENTY-SIX

I DECIDED I WAS fortunate to leave Ogden's place in one piece. As it was, I felt as though I needed a shower and a gallon of antifungal soap to get clean of him. Clouds were glowering overhead, and the air had begun to feel pregnant. A good cleansing rainstorm would help to clear things.

I found I was even disgusted with Barbara for convincing Lettie's folks to drop charges. Ogden was not a nice guy. I truly hoped Cammie would realize it and find someone else.

He was attracted to young girls, self-pitying, and refused to help out Barbara's son, even though she'd helped Ogden when he needed it. Why, I wondered, had I hoped for more from him? I winced when I figured out the answer. It was because I was not only sorry for Phillip, I was actually feeling maternal toward him.

The thought that I wanted to protect Phillip produced a myriad of feelings in me. Visions of myself as a mother were uncomfortably clear, sufficient to give me chills. And maybe a little longing. Perhaps Meredith's belief in the biological clock had some merit.

All that aside, even though I didn't have the killer figured out, I had figured out *how* Barbara's murder occurred, most likely *when,* and probably *why.* The play. It had different meanings for each of them, and for one, it was lethal. Barbara wrote the play and, intentionally or inadvertently, implied that one person had killed Lettie. Slither. Which meant Adrian could be the guilty one.

I had thought it was Ogden because of his involvement with Lettie. However, I couldn't get around the fact that he had been in King Soopers buying insulin at five past nine and in front of Alice Farrar's from nine-fifteen to about nine-thirty-five. Pretty tight alibi, *if* he had been the one in the car. I had this rotten little suspicion; what if Linc and Judd had driven the car over there for Ogden? That might explain why they were so afraid to talk to the police.

And what had Ogden meant by that sly reference to Rachel, that still waters run deep? Rachel had gone out of her way to set things up for Ogden. She'd even rented an apartment for him. I closed my eyes, forgetting that I was driving, and opened them seconds before I ran a stoplight. Rachel had rented that apartment a month before he even came. She'd have had all the time in the world to make a second set of keys.

She had been with the theater group from the start and had been a rather promising actress back then. She could have been extremely jealous of Lettie. She could easily have left the business office, made her way down, out the lobby door, in the side door, along the scrim to Barbara.

She was so much a part of the theater, she might have passed unnoticed, even. As far as that went, if she were athletic, she might have gone down the catwalk ladder and dropped down behind Barbara, but it wasn't too likely. She had been wearing a straight skirt and a twin set that night, and it's pretty hard to be athletic in an outfit like that.

On impulse I turned south. Rachel lived near the Denver University area, characterized by small older homes, many set on the back of the lots on quiet residential streets. I was a little curious about her house and what it looked like. The state of a house tells so much about the person. If you find a house with unrefrigerated mayo and animal feces, you find mental health problems. I was positive I would find Rachel had an impeccably tidy two-bedroom condo, all done in

beige and white with aqua accents, right down to the guest
hand towels.

Rachel didn't have a condo; she had a dark brick house,
set up from the street and midway back on the lot. It was
made gracious by a generous growth of ivy and mature ev-
ergreens. I climbed the steps to the walk, and then went up
the stairs to the little porch. I rang the bell, heard it echo in
the house, and waited. Rachel didn't answer. I rang again,
and when I still didn't get an answer, I tried the screen door.
I started to leave, then went round the back and peeked in
the garage. Her little green Geo sat right there.

I tried the back door, finding the screen unlocked but the
door locked tight. Finally I went round to the side and tried
to peek in. The curtains were drawn; I couldn't see a thing.

The neighbor to the south was peering out the door at
me, so I waved and walked over to her house. An older,
rounded woman answer my knock, a worried little frown on
her face. I explained I was from the theater and wanted to
find Rachel.

"I haven't seen her leave today," she said.

"You don't have a key for her house, by chance?"

"Well, yes. Do you think…?" She left the rest hanging
in the air as though she couldn't bring herself to say anything else.

"I think I'm worried about her, and she may need help,"
I said. I showed her my driver's license and repeated that I
worked with her at the theater, and that was adequate to
move her along. She took a key from a row of little hooks
and led the way to Rachel's front door. She unlocked it,
stepped inside, and yoo-hooed.

I went past her into the living room. I was wrong about
the decor. It was done in white with forest green accents
and framed Impressionist prints on the walls. I was right
about it being tidy, right down to the puffed green throw

pillows and the jade plant, whose leaves looked as though they'd just been polished.

The neighbor called out again, but there was no answer.

"Maybe she rode with someone else," I suggested.

The neighbor shook her head. "She always takes her car. I would have seen her leave. I'm up pretty early."

That was probably an understatement, I thought. I pushed open the door to a tiny side room, which turned out to be Rachel's bedroom. The bed was made, the room clean, the closet so orderly it could have been on exhibit. She even had her shoes in their original boxes.

We proceeded into the dining area, where a little square oak table and chairs stood. A sheet of paper lay there, a note handwritten, dated with the time.

To whomever,
In my closet you will find the drugs I gave to Lettie and Barbara and now myself. Jealousy led me to destroy Lettie. And Barbara stood in the way of my chance to be happy with Lawrence, and so did Adrian.
    But I can't make myself go on any longer.
                                                              Rachel

"Oh, no!" The neighbor began to shake. "She must be here somewhere....."

We rushed to the kitchen. It was sparkling clean, and empty. I noticed a basement door to the right and pulled it open. The stairs were littered with newspapers, bags of recyclables, and junk. Tidy stopped at the top of the stairs.

And so did life.

I yelped, and the neighbor screamed outright.

Rachel stared straight at us with unseeing eyes, sprawled at the foot of the basement stairs on her back, her head at an unnatural angle, her arms out as though she'd tried to

catch air on her fall down. I found myself stunned, unable
to move or even think straight for a moment. It was hard to
draw breath, and my knees felt rubbery.

The neighbor turned and shoved blindly past me to the
kitchen sink, where she gagged noisily. That seemed to jar
me out of my shock. Perhaps Rachel wasn't beyond help. I
started down the stairs.

Rachel hadn't thrown out a newspaper or magazine for
years. They must have been stacked in teetering piles on the
stairs, leaving only a thin trail down. Now most of them
had slipped and fluttered down the stairs as she fell.

The steps were so covered with papers that I slipped and
barely caught myself before I plunged down too. I had to
grab a broom and push them aside ahead of me; it seemed
to take forever to reach her. Her eyes were glazed and un-
blinking. It was eerie, and I was almost afraid of her. I knelt
beside her, called her name, and touched her cheek. A chill
started in my fingers and ran through my body.

I felt sick.

Rachel was very dead. No question. She was cold to the
touch and stiff. It was hard to believe; the other two had
survived. I touched her again, even leaned close to her face
to see if I could find any trace of breath in her. Nothing.

The old saw, Trouble runs in threes, ran through my
mind, but three "accidents" in one play was too many. She
was really the first. The first to die.

Through all the disbelief came one thought. Had she really killed herself? Had she taken drugs and then stumbled
over to the basement for some reason and fallen? Or had
someone pushed her?

For that matter, had someone come here, forced her to
write the note and take the drugs, and then pushed her to
her death?

Stokowski would believe she had fallen; I was willing to

bet she had been filled with enough drugs to drop a rhino in its tracks and then pushed. I felt as nauseated as the woman upstairs sounded.

A quick glance around the basement revealed all the left-over clothes and furnishings from a lifetime of collecting, saving, and storing. Not even pathways existed through the jumble. All the mess of her life was tucked away out of sight, until now, when death would reveal it all, the old, the useless, and the evil.

I climbed up the stairs to where the neighbor was still being very sick in the sink. Once I was sure she was under some control, I got her to the couch in the living room and covered her with a little crocheted coverlet that had been folded on the end cushion. I told her to stay put and not to touch anything, found the telephone and called the police, and then finally called Stokowski, who said he'd be right there.

Next, I went straight to Rachel's closet. Sure enough, on the floor in one of many shoe boxes I found a vast and lethal collection of prescription drugs and some innocent-looking herbal medicines. I left the box as I found it, careful to make sure I hadn't left a fingerprint or damaged anyone else's prints. In the bathroom four old prescription bottles of varying dates lay in the sink, empty. It looked as though she had taken, or been given, a vile mix of painkillers and downers. How convenient.

The medicine cabinet door was ajar, too conveniently. Carefully, using a ballpoint pen from my bag, I opened the door wide enough to see inside. A rather boring collection of toothpaste, aspirin, and sleeping medications stood on the shelves. I closed the cabinet door to its original position and returned to the dining area and table to reread Rachel's note.

I tried to figure out why I felt so disbelieving and distant from Rachel's terrible end. I felt no flood of anger or overwhelming grief, simply numbness at the scene. For reasons I wasn't sure of, I was certain she had fed drugs first to Lettie and then to Barbara. A long-ago sin had risen to strike again—but why now?

I thought of her apparent devotion to Lawrence. Had she been led on by some promise from Lawrence? Or had she overheard, as everyone did apparently, the argument between Lawrence and Barbara when Lawrence asked for the divorce, and assumed that Lawrence was in love with her? I thought back to her appearance at the Steadmans' when Barbara was in the hospital. She had been so very there, so doting on Lawrence. It was entirely possible that she had assumed he loved her.

And when she learned he'd been with another? What then? Despair? She hadn't mentioned it in her note, though. I reread it, this time looking at the curious wording, at once too little and stiff, even for Rachel. Even under stress.

There had been now three people attacked, one fatally: Barbara of an initially suicidal-appearing act, Ogden of an apparently accidental insulin mis-dose, and now Rachel of an apparent suicide. I was suddenly frightened. All three of these people had been in the theater group with Lettie, and very involved with her. Of the group, only Lawrence and Adrian remained. And while Lawrence, at least, appeared to have a decent alibi, Adrian was there the whole time. And the boys were dedicated to him; even Phillip would be loath to say anything against him, even if he'd seen something.

But it was all so pat, so easy. Too easy. The note, the confession, the suicide. Not all that different from Lettie's death sixteen years ago and the attempt on Barbara.

I thought of Ogden's sly reference to Rachel. Had he sent me here, knowing I'd find her? Had he set it up? Had the whole insulin accident been engineered by him to cover, while he was actually getting revenge for Lettie's death? Or was Adrian the one who was stalking the cast, in some misguided devotional revenge?

I felt sure that Linc and Judd knew something, remembering the discomfort I'd seen in Linc's face when I'd talked to him at Adrian's. I was guessing that they had Ogden's car to watch Lawrence. Hoping I could convince him to talk, I dialed Linc's house and asked to speak to him.

"Didn't they get there? They said they were going to meet you. He said you called him."

"I didn't call them. Where were they going?"

"I thought they said the theater, but maybe it was Adrian's. They're worried about Adrian."

"So am I." But for different reasons now. I had the panicky and ugly feeling that the entire theater company was slowly being eliminated or set up to take a fall.

Ogden had steered me over here. If he had killed Rachel, he could have sent me knowing I'd find her and call the police, and would then have to spend hours answering their questions. That would keep me out of the way while he lured the boys to Adrian's. To kill them, too? And Adrian? Or to kill Adrian and pin it on them? In spite of Ogden's protests of innocence, he had probably been there; he had the opportunity and a motive.

If I waited for Stokowski, I would definitely be here all afternoon and possibly part of the evening. And the boys could be dead or neatly framed by the time I convinced Stokowski. Sirens sounded in the distance. I made a quick decision.

I ripped a deposit slip out of my checkbook, tore off the account numbers, and handed it to the woman on the couch. "Give this to the police and ask to speak to this detective. Detective Stokowski. Tell him the boys were lured to the theater by someone pretending to be me and to come ASAP."

The sirens were nearly here. I ran from the house, dove into my car, and pulled away. I reached the corner of the block as they rounded the other end. I didn't wait to see them pull up in front of Rachel's.

As I drove, I pulled out my cell phone, punched in Stokowski's numbers, and left him a long message, telling him what I had figured out. Then I called my voice mail at the *Daily Orion* and found I had two messages. The first was from Zelda, saying that Mr. Gerster had told her he was closing the paper as of the first of June. I gasped and felt a distinct pain in the region of my heart. The *Orion* closing! How could that be?

I barely heard the second message, I was so shocked about the first. The second was from Jason. He'd decided to come back to Denver; the job in New York wasn't fun without me. He wanted his old job at the *Daily Orion* back!

I pulled to the side of the street and made a quick call to New York. His office said he'd already gone. When I asked for his voice mail, they said he didn't have it anymore.

Now I had a no-refund ticket to New York, and Jason was coming back. Neither of us had jobs. And the *Orion* was closing.

I took Logan north, then turned on Alameda, crossed Broadway, and decided, since I was nearly at Adrian's, I'd stop there and check things out.

I slowed and cruised past to the next house east. Adrian's house was closed and the shades drawn. Most noticeably, the porch light was burning—in the afternoon. I had a real bad feeling about this. I parked briefly across the street and called Stokowski again to leave a second message about Adrian, so he'd know where to go if I never reappeared. The phone went dead as I was explaining that Adrian's porch light was on. I hadn't paid the telephone bill. Poverty is so infuriating. And expensive!

I packed my phone in my bag, got out of my car, and ran to Adrian's. I banged on his door, rang the bell, peeked in the window, and ran to the back door. Locked. The kitchen was tidy, no signs of life—or previous meals. I ran around the other side of the house, peering in the windows as I went, and roused the neighbor's dog to hell-hound fury, but I couldn't see a thing amiss. I checked the garage. Adrian's car was gone.

I jumped into my car and drove as fast as possible through the neighborhood to the theater. The sun was completely covered by clouds now, and I could almost smell rain. The wind was picking up; it probably would blow the storm on to Denver in another hour.

Adrian's car was the only one in the theater parking lot. I pulled in next to it, killed the engine, and got out. I left my car doors unlocked, just in case I needed to leave in a hurry.

The hood of Adrian's car was warm, but the sun had been shining on it earlier that morning, so the warmth meant nothing. I was very nervous about this. The stage door was locked. Someone had painted out the obnoxious graffiti.

I headed around to the front door.

"Yo, Stella, wait!"

On the rooftop, Linc waved, then temporarily disappeared. I walked toward the rear of the building. Linc raced down the steps and jumped the last three athletically. "Stella, what are you doing here? You're supposed to be inside."

"What do you mean?"

"Phillip said you called him to come here. He's in there, looking for you."

A chill ran over my neck and down my arms. "I didn't call him."

"Well, someone did. We were there. It was a woman's voice."

Or someone imitating a woman. A really good actor, like Adrian. "Oh, no." I started for the front door.

"Wait! I got a key," Linc said and pulled out a ring of about twelve keys. He flipped through them, selected a brass Kwikset, and handed it over. "This one."

"When did he go in?"

"About ten minutes ago."

"Anybody come out?"

He shook his head. "Trouble?"

"Big time. Go call the cops."

"Yo," he said and started off. "Oh, Stella?" I turned to him. "Take this." He threw me his lighter. "There's a can of hair spray on the floor just inside the door. In case you need it—" He took off.

I fitted the key into the lock, turned it, and pushed the door open slowly. Once in, I wedged the door open with the brick and moved into the shadows. I stooped and groped along the wall for the hair spray but couldn't find it. Too bad. In my experience hair spray is about the most useful stuff around.

The sound of radio music filtered out from the workshop.

I crept through the dark, musty backstage, following the wall. Listening for other sounds, any other sound. The radio announced its station, KEZW. The scent of raw pine wood and paint grew stronger. There was no light on in the work-shop. What could Adrian be working on in the dark?

The tune playing on the radio was Sinatra's version of "Send in the Clowns," and it occurred to me that it was oddly appropriate. I crept along the wall, rounded the cor-ner, and saw in the dim light coming in around the edges of the blackout shades in the windows a tall, lanky figure standing stone still, arms behind him.

"Phillip?"

He turned toward me. I reached for the light switch, flicked it on, and saw his face was waxy pale and tear-streaked. "Phillip?" I asked. "Phillip, what are you doing here?"

"You asked me to come."

"No." I stopped. He brought his hand around in front of him. In it he held a deadly little pearl-handled pocketbook gun.

"Put the gun down, Phillip."

He looked at it as if he didn't recognize it. "Stella, I didn't do it."

"What, Phillip?"

He pointed. I followed the line of his finger and saw in the darkness a pair of feet in men's shoes, protruding from beneath the workbench. "Oh, no."

My first thought was that they were Lawrence's and that Phillip had killed him. Ignoring the gun in Phillip's hand, I knelt beside the prone figure and realized it was Adrian. I reached for his wrist. "Phillip, what happened?"

"I don't know. I came here as fast as I could. I came in, and it was all dark. I called out, and then I heard the music and came in here. He was here. He had a gun in his hand…"

I felt the flutter of a rapid, shallow pulse—but at least it was a pulse. "We've got to call an ambulance. Phillip, get the phone. Now!"

Phillip was shaking his head in shock. "He was lying here, with this gun. There was blood, and his eyes were open. He lifted his hand and the gun, like he was giving it to me. I took it, then he…it was so weird. Like slow motion. Like it wasn't real."

"Phillip, put down the gun and call nine-one-one."

Phillip looked at me, tears starting down his cheeks. "He wasn't trying to kill me. He tried to say something to me.

I could see it in his eyes. But I couldn't hear him. I got real close, but I still couldn't hear, and then he stopped talking. His lips stopped moving and...and his eyes closed.''

"We've got to call for help, Phillip." I stood, stepped over Adrian, and reached past Phillip for the phone. I punched in 911 as I lifted the receiver to my ear. I wasn't sure what he was going to do next, but I didn't want to struggle over the gun and risk it going off, so I figured I'd keep him talking while I dialed. "Why do you have the gun, Phillip?"

"The gun? I don't know."

I put the receiver to my ear. No ringing. I depressed the switch hook a couple of times. There was no dial tone. I traced the cord. It had been ripped out of the wall.

Phillip hadn't paid any attention to me. He looked at the gun in his hand, surprised, and dropped it immediately. I flinched. Fortunately, it didn't go off.

"I...I took it from him," Phillip stammered, his eyes filling. "Adrian was a good guy. He didn't hurt anyone. Why did he do this?"

I glanced at the workbench. A yellow invoice sheet lay on it, Adrian's rough printing scrawled across the top: "I can't stand this. Too much!" But that had to be a protest over the price of the wood on the invoice. "Phillip, Adrian didn't do anything. We've got to get out of here and get help."

He seemed to wake up. "What?"

"We've got to get out of here." I grabbed his elbow and tried to steer him toward the door. I kept up a running dialogue to try to orient him. "Adrian was shot because he figured out who tried to kill Barbara. Come on."

It was all falling into place now. I'd had the whole thing figured out almost right, but I'd been looking at it as one long crime, rooted in the play. Instead, it was rooted in

Lettie, and it was two crimes. Lettie's death and Lettie's revenge, two different crimes. "He didn't shoot himself, Phillip. You were set up to take the fall." I'd pinpointed Rachel as the killer. "A long time ago, Rachel—"

Phillip looked at me, stunned. "Rachel?" He shook his head. "Why would Rachel kill Adrian?"

"She didn't shoot Adrian." I dragged him toward the side door. His gaze lifted to a spot behind me. A footstep sounded behind me.

A harsh feminine voice rang out. "Freeze. Drop the gun."

Thank God. The police. My heart seemed to suspend action. "Don't anyone shoot. He doesn't have a gun." It was my voice, although I don't remember saying a thing. I only remember feeling the most profound sense of relief that the police had got there in time.

Phillip's face seemed to bleach to an even more unhealthy shade of gray. His gaze was fixed on the person behind me, terrified, then he tore it away, looked at me deeply. I didn't understand his reaction. It seemed too extreme.

"Now move very slowly so I don't get nervous and shoot you both right here." The voice was softer this time, familiar. My heart did a skip beat, and a clammy sweat slicked my palms.

I turned. Cammie stood in the workshop doorway, a rather large, ugly gun in her hand.

TWENTY-SEVEN

THE GUN LOOKED even bigger when she waved it at us. "I can use this if I have to. Now come with me." She stood back, motioning for us to go toward the stage.

I could feel the lighter in the pocket of my slacks and hoped it didn't show. "I'm feeling a little dizzy, Cammie," I panted.

I walked unsteadily, staggering a bit, close to the shelving where Adrian kept his ether, glue, spirits, and paints. I wanted to lurch closer to the shelf and snag one of the aerosol sprays, preferably paint. I figured it would flare nicely if I could get the chance.

"Get away from the shelves," she said and waved the gun at me.

I nodded, then, raising my voice a bit, I said, "You see, Phillip, Adrian came back here to check his files. He had recognized the torn bit off the voucher, and he came back here last night to put it all together. And he did, didn't he, Cammie?"

"You're the one who caused all the trouble; now move. We're going to take a little walk here."

Phillip, very confused, seemed unable to move. "I don't understand. If...?"

"It's a long story, Phillip. It starts back when Rachel was very young and, I think, in love with Ogden. I think she was jealous when Lettie Starling, barely fifteen years old—"

Cammie interrupted. "She was only fourteen when she joined the cast of the theater."

"Lettie was a wild girl, willing to try a lot of things, including an older man for a boyfriend. You see, Phillip, Cammie didn't know about all this until she saw the play your mom wrote. Until then she simply thought that her sister had killed herself accidentally with drugs. That was bad enough, but when she saw the play, she figured out Rachel was in fact the snake, right, Cammie?"

"I adored Lettie. She was so smart and pretty and talented. Her death devastated my parents. They were never able to recover. My father died of a stroke three years later, and my mother followed him with a heart attack. At sixteen I was orphaned. Rachel didn't just kill Lettie, she killed my whole family."

"And you decided to avenge it."

"Rachel kept Lettie supplied with drugs." Cammie's voice shook lightly. "She never realized what Rachel was doing. How she was killing her."

"And Rachel probably started the scandal that drove Ogden out of Denver, and then either she overdosed Lettie or she helped her to commit suicide. And she got away with it."

"Not quite right. Rachel knew Lettie was crazy in love with Ogden. The night Ogden left Denver he tried to reach Lettie, but he couldn't. So he gave Rachel a note for Lettie, explaining why he was leaving and how and where to meet him. Rachel never passed it on. Instead, she told Lettie that he'd run away from her. Then Rachel gave her the drugs, deliberately overdosing her. She murdered my sister."

"And when you grew up, you joined this cast as Lettie had done. And you persuaded Barbara to hire Ogden."

"It didn't take much. Once I suggested it, she was unstoppable."

"And you planned to avenge Lettie, but instead you fell in love with Ogden."

"That was a bit of a complication. He's really quite attractive. Now, enough of this. Move."

The gun in her hand wavered back and forth between Phillip and me. "Move!" She pointed toward the stage door.

Phillip looked completely bewildered. "But why hurt my mom? She didn't do anything."

Cammie frowned. "I didn't hurt your mom. Rachel did that."

I thought for a moment. "When you went up to fix the lights, you saw that Rachel wasn't in the office, didn't you?"

"I didn't think about it at first, but by the time I got home that night, I realized what Rachel was up to. She's been in love with Lawrence for years. Everyone knew it—that puppy devotion. Nobody cared, Lawrence wasn't reciprocating; in fact, he seemed oblivious to her.

"Nobody ever paid attention to Rachel, but they should have. She's been giving Barbara little pills for months, just like she did my sister. I saw her, but I didn't realize what she was doing until I saw the play. She was hooking her slowly. Then two things happened. She saw the play, and she overheard Lawrence and Barbara arguing onstage. When she heard Lawrence say he wanted a divorce, she figured Lawrence had fallen in love with her at last. She knew she had to kill Barbara, so that night she gave her a double dose. When you made Barbara go stand by the Venus's-flytrap, Rachel simply went down, sympathized, got close, and put ether over her nose. Barbara was too groggy to fight much. Then Rachel slipped the rope around her neck. That's all it took. I figured it out after the police had talked to me."

Where were the police? Linc should have reached them by now. "Cammie, why try to kill Ogden?"

Her gaze dropped momentarily to the floor, but before I could move, she was glaring at me again. "I thought he loved me. When I realized he was still in love with Lettie, that I didn't mean anything to him, I was furious. For a few weeks I'd actually been happy, felt loved and important, and then he took it all away. I was there with him on Saturday, and he didn't care about me. He's still in love with Lettie, or he thinks he is. Anyway, it was as if my whole world caved in. I was even more alone than before. So I helped him overeat, got up that night while he slept, and diluted his insulin."

"But he didn't die."

She looked straight at me for a cold minute. "He will. It's only a matter of time."

"You were there before I was today. You diluted his insulin again?" Her slow smile answered my question. "All this to avenge Lettie's death?"

Phillip shook his head. "I don't get it."

Cammie turned to him and snarled, "You don't have to. Now come on. Out the side door, and hurry."

"This is broad daylight, Cammie, where are we going?"

"Never mind, just go! Phillip, lead the way. Anything funny, and Stella will be a thing of the past."

Phillip walked silently to the side door and pressed the break bar. The door opened about two inches, then bumped against something.

Phillip shoved it again. It didn't open. "There's something there." The skies were darkening, and rain-heavy wind and grit whistled in through the crack. He pressed his face against it to see out. His eyes watered. "Someone's moved a car up against it. We can't get out this way."

Judd, I thought. Judd had decided to make sure no one left, but it didn't make it any safer for us. I could feel Cammie deciding to kill us on the spot.

"Cammie, don't shoot us. You need us. Think of our hostage potential. We're cash on the hoof. Good for your freedom."

Cammie knew the building. Maybe she would kill us and crawl out some back window, or, or...I realized I didn't know anything about the place. All the time I'd spent in it, I'd never fully explored it. All I knew is that the basement was filled with all the leftover costumes and sets, and Zelda maintained there was an entire ecosystem in place there.

I wondered if Cammie was afraid of rodents. I hate them, but maybe we could scare her to death. Unlikely.

I was running out of options. "The front door, Cammie. Let's try the simple way out."

She wavered, then made up her mind. "Go. Nothing funny, and hurry up."

"You could send Phillip. He could check on it and report back."

"Hah! Not on your life."

It *was* on my life, but I didn't mention it.

We walked hurriedly up the aisle. Phillip shoved on the break bars of the double doors. They moved about an inch, no farther. Locked down.

"That can't be. What's in the way?" Cammie's voice was rising. Phillip stood on tiptoe, peering out the glass window in the door. "Someone put a bar through the door handles."

"Move out of the way," she said and pushed to the door. "Either of you moves, I'll blow the other one away." She glanced outside, then back before I could figure out anything to do. She was furious. "Shit!"

Lightning flashed outside, thunder cracked. The lights flickered. Out of the corner of my eye, I saw a movement in the cloakroom curtain. I glanced sideways, trying not to move my head. The curtain of the cloak closet was moving.

I spotted shoes below. Men's desert boots. Lawrence. It had to be Lawrence; no teen would be caught dead in them. What was he going to do?

Cammie waved the gun. "All right, move. Back to the stage."

"Cammie, I'm getting dizzy. I don't think I can walk."

She raised the gun straight up and fired. "Now see if you can walk."

I could, of course.

I clutched my bag under my arm and tried to think. But it's so hard when you're scared witless. Funny, I thought, how even with my life hanging by a thread, I was still clutching my purse to my side.

The wind was rising outside, whining around the roof. The sound was unnerving. There's something essentially unpleasant about high winds and rain. I sniffed. There was a smell of sulfur. It could have been Cammie. She was the devil herself.

Cammie smelled it, too. And Phillip raised his chin, looking around. His gaze caught on the curtain, the shoes. Amazement crossed his face. He recognized the shoes. He glanced at me. I nodded, raised a brow, and shook my head. "Come on, Phillip, let's go to the stage." I was afraid Cammie would see the feet.

Phillip caught on. He turned, seeming now to take strength from his father's presence. He moved slowly, though. The smell of sulfur was stronger the closer we got to the stage. My eyes began to burn.

Smoke.

But not the smoke of fires. It smelled like the Fourth of July. Like the snakes we used to burn on the sidewalks that made clouds of sulfur smoke. Judd. Judd and his smoke bombs. It would set off the sprinkler system, and we might be able to surprise Cammie.

"Cammie, the place is on fire!" I said. I figured the sprinkler system would come on, the shock of the cold water would startle her, and we could drop to the floor and...and get shot on the floor. Not a good idea.

Phillip caught on. "Cammie, you know how it will burn—we've got to get out. Our only chance is through the shop windows."

Cammie snorted. "We've got a sprinkler system. Keep moving."

I walked as slowly as possible. "My eyes are watering. I need to get a tissue from my bag."

She didn't respond. I moved my hands slowly, dipping into the purse. I fished inside it, found a ballpoint pen, and tried my best to hide it behind a wad of tissues. My eyes really were stinging and watering from the smoke. So much for the alarm system. We were dry as a bone.

"Give me one of those tissues," Cammie said.

I handed her one over my shoulder. I kept the pen in my left hand. What I could do with it, I didn't know, but I felt a lot safer now. That helped my thinking.

The storm outside seemed to have subsided. It was very quiet. *Now, Saint Don Bosco, now is the time for a huge clap of thunder.* Nothing. Why didn't the sprinkler system turn on?

What was Lawrence going to do? We were partly down the aisle now, walking as slowly as we could.

Smoke blanketed the house, dimming the lights, but it was heaviest along the floor. It wasn't reaching the alarms on the ceiling. In fact, the air was clearing.

"Hurry up," she said.

We stumbled up the stage steps. I noticed the breaker box on the wall. If I could reach the main switch—

There was a rumble of thunder, but no startling clap that would distract her. Out of the corner of my eye I saw movement on the far side aisle. Lawrence had slipped down unnoticed almost to the stage. If she turned even a hair, he'd be seen.

"Cammie!" Lawrence called out, then ducked behind the curtain. His voice was muffled, but it sounded as though he was moving. "Cammie, stop this. Don't shoot them. He's my son. The only thing I have left. There's no evidence against you—"

She shot wildly at the curtain.

Lawrence shouted, now from the back of the stage, behind the scrim. She shot again.

I lunged for the breaker box, praying the black leg hid me just enough that she couldn't aim well. The breaker box creaked and screeched as I jerked it open. I yanked on the broad-handled switch, hard.

The lights went out.

"Duck, Phillip!" Lawrence yelled.

I threw myself to the right toward the stage, stumbled, and fell to the floor. I heard footsteps.

One shot, two. A grunt. Lawrence.

More footsteps. "I'll kill you all," she shouted. She was practically on top of me.

I kicked out. Connected. My foot struck her leg.

She yelled. And fired again. I rolled and kicked. She fell. The gun clattered to the stage floor. I threw myself toward her. Caught hold of her hair and yanked, hard. Both her hands were on me, clawing. Then pounding. She had the strength of a madwoman.

I had the strength of terror. We struggled. Using the advantage of weight, I rolled onto her, pinning one of her arms beneath her. My hand was still entwined in her hair. I yanked up and down, pounding the back of her head against the stage floor again and again, until I felt her relax. Then I did it again, to make sure she was out of commission.

The lights blazed on, blinding me. I heard Phillip run back to Lawrence's side.

"Phillip, get me a cord or something to tie her with." I put my forearm across her throat, tight but not choking. I didn't want to risk her getting away. I lay on top of her, pinning her to the floor. I had no strength left to protect myself if she got any advantage. Her gun lay barely two feet away.

Cammie stirred. I pressed my forearm down on her throat until her breathing was hoarse. I thought about grabbing the gun, holding it on her. Then I remembered Stokowski's comment: Don't point the gun if you can't shoot it. It'll only be used against you.

I looked at her—still seemingly unconscious, her cheeks pale with bright spots of red, and a long scratch across her chin. Blood ran down the side of her face. I frowned. She hadn't been cut. Then I realized it came from my head. I didn't remember hitting my head during the struggle with Cammie. Drop by drop it ran down her face. I began to feel dizzy. And sick.

She looked so young, so baby-faced. She had coldly planned to do away with all of us out of some warped sense of justice. Revenge. She had seemed so vulnerable when I met her, I'd immediately liked her and felt protective of her.

She moaned softly. My arm was beginning to tremble, the aftermath of my adrenaline rush. I twisted around, aimed, and kicked hard, sending the gun spinning off into the far wings.

Where were the cops?

I glanced away from Cammie. Phillip was bent over Lawrence, stroking his face, murmuring to him. Lawrence was sprawled on his back. Blood streaked his shirt, a huge patch on his upper arm and shoulder and other streaks down his arm, on his trousers. I didn't see how he could still be alive with so much blood leaking out of him.

I heard fumbling at the stage door. It flew open.

Cammie moved. I banged her head on the floor again, very hard, and pressed against her windpipe. She lay still.

I was beginning to feel very cold. There was a lot of blood on her face now.

I recognized the battered brown shoes at my side. "You can get off her now, Stella." Stokowski knelt by my side.

I looked at him. My teeth had begun to chatter. "She's not dead."

"She will be if you don't get off her. C'mon."

I rolled to the side.

She coiled and sprang up. I kicked with both legs. She fell heavily on her back.

Stokowski wrestled her down and snapped cuffs on her this time, then came to me. "You all right?"

Blood was streaming down the side of my face now, dripping on my shirt. My head and scalp stung, but I felt better. "I'll live. Look after Adrian. I think he's still alive. He's in the workshop under the bench."

"The paramedics are working on him now. He's still breathing, barely. You feel okay?"

"Yeah. Oh, you'd better get word to Ogden— Cammie messed with his insulin again."

"Right, and let me tell you, if you ever do this again, I'll put you behind bars until you're too old to move."

I smiled slightly. This was the Stokowski I knew and Zelda loved. I looked up at the ceiling. Smoke hung like a tent over us. The sprinklers still didn't turn on.

I WENT WITH Lawrence in the ambulance to Denver General, now called Denver Health Medical Center. It would be a while before we could see Adrian, but they said they were "guardedly optimistic."

After they put a few stitches in my scalp, I joined Phillip in Lawrence's room. Lawrence's wounds turned out to be much less serious than they had first looked, although he'd bled considerably. My wound had been a very low priority in the emergency room, so he was in bed drifting in and out of sleep by the time I got there. Phillip was at bedside.

"How're you doing, Phillip?"

He smiled ruefully. "I'm okay." He looked at his dad. "Did you see Dad? He came down and nearly got killed for me. Uh, us. He was awesome."

"Yes, he was, Phillip. He saved our hides."

Lawrence opened his eyes and smiled the tiniest bit. "Had to. You're...my kid. Proud of you."

Phillip blinked back tears. "I'm proud of you, too."

"Think...we can...work on making things work out?"

"Yeah," Phillip said. "Think so."

There was a commotion at the door. Linc and Judd stood there, grinning. And behind them, Jason. "Well, come in. Standing room only."

Jason came over and wrapped me in his arms. Nice and warm and strong. He gave me a nice warm, loving kiss and then said, "Goddamn, I'm glad you're all right. Please don't do this again."

"Excuse me—" A nurse was at the door. "Dr. Whistler asked me to tell you that Adrian Foster is out of surgery, and doing well in recovery."

Linc and Judd sat very still. Then slowly a huge smile crossed Linc's face. Judd, the wiseass, leaked a tear down his cheek and said nothing. We all cheered.

"Judd," I said later. "Something's bothering me. Why didn't the sprinkler system work?"

He sucked in his lips. "Uh, well, we were smoking in

the basement, and I didn't want to set it off, so I took it apart. I'm real sorry.''

"When's your birthday?"

"November tenth." He looked funny.

I smiled. I thought so. He had written the letter. "You were really Scared, weren't you?"

He nodded. "Zelda told me you helped people, and when I heard you were going to work at the theater, I thought…maybe you could help us.''

"Scorpio's a good sign."

WE LEFT LAWRENCE and Phillip together, and Linc and Judd decided to wait to see Adrian. Jason drove me to the town house, where we put on some Chopin because it's Fluffy's favorite and then settled down on the couch. He wrapped an arm around me and pulled me close. "Stella, I quit my job.''

"I know. I called to talk to you. They said you left.''

"You had doubts about that job all along.''

"That's why you left?''

"I resigned because I wanted to be with you. And as soon as I did, I found out that I was the guy for whom the job was wired. I was the board member's son. My dad manipulated the whole thing so I'd have a job in New York.''

"He wanted you closer.''

Jason's gaze lowered. "Well, maybe. I decided that I'm ambitious, but it has to be my ambition, not his. I don't want him to do it for me. That only makes me less than I am. I have to do it myself. I need to live my life, not his.'' Then he paused, looked into my eyes, and smiled. "Now, tell me. Why did you call me?''

I felt ill. "Because Zelda told me that Mr. Gerster is closing the *Orion*. There is no job for you to come home to.''

"Why? Why is he closing?"

"She said he was too tired to run it by himself, and he didn't have the heart to try to teach Andy what to do. He's lost too many people."

Jason rubbed his neck, thinking. "Well, I'll bet if we suggested that we'd both come back and work with him, and buy the paper, I'll bet he'd come around."

He might not be thrilled to work with me, but I knew he'd love working with Jason. "All we need is money. But, Jason, I spent my last on a nonrefundable ticket to New York."

He grinned. "One-way?"

"Well, no. I could only afford round-trip. Does it still count?"

"That's commitment, you know."

"For both of us?"

"For both of us."

I buried my face in his neck, feeling tired, surprisingly contented, and at peace. He shifted to get more comfortable. "Do you think Fluffy and Lips will mind sharing?"

Fluffy was bright green and quite cheerful. "Even Lips is out from under the log and looking pleased. I think she likes me." He continued to gaze into the terrarium. "Stella? A plant leaf blinked at me."

I thought about that for a minute. "Probably a cricket sitting on a leaf."

"A green cricket?"

"The crickets are light brown."

"The leaf blinked again." He let go of me and pressed his face close to the terrarium. "Oh, my God, it's a little tiny lizard. Stella, they had a baby."

I don't even remember getting to the terrarium.

Sure enough. There, almost impossible to see on a Swedish ivy leaf, sat a tiny little green anole. Blinking at me. I could not believe it. Fluffy and Lips's egg hadn't been eaten by the crickets. It had hatched.

"What are you going to name it?"

Before I could answer, the little guy darted to another leaf. "I'm going to call him Scooter." And then I started to cry.

"It's all right, Stella, we'll find wingless fruit flies somewhere."

"It's not that—" I leaned into him. "It's just so nice to see life starting again."